"Hey, it's okay.
Jake soothed

Cynthia's breathing was still ragged, so he reached over in the car to give her a comforting one-armed hug. He let his comforting hand slip between her legs. She was hot, wet and ready. "You're not scared. You're turned on."

"I'm sorry," she gasped, and squirmed. "I can't help it."

He increased the pressure of his palm "You're a danger junkie."

"Are *you?*" she whispered.

For an answer, he took her left hand and placed it in his lap. She found and grasped his erection and heard the breath hiss out from between his teeth.

"I have to go home and shower," she said, her hand moving in light strokes that burned through his slacks.

"I'll bring the soap." If they made it that far. He cupped her more intimately.

"Isn't it dangerous to drive with only one hand on the wheel?"

"Not as dangerous as driving with no blood in my head. It's all drained down south."

Dear Reader,

The way two people make love is unique—a kind of fingerprint of their relationship. Put those same two people with different partners, and their lovemaking will change, just as a favorite recipe changes when you add new ingredients. I suppose that's why I enjoy writing love scenes so much, and why I'm really excited to be part of Harlequin Blaze.

Live a Little! explores one woman's sexual fantasy—and what happens when that fantasy comes true—but it also takes a look at how liberating it is to find the right partner. This book also contains the love scene that won Harlequin's 2000 Summer Blaze Contest—and launched my career. I think it's fair to say I have great fondness for this book!

Sexy books are very fashionable right now. But, in my opinion, sex without love is like dessert without dinner. It might be fun for a while, but as a steady diet you'd soon get sick of it. I love to write hot scenes, but a lot of the heat comes from the emotions and vulnerability of the characters as they open their most secret parts to each other. As they fall in love.

I hope you enjoy Cyn and Jake's sensuous—and sometimes bumpy—journey just as much as I did. I also love to hear from readers. Visit my Web site: www.nancywarren.net or write to met at Nancy Warren, P.O. Box 37035, North Vancouver, B.C. V7N 4M0. And don't forget to check out www.tryblaze.com.

Happy reading,

Nancy Warren

LIVE A LITTLE!

Nancy Warren

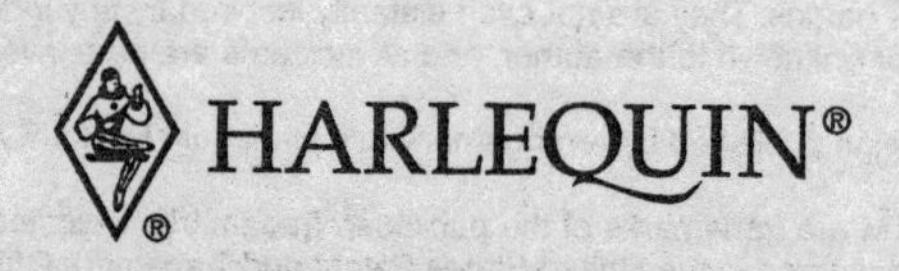

TORONTO • NEW YORK • LONDON
AMSTERDAM • PARIS • SYDNEY • HAMBURG
STOCKHOLM • ATHENS • TOKYO • MILAN • MADRID
PRAGUE • WARSAW • BUDAPEST • AUCKLAND

For Rick, who always believed. With love.

ISBN 0-373-79023-6

LIVE A LITTLE!

This edition published by arrangement with Harlequin Books S.A.

Visit us at www.eHarlequin.com

Printed in U.S.A.

1

IT'S TOUGH TO SCRATCH your stomach when your hands are cuffed to the bed Cynthia Baxter discovered to her intense frustration. She twisted and rolled her naked body, but the elusive itch was an inch or so north of her belly button. Her feet couldn't reach it, her knees couldn't reach it; she couldn't twist it away.

The sound of metal scratching the mahogany four-poster, which had been handed down in perfect condition through generations of Baxters, only added to the guilt she was feeling.

"Walter!" she yelled, but got no reply.

She'd carefully followed the instructions in *Raunch Magazine*'s fantasy issue in a bid to put some passion into her relationship. Here she was, enacting "Helpless Virgin Ravished by a Dark, Dangerous Stranger," and her fiancé, who should be overcome with lust while performing on her body all the outrageously kinky acts she'd read about in the magazine—and highlighted for him in yellow so he couldn't miss them—was in the living room, attached to his cell phone.

She listened hard, but couldn't hear his voice. Maybe he was too put off by her naked body in daylight to come back.

"Walter?"

Silence.

"Walter!" Her voice echoed through the house. Why couldn't he hear her?

She took a deep breath, and her nose wrinkled at the smell of the new perfume she'd splashed all over her body. In the department store it had smelled spicy and exotic, but now that she'd been wearing it a few hours, it smelled cheap and cloying. "Walter! Are you there?"

Nothing.

A terrible suspicion dawned. He tended to be obsessive about his work, which made him forgetful about other things. Was it possible he'd forgotten her and left?

Helplessness was part of the fantasy, according to the September issue of *Raunch Magazine.* The "sexperts" had been quite clear on that. They gave very specific instructions for fulfilling every woman's wildest fantasies, instructions that left Cynthia hot and squirming and eager to create "her own personal erotic drama, leading to an orgasmic orgy of legendary proportions." She wasn't greedy; she'd be happy with a single orgasm. So she'd lapped up the magazine pages with the same eagerness displayed by "Concubine Washing her Master's Plinth."

Fortunately, the magazine had helpfully categorized the fantasies into "Boudoir Beginners," "Intimate Intermediates" and "Erotically Advanced." Of course she'd read through the advanced pages, but frankly, even if she could afford all the equipment, she didn't imagine ever wanting to play games such as "Whorehouse Dominatrix and Groveling Schoolboy" or anything that involved a cast of more than two.

Exposing her naked body in anything but utter darkness was intimidating enough, even in front of Walter, who didn't see all that well without his glasses. No, Boudoir Beginners was plenty exciting enough. There wasn't one scenario that didn't speak to her in some way, but "Helpless Virgin Ravaged by a Dark Dangerous Stranger" was her favorite.

In the privacy of her own bedroom who was going to care if she was politically correct? She was free to imagine being imprisoned by an exotic stranger, a masked Zorro or a ruthless pirate. Whoever he was, this stranger was dark, tall, lean and muscular. She was his prisoner to do with what he pleased, and he was very imaginative.

It was an exciting fantasy. Not that Walter was a Dark Dangerous Stranger, not by a long shot, but then she wasn't a virgin, either, although some of the stuff in *Raunch* made her feel like one.

She wasn't a virgin, but she was definitely helpless. Bondage of a more pretend kind—by a loosely tied silk necktie for instance—was heavily frowned on by the sexperts at *Raunch,* who advised using real handcuffs. Since Cynthia was a person who always followed the rules, handcuffs now bound her.

So far, a kind of determined desperation had pushed her into actually following through with this crazy idea to become sexually exciting. But now that she'd bullied and begged Walter into acting out the fantasy, now that she was actually lying here staked out, naked and helpless, in a respectable suburban neighborhood in the middle of the afternoon, it wasn't erotic excitement she felt.

It was embarrassment.

Who was she trying to kid? No wonder Walter had wandered off. She didn't look a bit like the models in *Raunch,* with their breasts thrust upward like mountain peaks, their tiny waists, ever so slightly rounded hips and long Barbie-doll legs.

Cynthia's breasts just sort of sat on her chest like

lumps of unrisen bread dough with raisins on top, while the rest of her was far from voluptuous. Once she got out of these handcuffs she'd never ever suggest they depart from their standard quick couplings under the sheets in proper darkness.

She yelled a few more times, until her throat hurt and she heard an edge of hysteria in her tone. No use yelling herself hoarse; she'd have to calm down and wait. He'd remember her eventually.

Breathing slowly and deeply, Cynthia contemplated the ceiling. There was a shadowy streak in one corner that looked suspiciously like a cobweb. She'd have to take a broom to it as soon as she had a free hand. Which brought her back to her ridiculous predicament. She had no idea how long she'd been here, but her arms ached. She was cold, she was hungry and she had to go to the bathroom.

Where the hell was Walter?

She watched the time tick slowly by on the bedside clock while her anger mounted. Friday afternoon dimmed to Friday evening before true fear began to set in. She could starve to death, freeze to death or die of a bladder infection before Walter remembered her.

After seventeen eons, she heard the sound of gravel crunching outside. But her first thought—that Walter had remembered her and come back—was squelched when she heard the snuffle of a canine nose and the telltale hissing sound among the dahlias under her bedroom window. Thank God, it must be Mrs. Lawrence and Gruber, her overweight poodle, from next door.

Should Cynthia call out?

Embarrassment warred with physical discomfort, but it was a short battle. Her bladder won.

If she had to be rescued by someone off the street,

at least it was a woman. "Mrs. Lawrence," Cynthia yelled as loudly as she could, hoping her neighbor had her hearing aid turned up.

"What's that? Who's calling?" The wavery voice sounded uncertain.

Always excitable, Gruber started barking.

Cynthia yelled, "I need help. I'm tied up in the bedroom. Use the spare key, and please hurry."

"Oh, my dear. Oh...it's Cynthia. I hope it's not a home invasion," the wavery voice continued. Cynthia wished her sweet elderly neighbor would quit talking to her dog and get the key.

"Mrs. Lawrence? You remember where the key is? Under the third geranium pot?"

She heard the crunch of gravel and the muttering of her neighbor while she lay there hoping poor old Mrs. Lawrence wouldn't have a heart attack when she saw her naked and in the most humiliating predicament of her life. At least her feet weren't bound. Not that it made a lot of difference. If she brought her knees up to cover her breasts she'd expose the lower part of her body, and the added pressure on her bladder might turn her into a human water pistol.

So much for taking chances. So much for trying to be a sensuous woman. She might have known she'd fail.

Minutes dragged by, each one a painful battle for mastery between herself and her bladder. Cynthia thought she heard a scraping noise from outside, but couldn't be sure. If she didn't get to a bathroom soon she was going to have an accident.

After about three more stretches of eternity, she heard a tiny sound from inside the house. "Mrs. Lawrence, I'm in here, in the bedroom."

But it wasn't Mrs. Lawrence's worried face she saw

in the doorway a few quiet seconds later; it was a cold and deadly black revolver, in a large and very male hand.

Too frightened to scream, Cynthia stared at the terrifying thing. She pulled frantically against the handcuffs, but she was helpless—an occupational freebie if the guy with the gun was some kind of rapist pervert.

A dark shape leaped across the doorway. She had the impression of bulk and purpose, then the gun was pointing across her and into the room.

The man attached to the gun threw himself through the doorway, sailing like a missile, the gun held stiffly forward. Cold blue eyes, focused and deadly, swept over her and scanned the room.

It was the sight of those eyes that finally made her scream.

He hit the floor rolling and disappeared into the en suite bathroom.

She was going to be killed by a madman, and Walter had trussed her up like some twisted sacrificial offering. The chains of the handcuffs clanked against the mahogany bedposts over and over as she jerked frantically against her bonds.

In seconds the man was standing by her head, gun lowered slightly. He kept his eyes on the doorway. "To the best of your knowledge, are you alone in the house?" The hoarse whisper sounded as corny as a bad cop show.

A bubble of hysteria caught in her throat. Keeping her eyes on the gun, which was so far still pointing toward the door, she croaked, "I was."

His hard glance flicked to her face, questioning, forcing her to clarify. "Until you showed up."

He pulled something from his pocket and thrust it

toward her face. She cowered, thinking of chloroform, or some instrument of horror, but the object in her face was an identification badge. "I don't—"

"Jake Wheeler, FBI." The curt words sent a new shiver of fear through her. He towered above her, black hair cropped short, his face so lean and chiseled it would surely splinter if the grim mouth ever smiled.

His eyes were a smoky blue and fringed with ridiculously thick, curling black eyelashes. They'd be gorgeous on a porcelain doll. On him, with the deadly expression in their depths, they were terrifying. He wore a black sweatshirt and jeans; she wondered absurdly whether they had casual Fridays at the FBI.

At her nod, he thrust the small black folder back in his pocket. "Do you know who did this to you?"

"Walter Plinkney. And I hope you find him," she said bitterly. "The electric chair is too good for him."

A flicker of doubt crossed the lean, hard face. "You know the perpetrator?"

She nodded stiffly. "My..." No way she was telling this frightening man that her own fiancé had wandered off in the middle of sex. "Ah, my date."

He gazed more carefully down at her, as if her body was a crime scene and he was searching for evidence. "Did he hurt you in any way?"

Knowing he was just doing his job, she resisted the urge to squirm. "Only my pride."

"He didn't do anything you didn't want him to?"

"Yes," she wailed. "He left me here, before we even had sex."

She thought he stifled a grin. His face softened for an instant, making him appear almost human. "But you were a willing participant?"

She had heard of a full-body blush, but never believed she'd experience one, until now. Even her toes felt like they were turning red enough to match the scarlet nail polish she'd applied to her toenails. "It was my idea. Do you think you could get me out of these things?" She indicated the cuffs with a jerk of her head.

"Where's the key?" He glanced around the bedroom, neat and tidy as always. No key ring marred the gleaming bedroom furniture.

"Walter had it last...."

"Where is he now?"

Cynthia wouldn't have thought it was possible to experience more humiliation than she already felt, until he asked that question. "He had to leave," she mumbled.

"Maybe we could phone him?" He looked at her doubtfully. He was clearly wondering what on earth would prompt a man to chain a naked woman to a bed and then leave her there. It was a fair question; Cynthia was wondering about that herself.

"I really can't wait much longer. I have to use the bathroom."

Bending over, he fingered the handcuffs. "Are they regulation?"

"I don't know, they came from a sex shop!"

"Probably not regulation, then. I'll see what I can do."

"Would you hurry? Please?"

Some of her agony must have got through to him. He sped out of the room and returned a couple of minutes later with a pair of shears she recognized from the workshop. Her poor father would roll over in his grave if he knew how they were being used.

The man fitted the blades to the chain of one handcuff. "Hold very still," he ordered.

She did.

She watched the bulge of his biceps, the set of his jaw and his reddening face. Heard the grunt of effort and then the blessed sound she'd been waiting for. *Snap*. He walked around the bed and started on the second cuff.

Belatedly, Cynthia wondered what had happened to her neighbor. The last thing she needed now was the arrival on the scene of one of her mother's oldest friends. "Where's Mrs. Lawrence?"

"She went next door to call 9-1-1."

With a little cry of horror, Cynthia stared at the icy blue marbles he had instead of eyes.

Muttering a curse, he shoved the cutting tool under his arm, reached into a pocket and hauled out a cell phone. Even as he pushed a button, she heard the siren, and seconds later saw the sweeping pattern of red light play across her bedroom ceiling.

The glance Agent Wheeler gave her could have contained pity, except she didn't think he kept any in stock. He ignored the commotion outside long enough to snap the second chain.

Too desperate even to stop and thank him, she wrapped herself in the bedcover and shuffled to the en suite, almost tripping in her haste.

She emerged a few minutes later in her oversize white terry robe with the belt knotted tightly around her waist. She crept to the window and peeked out. The FBI man was there, talking with a local police officer in uniform. Both leaned against a squad car, as casual as could be. She heard male laughter and then, with a slap on the back, Agent Wheeler sent the uniformed officer on his way and headed back up her front path.

She grabbed panties out of her drawer and hauled them on under the fluffy robe. The handcuffs were still around her wrists, the severed chains hanging down a few inches. She pulled the terry-towel sleeves over them and took a deep breath.

She hazarded a glance in the mirror above her dressing table and wondered again just what the hell she'd thought she was doing acting out a torrid sexual fantasy. She was boring and dull Cynthia Baxter—an accountant, for God's sake.

She sighed, pulling a brush through her nondescript midlength, midcolor hair. Hours earlier, it had looked pretty good in big soft curls courtesy of her hot rollers. But all that thrashing against the pillows had turned her sexy do into a cross between Audrey Hepburn in *Breakfast at Tiffany's* and David Bowie as Ziggy Stardust.

"Why did you do it?" she wailed to her own reflection as she dragged the brush through another snarl. But she knew. She was staging an adolescent rebellion fifteen years too late.

She was exactly what her parents had wanted her to be—except for her unmarried state. "You'll be left on the shelf, dear, if you leave it much longer," her mother used to predict. It had made her feel like stale peanut butter. As if Cynthia could magically make men find a mousy, old-fashioned girl attractive.

Surprisingly enough, Walter did. Or maybe it was a case of one stale-dated jar of peanut butter gravitating to another. He wasn't much to look at, but he was male, and single, and a doctor. Her mother was delighted, and Cynthia hoped she might at last experience some of the physical pleasures she'd read about at night in secret.

Sex with Walter was like a Pap test, only not as much fun.

She wondered if his being a gynecologist was the problem: he got the two mixed up.

They'd been engaged for six years. It salved her conscience, and her mother's. Not that she'd ever spent an entire night at Walter's, of course, but the unexplained hours didn't have to be explained.

Cynthia hadn't imagined how lonely she'd feel when her mother died. Or that within the year this jumpy kind of panic would set in, as though her youth was slipping through her fingers. She'd imagined her life in bright colors, not this uniform gray. There had to be something wild and unpredictable she could do. She decided to start in the bedroom. In private.

Nowhere in her fantasy had she imagined having to be rescued by an FBI agent.

She hadn't been this mortified since sixth grade, when Daniel Prewitt asked her, in front of the whole class, if she wanted a stiffy, and she'd thought he'd asked her if she wanted a Slurpee and said yes.

Face it. You were born to be a boring accountant married to Dr. Dull. Her career as a femme fatale was definitely over.

Her makeup looked garish in the mirror, and she remembered in horror that she'd rouged her nipples like the magazine suggested. She hoped to heaven FBI Agent Wheeler hadn't noticed.

She remembered the way that cold, hard gaze had just flicked over her without any hint of emotion. Her naked body hadn't kindled the fires of lust in him any more than it had in Walter.

She could have spray painted the Stars and Stripes across her chest and it wouldn't have raised his flagpole.

Being found handcuffed naked to a bed by a strange man was bad enough. To be in that predicament and leave him unmoved... No, wait a minute. She remembered the flicker of humor that had flashed in his eyes when he found out it wasn't a criminal act but a sex thing. He hadn't been unmoved at all. He'd been amused.

Her naked body struck him as funny.

She wanted to die.

But first she had to get rid of the FBI.

He was sitting in the living room. Her living room. Completely at odds with the antique furniture and her mother's collection of Hummel figurines.

"Sit down," he commanded. There was no sign of the gun, but just knowing he had it on him somewhere gave her a fluttery feeling in her stomach.

She sat.

Polite as always, she remembered to thank him. "Thank you for..." She cleared her throat. "Releasing me."

He gazed at her for a long moment. "What's going on?" he finally asked.

"I beg your pardon?" *Could this day get any worse?*

"I don't have time to play games. Whose house is this?"

"Mine."

He snorted. "Look, honey, I sent the cops home. You're a hooker who makes house calls. Fine with me. I'm not the vice squad. I just want to clarify the situation before I escort you out the door."

Her mouth dropped open and the first ray of sunlight brightened the worst day of her life.

"You think I'm a prostitute?" He believed men would *pay* to have sex with her?

He sent her the kind of look she imagined an FBI guy would give a hooker. She might even have played along with the idea except for the part where he was planning to lock her out of her own house. "I'm not—"

"Save it. Where's the john?"

"Down the hall to your left," she answered primly.

He chuckled. "You're good, you know that? If I hadn't given up the wild stuff..." His gaze wandered her body lazily, and she had her second pleasant shock of the day. Back when he used to be wild, he might have paid to have sex with her. "Where's the guy?"

Belatedly she realized he had used the term "john" as in paying customer, not bathroom. "He was called away. To deliver a baby, I imagine."

"What?"

"Walter's an OB-GYN. I'm assuming he had to attend a birth. This really is my house."

He shot her a skeptical glance. "And you can prove this?"

"The lady next door knew my voice."

"She's half-deaf. She heard a woman's voice. You'll have to do better than that."

With a sigh, Cynthia said, "I'll get my driver's license."

She strode to the bedroom to get her purse, and he dogged her footsteps. "Do you mind?" she asked in annoyance.

"Don't want you hijacking the family silver."

With an irritated huff, she grabbed her black leather purse and fished out her driver's license. "There."

He glanced down at it. "This isn't you."

"Of course it is."

He took the plastic folder from her hands and looked more carefully—at her, then at the photograph on her license. "You should get that picture updated," he said.

The photo was less than a year old. It was the *Raunch* version of her that was different. And once you took Walter Plinkney's admittedly disappointing reaction out of the equation, she quite liked the *Raunch* version. It made a dangerous, gun-toting FBI agent talk about sex and her in the same breath.

At that moment she vowed to keep some part of her *Raunch* look. Not the rouged nipples, probably, but, well, part of it.

"Hold out your hands."

"This is my house. Stop ordering me around." She stuck her hands behind her back. Once she got the remnants of the handcuffs removed, no man was going to touch her hands for a very long time.

He plucked a pair of keys out of his pocket and dangled them in front of her. "I found them in the candy dish."

With a relieved sigh, she gave him her hands.

Swiftly, he unlocked first one cuff, then the other. While he worked, he asked, "If you're not a hooker, what do you do? For a job, I mean," he amended hastily.

Well, it was nice while it lasted, she thought. "I'm an accountant." She watched him from under her lashes, waiting for his eyes to glaze over in boredom.

Instead, she got a curious reaction. He blinked slowly and stared at her, hard. "You're putting me on."

"I'm serious. No one lies about being in accounting."

"An accountant. That's fantastic!"

No one, but no one, got excited about accounting except for one reason. Her mind fogged over with depression. "Don't tell me, you have a thorny tax problem you'd like me to solve?"

"No, not at all. Let's sit down. Why don't you tell me about yourself."

"You can't be serious." She pulled the terry robe

tighter around herself, and was reminded she had nothing on underneath but mint-green cotton panties.

"I guess I should have introduced myself properly." He shot her a killer grin, one that completely transformed him from scary law enforcer to incredibly attractive man. "I'm Jake Wheeler. I just moved into the neighborhood."

"Cynthia Baxter." She shook his hand automatically, while cold dread filled her. "Did you say you were a neighbor?" He'd seen her naked; now he was going to say "hi" over the fence? She'd bump into him on garbage day and at the Fourth of July neighborhood barbecue.

She felt like she needed to stick her head between her legs to stop from fainting with horror.

2

CYNTHIA BAXTER was the answer to his prayers. A sexual wildcat with a head for numbers.

Jake wanted to stand up and cheer. Making himself slow down, he vowed to check her out thoroughly, but he had a feeling Mrs. Lawrence and her daisy-watering dog had done him a huge favor when they'd recruited him to help one of his new neighbors.

He was getting absolutely nowhere on the Oceanic investigation. No chance of getting an agent inside; Neville Percivald was too smart and too careful.

In spite of his sissy-boy name, old Neville had a fondness for wild women. It was the only exploitable weakness Jake's relentless research had uncovered. Percivald had been followed to a couple of underground clubs that catered to the leather and whips set. If Jake could trust her, and get her inside Oceanic, Ms. Baxter might just be able to find the evidence he needed to launch a full investigation.

Jake had a hunch Neville and Cynthia would go together like leather and studs.

"Where do you work?"

"A cement company."

"Really?" He led the way back into her living room, away from the distracting scent of heavy perfume and the sight of that bed, which reminded him of her trim little body naked and ready... He cleared his throat. "How long have you worked there?"

"Nine years. Do you have to fill out a report on me or something?"

"No," he reassured her, "I'm just being neighborly."

Cynthia Baxter wasn't a cop or an agent. She'd worked at the same job for almost a decade, as an accountant. And they just happened to be short one accountant at Oceanic Import-Export. Cynthia was perfect; not only was she qualified for the job, but, if his hunch was correct, she'd check out cleaner than the laundry waving on Mrs. Lawrence's line.

And to debrief her after work each night, all he had to do was jump a couple of fences.

"How long have you worked at the FBI?" She sounded like a society hostess, but he heard the snotty undertone. She wouldn't intimidate easily. Good.

"Twelve years. Guess we're both heading for a gold watch, huh?" If she really loved her job at the cement company, they might be able to work something out, but the fewer people who knew anything about his plan, the better. And it was a good plan. He was getting a feeling he'd finally caught a break.

If Cynthia landed the job at Oceanic, she'd be his own personal Mata Hari, working there by day and passing on what she heard to her new neighbor. It was so perfect he wanted to kiss her red, red hooker lips.

They were full and pouty under the not-so-subtle makeup job. If more accountants looked like her, no red-blooded male would ever get behind on his year-end tax return. Neville Percivald certainly wouldn't.

Excitement churned in Jake's gut. "May I call you Cynthia?"

She stared down at the driver's license still in her hand, then jerked her head up. "You can call me Cyn! Cyn's my name and sin's my game."

He chuckled softly. It just got better and better. If he hadn't sworn off her kind of woman, he could go for her himself. Something about the way her trashy looks were so at odds with the innocent expression in her wide-spaced, green eyes...

A devastating combination, all right. But, Jake reminded himself firmly, Neville Percivald was the one who was going to end up tied in knots over her.

Not him.

CYNTHIA ENTERED the swooshing glass door of Très Chic! feeling like a bag lady at a Parisian catwalk. Her bemused gaze caught leather, lots of leather, faux animal prints, patterned boots and clothing she couldn't even identify.

She was chewing on her thumb, ready to bolt, when a young woman strode up. Her jet-black hair had a dramatic white streak in the bangs and she wore skintight leather pants with a cowboy kind of fringe on the bottom, a slinky orange top and what looked like go-go boots. "Can I help you?" she asked in a tone that suggested Cynthia was way beyond help.

She took a deep breath. "Yes. Yes you can." She glanced helplessly down at her tweed suit and sensible pumps and stated the obvious. "I need a miracle."

"You looking to update your image?" The girl appeared doubtful she could pull it off. "Looks like whatever catalog you shop from's out-of-date." The girl glanced past her out the window, doubtfully. "You might try—"

"I've been living in Moscow."

"Huh?"

The girl had been going to throw her out of Très Chic!, and Cynthia would never have the nerve to come in here again. It was now or never. Desperation lent her ingenuity. "In Russia?" She shrugged. "I've been living there for the last ten years, as a—as a secretary in the American embassy." She gestured to her suit. "This was all I could get, and I had to trade three cartons of Marlboroughs just for the skirt."

"Shoulda hung on to the smokes," the girl muttered.

"I missed the American fashion—uh—scene so much!" Cynthia gushed. "In Moscow, they think Prada is a car!" She laughed at her own joke, gaily.

The girl gazed at her blankly.

"You know, like Lada?" She imagined Muscovites were ten times as fashionable as she, but her ploy seemed to be working. The girl had stopped gazing down the street, looking for another store to pawn her off on.

"That's tough. I've seen those fur hats on TV, and they're like..." She grimaced. "So, how do you want to look?"

Cynthia took a deep breath. "Sexy."

The girl chuckled and eyed her more carefully before nodding slowly. "Sexy's my specialty. Come on."

Two hours and a whole lot of bags later, Cynthia's credit card carried a hefty balance and she owned leather, faux animal skin, boots, bags, costume jewelry. The works.

She was still wearing the last outfit she'd tried on, a tight paisley skirt and a little white cotton shirt that looked to her like underwear. On her feet were chunky black shoes.

"You look awesome," the girl assured her.

"Would you do me a favor?"

"Sure."

"Pass me that garbage can." Cynthia thrust the two-piece tweed suit and the color coordinated blouse in the wastepaper basket and dusted off her hands briskly, as though she could trash all her dowdiness at once. "Thanks, I needed that. After I'm gone will you take that out and donate it to charity?"

The girl laughed. "You got it. Come in anytime for advice. You look great, you know? Once you get your hair cut—"

"Hair cut?"

"I just assumed...um, I'm sure they cut hair real good in Moscow, it's just that here, styles have changed a bit in the last ten years."

Cynthia put a hand to her chin-length bob. "Oh, of course."

"I know a great stylist. Michael. He's a genius with hair." She dug out a dog-eared card for a place called Ecstasy. "Put yourself in Michael's hands. He's the best. And..." The girl paused, looking anxious. "I hope you don't mind me saying this, but if you're going for the complete new look...?"

"Oh, I am."

"Those glasses just scream eighties."

"The glasses, of course. Thank you. Um, anything else?"

She shook her head. "You make sure and come back when you're all done. I bet I won't even recognize you myself."

Since Cynthia was a big believer in never putting off till tomorrow what you could do today, she immediately went home and made appointments, with her eye doctor and, after a good talking-to about taking risks, with

Michael at Ecstasy. She just hoped she didn't come out of the salon with black-and-white hair. She wanted to look different, but not like Cruella DeVil.

Michael turned out to be a flamboyant trivia buff with a passion for tropical fish. After putting herself in his hands, Cynthia forgot to watch what he was doing as she tried to keep up with his conversation.

"My God, what did those Russians do to you?" he gasped, as he turned her this way and that in the mirror. "This is enough to restart the Cold War!"

She grinned weakly.

After she'd been shampooed and returned to his chair, Michael picked up a pair of scissors and started snipping. "Julia says you used to live in Moscow."

Cynthia made a noncommittal noise.

"You know, ten years in Russia has probably faded your hair color. I'm sure it wasn't always this mousy."

"No," she agreed with a straight face. "It used to be much nicer."

"I'll give it a rinse. Kind of mahogany with a touch of burgundy in it. How does that sound?"

Anything that wasn't in zebra tones sounded good to her.

When at last he was done, she could barely believe it. Her hair was wild, young. It had spiky bits, but an overall softness. "I love it!" she cried.

The stylist nodded. "I went with Sex-and-the-City hip, not I'm-an-MTV-music-awards-presenter hip. I think it works."

"I think so, too." She giggled happily, tugging at a mahogany-with-a-touch-of-burgundy spiky bit. "I definitely think so."

"Got a hot date tonight?"

She had a date with Walter, but as to the heat level...

She forced herself to be optimistic. She'd surprised him with the magazine; maybe she should have updated her appearance first.

"I don't know. But I hope so."

"WHAT HAVE YOU DONE to your hair?" Walter's eyes bugged out when she opened the door to him.

Her smile faded slowly. "Don't you like it?"

"It's red. It's too young for you. It's—it's..." Although he couldn't seem to find the words, the horrified expression on his face sent a clear message.

She turned away, stalked into the living room and began rearranging the Hummel figures, putting Fishing Boy beside Choir Girl instead of beside Hiking Boy where he belonged. Let anarchy reign, she decided. Better still, she should pack the little pottery figurines away in a box and redecorate—entirely in animal prints and edgy avant-garde sculptures.

But the Hummels had been her mother's, and Cynthia was sentimental. With a sigh, she put Fishing Boy back beside Hiking Boy and snapped on a lamp.

All her life, except when she'd been away at college, Cynthia had lived in this house—first as a child, then after her mother was widowed. Maybe she just needed a change.

Walter stood warily at the edge of the British India rug, obviously uncertain how to handle her. A worried frown played around his eyes.

How well he fit into this room, she thought. An old-fashioned man in an old-fashioned room. He probably had no idea his tie was too narrow, or that he'd been wearing that sweater so long it was almost back in style.

She used to belong in this room, too. Now she no longer did. In fact, for a while she hadn't felt like she fit into her own body. But in the last week, despite the ghastly disaster of the sex thing, she felt like she was starting to get it right.

She hadn't seen Walter since Friday, when he'd left her naked, tied up and forgotten. Oh, he'd called later that night, sounding tired and harassed. The delivery had been difficult. He was sorry he'd had to leave. He was doing hospital rounds for the next few evenings, but why didn't they have dinner at her house Tuesday?

Cynthia thought about the mother and baby; she was glad they'd survived and Walter had made it happen. She forgave him, of course, but still felt he should grovel a bit after what she'd been through.

Now here he stood. No flowers, no apology, no wine. Not even an invitation to a restaurant. As usual, she was cooking dinner for Dr. Tightwad. If he'd come across the room, take her in his arms and whisk her off to bed, she'd forgive him completely.

She glanced toward him with what she hoped was a sultry, come-hither look.

He rubbed his hands together with enthusiasm. "Is that pot roast I smell? I'm starved."

Her mother, who'd been over forty when her only child was born, had a rule about controversy at the dinner table: it was bad for the digestion, bad manners, bad, bad, bad. So Cynthia, who had spent her entire life until last Friday being good, made polite conversation while inside she was more stewed than the pot roast.

She did the dishes while Walter read the paper. After the dishes were finished, she made coffee and they drank it in the living room like a normal pair of seventy-year-olds.

She gazed down at the cup and saucer in her hand. Red cabbage roses covered the china, faded after thirty years to old-bathrobe pink. Cynthia made a discovery. She didn't like the china.

Not only was she drinking out of her mother's china, she was living her mother's life. Only she'd skipped the part about being young, and morphed right into advanced middle age.

The cup began rattling on the matching saucer, like frenetic castanets. The body-hugging little top felt a couple of sizes too small. She couldn't seem to get her breath.

Across the room newspaper rustled as Walter turned a page.

A scream built in her throat. It was a year since her mother had died. And Cynthia had this sudden *Twilight Zone* vision of herself returning from the funeral service to *become* her mother.

She'd loved her mother. And her father. But somehow she'd lost herself, and she had to do something to get back on track. Maybe it wasn't Walter and her sex life that was the problem.

Maybe it was this house.

"I'm thinking about selling the house." She said it aloud, rolling the idea in her head as the words rolled off her tongue.

"Hmm?" The paper rustled again as Walter neatly folded it in quarters and placed it on the table beside him.

"I'm thinking about selling the house."

After staring at her blankly for a moment, Walter smiled. She recognized that smile. It was the patronizing don't-worry-everything-will-be-all-right-I'm-a-doctor smile that always made her want to smack him. "That's perfectly normal."

"Pardon?" Maybe she hadn't heard him correctly.

He rose and crossed the room to settle beside her on the gold damask couch. He gazed right into her eyes and spoke soothingly. "You're a woman in a delicate stage of her life. You're approaching your mid-thirties—"

"I'm thirty-one!"

He carried on as though she hadn't spoken. "Your biological clock's ticking." He brushed his finger across her nose as though she were a fretful child. "I think we should move up the wedding date."

The tightness in her chest was becoming a burning. "Why?"

He patted her knee. He actually patted her knee. "You're acting out, exhibiting behavior that's out of character. I think you're sending me a pretty clear message."

"Stop talking to me like I'm a postpartum patient. I'm your fiancée." And where were the words of love she equated with choosing a mate? The romantic gestures, the sex?!

"I just want to help you, guide you."

Control me, she thought, and the burning intensified.

He took her left hand, where a tiny diamond gleamed weakly. She'd tried to convince herself the ring was tasteful, but really it was just cheap. "I could make some room in my schedule in April. We could get married then." He glanced at her head doubtfully. "Will your hair have grown back?"

Maybe she wasn't being fair. For him, deciding on a wedding date a mere seven months away was being spontaneous. She tried to kindle a little enthusiasm. "We could take some of the money I get from the house and go on a really great honeymoon."

He gave her that smile again. "Do you have any idea

how property values are rising in this neighborhood? We're only forty-five minutes outside Seattle. The house is close to my practice and your job. It's a wonderful place to raise a family. After we're married you'll settle down."

Their clasped hands were starting to sweat. Visions of Venice and Aruba faded. "What about our honeymoon?"

"It's already arranged. I'm swapping Myron Slavinsky an extra week of hospital rounds for a week at his time-share in Palm Desert."

"Practicing your golf game for your retirement?" She pasted on a phony jovial smile. The burning was so bad she gasped. Maybe she was having a panic attack.

He pushed his glasses back on his nose. "Golf is growing in popularity with younger people, too. You'd be surprised."

She pulled her hand away. "I can't do it, Walter." Funny how calm she felt now she'd made her decision. If she married Walter, she wouldn't just be settling, she'd be sinking to subterranean depths. She'd be buried alive. No wonder she couldn't breathe.

"But Myron says the course is very good. And anyone staying in the time-share gets a discount on the golfing."

"Then maybe you and Myron should go, since you both like to golf and I hate it." The burning was spreading, from her chest to her whole body. Kind of like a heart attack, she supposed, except instead of blocking, her arteries felt like they were unclogging. New life pumped through her veins. She jumped up.

"Since when do you—"

"Since always. I've always hated golf. And bridge.

Only you never listened to me. I think you should listen now, and listen carefully. I'm not marrying you, Walter. It would be a disaster."

To her absolute fury, his patronizing smile didn't falter. "You're upset, irrational."

"I'm angry!" And she was, angrier than she'd ever been. She stalked across the living-room carpet, energized by her fury. She felt sharp, as if all the fuzzy edges of her brain had burned clean. "I'm so angry I want to throw things, swear, have sex with a stranger."

Walter cleared his throat. "It keeps coming back to intercourse, I see. I don't want to hurt you, Cynthia, but perhaps I could arrange for you to speak with one of my colleagues who, um, understands these stages women go through—before you do something you regret."

Her pacing stalled for a moment. "Talk to a colleague? You mean a psychiatrist?"

"There's no need to use that tone. It's perfectly all right to seek professional help when you're feeling confused, and acting...different."

"Don't you see, I'm not different. This is the real me. I've only just realized it. And I've also realized we'd be terrible together, Walter. I—I want different things. Excitement, romance, travel. I don't want to spend my thirties saving for retirement."

She'd hit him where he lived, she knew. The man was obsessed with money and security. She had a hunch it was her accounting background that had first attracted him to her.

He looked lost for a moment, sitting there staring at her. "Don't do anything rash. Take a week or so to think things over and we'll talk again." He gazed at her, looking truly troubled, and for a moment she thought maybe he did love her after all. Then he said, "Promise me you won't put this house on the market."

"Goodbye, Walter."

After he left, Cynthia felt as if she'd come out of a tunnel into fresh air. She was bursting with the need to get started on her new life.

No wonder the FBI agent hadn't believed this was her house. It didn't reflect her personality at all. The Hummels stared at her from their big-lashed innocent eyes, as though anticipating their doom. "Sorry, guys," she said. "You're the first to go."

She ran down to the basement and collected a few boxes and mounds of tissue, then ran back up to the living room. She wrapped each little figure carefully before stowing it in the box. Aunt Lois, her mom's younger sister, would love them.

Cynthia packed up the cabbage rose china, the hand-crocheted doilies, the pinwheel crystal and her mood rose. Music, she needed music.

She put on Shania Twain, bounced, bumped and swayed as she worked, and reminded herself to feel like a woman. A woman in charge of her life.

After Cynthia finished in the living room she had four boxes neatly packed and labeled.

Next she hit her bedroom. Ruthlessly she dragged out every suit more than twenty-four months old, and a few that were newer. If her colleagues at the cement company didn't like her new image, that was their problem. She gazed at the stifling array of suits, which had most likely been designed for middle-aged women. She must have been crazy to have bought them. She chucked the works in a big green garbage bag to be donated to charity.

She dragged the bulging bag into the living room to

join the boxes. She was just wondering whether she had enough energy to haul it out to her hatchback when the doorbell rang.

Her lips thinned. She'd made Walter return her house key before he left—she glanced at her watch—less than two hours ago. He'd been smugly certain she'd change her mind and resume their engagement, but did he really think she was going to change it in two hours?

It wouldn't take her two minutes to set him straight.

She marched to the door and flung it open.

Jake Wheeler stood there, all he-man tough and semi-dangerous, lounging in her doorway, a quizzical expression on his face. "You should have checked through your peephole first," he said by way of a greeting.

"How do you know I didn't?"

"Your jaw's hanging open. Either you have an advanced case of lockjaw or you're surprised to see me. I'm guessing you get a regular tetanus shot."

It flashed through her mind, as she took in the blue, blue eyes and the black hair, the craggy face and the body, that he could have been a model for *Raunch Magazine*'s fantasy issue.

Even as the thought germinated, a blush began on her cheeks and spread. This man had seen her naked. She shut her mouth with a snap. "You're right. I wasn't expecting you."

"I like the hair."

"You do?" The color probably matched the full-body blush.

He chuckled. He had a very attractive chuckle. "Let me guess—you change your hair color as often as you change your men."

She laughed back, realizing it was absolutely true.

She'd colored her hair once and dumped her first boyfriend. In only thirty-one years. "You've got me pegged."

"You going to invite me in or are you already entertaining?"

"Oh, I'm sorry. Of course. Come in." She stepped back, and he walked into her house and straight into the living room, where he jerked to a stop.

"You're not moving, are you?" He sounded almost panicked.

"I'm thinking about it. No. I'm finished thinking. I've decided. I'm moving. Yes. Yes I am."

"But this is a great neighborhood, safe, stable, a—"

"Great place to raise a family? I know. I was raised in this house." She sighed. "I just need a change, that's all."

"So redecorate. It's a lot easier."

"You sound like Walter."

His eyes crinkled. "The doctor who makes house calls? I get the impression that's not good."

Why would he care if she moved? He wasn't planning to arrest her or something—was he? It hadn't been illegal, what she'd done. Criminally embarrassing, yes, but surely she and Walter were old enough to…to what? They hadn't even got started. She crossed her arms over her chest as she shook her head. "I'd rather move."

"Look. If it's about me seeing you naked, I barely peeked."

The hot sweat of embarrassment prickled her neck and underarms. "What exactly do you want?"

"Just being neighborly."

"You're new to the neighborhood. *I'm* supposed to call on *you.*"

"I've been waiting for you to show up at my door

with a Bundt cake. I was getting lonely." He rubbed his stomach. "And hungry."

In spite of herself she had to smile. When he wasn't scaring her, he had an odd sort of charm. "I'm all out of cake, but I do have some double-chocolate ice cream in the freezer."

"Sold."

When she returned with two bowls of ice cream, she found him relaxed on the gold damask couch, staring down at a single Hummel figurine. The little girl feeding birds looked absurdly small and frail in his big hands. "What happened to all her buddies?"

Cynthia pointed to the neatly labeled box.

A glimmer of amusement threaded his voice. "How come she's missing the party?"

A shaft of guilt shot through her. "Mother bought that one when I was a child. She said she reminded her of me. I didn't have the heart to get rid of her."

He gazed at Cynthia consideringly. "I wouldn't have pegged you as the sentimental type." He placed the little figure back on the antique piecrust table beside the sofa and accepted the bowl of ice cream. "Please don't leave the neighborhood."

"Why would you care?"

"You're the only other person around here who's both single and not collecting social security."

Her heart rate increased. He'd mentioned they were both single and that he didn't want her to move. Could a gorgeous guy like this be interested in *her?* She gazed at the stunning tough-guy. No. He must have an accounting problem.

"It is mostly young families and older people," she said. "Why did you move here? There are plenty of condos downtown. That's where the single people live.

That's where I'm moving." She stuck her chin out a little, just so he'd know she could fit in just fine in a swinging condo block.

"I moved here because I hate living in a concrete cube. I like the character of these homes. I bought mine from my great-aunt when she moved into a nursing home."

"Moved into a nursing home...Mrs. Jorgensen is your aunt?"

He nodded.

"But she lived only two doors down. Beside Mrs. Lawrence."

He nodded again, as if he were enjoying a private joke.

"You won't tell her...please don't tell either of them..."

"That I found you buck naked, chained to your own bed?" He chuckled, a richly evil sound. "I don't want to send either of them to the ER, so don't worry."

Her hands trembled as she realized how truly ghastly that experience had been. Every time she saw Agent Wheeler she'd be reminded of how they'd met. "I'm definitely moving."

"You'd hate a condo after all this space." He glanced around the living room. "You just need to re-decorate. I'll help. I could be your own personal painter."

"Just what I need. A nosy guy in overalls to come home to. Anyway, I thought you already had a job. Or was that FBI badge fake?"

"No. It wasn't fake." Suddenly his face grew serious, and she recognized the man who'd terrified her when he'd burst into her bedroom with a gun. He put down his ice cream and leaned forward, hands clasped loosely between his knees. "All right. I'm not just being neighborly."

For some reason, goose bumps danced up her spine.

"I need your help, Cynthia. The government needs your help."

"What?" Her eyes widened, and her heart began to pound. She'd feel just the same if a guy from the Internal Revenue Service sat here and said, "It's about your taxes."

"You could be instrumental in helping the FBI crack a drug smuggling operation."

"Drugs?" Her voice rose. "In this neighborhood? The only drugs you'll find around here are blood pressure and bladder control medication. Hardly illegal. But very funny, hah hah." Jerk. He'd got her all scared for nothing. She scooped up a spoon of melting ice cream and let the delicious flavor soothe her.

"It's not in this neighborhood." He hadn't cracked a smile, so maybe he wasn't joking after all.

Jake didn't know how to approach this. He'd checked Cynthia Baxter out. She might be a sexual adventurer, but she'd never been arrested. She was a certified accountant who had indeed been with the same employer her whole working life. His original hunch was bang on the money. She was perfect. She was the rosy answer to a thorny problem and she lived two doors down. Now he just had to convince her to quit her job of nine years, take a new one and spy on her boss.

He had to figure out what would tempt her. He stood and began to pace while she watched him, her hair gleaming like old copper.

Everybody had a hot button. Money? Danger? Excitement? Patriotism?

What was hers?

Her big green eyes were huge in the lamplight, and somehow guileless. Must be a big turn-on to guys that a woman so innocent looking went for the kinky stuff in bed. He swallowed a mental image of her naked and helpless, the way he'd first seen her, lying there like an open invitation.

Except he didn't attend those kind of parties anymore. Not since he'd walked in on his wildly exciting girlfriend getting wildly excited with two other men and another woman. She was his ex-girlfriend now.

Cynthia Baxter reminded him of his ex. It wasn't so much the kinky stuff that put him off, it was the revolving door to the bedroom. He was already the second man through Cynthia's door tonight. Who knew how many were on their way? He paced. "I saw your boyfriend leave earlier."

Her lips pinched. "He's not my boyfriend."

"Why am I not surprised?" *Chew them up and spit them out like grapes. She probably ate them in bunches, too.*

She gasped. "Walter's not involved in some kind of drug thing, is he?" She answered her own question even as Jake shook his head. "No. Not Walter."

He had to forget the way she intrigued him, one minute sexy as a centerfold, the next as innocent as one of those damned big-eyed pottery figurines. It didn't matter what she did in the privacy of her own bedroom, so long as she didn't do it with him.

How to reach her. She didn't need money. He'd done his homework and knew that, in addition to this house, she'd inherited a nice chunk of change from the folks, had no siblings to split it with, and had managed to accumulate a pretty impressive portfolio of her own.

His eyes scanned the room, which resembled a half-dressed woman with so much of the stuff packed away. She hadn't touched the bookshelf, though. A full set of leather-bound matching classics that must be from some club were mixed in with books of poetry, modern novels, a few paperbacks and a line of glossy hardcovers as new as her hair color.

He moved closer and squinted: *Me, Myself and I, Flying Solo and Loving It,* was shelved next to *Time for a Change!* and *Be the Change You Want to See Happen.* Hello! Apart from supporting an entire industry of smarmy pseudo-shrinks, she was sending a definite message here.

Change. The woman was looking for change. He couldn't figure out why she hadn't quit her job in nine years when she'd obviously changed her hair color and men more often than he changed his razor blades.

She wanted change and he was the man to give it to her. "I want to offer you a job."

"The FBI needs another accountant?" She licked the last of the ice cream off her lips, her pink tongue teasing the glossy copper lipstick. No wonder they called her Cyn.

His own lips felt dry. "It's undercover work. Very hush-hush." The James Bond script people would be embarrassed to use a line like that, but it brought a gleam of excitement to her eyes and she jumped up to face him.

"Undercover?"

He was going with his gut, but it sure seemed like he'd punched the right button. He nodded gravely, glanced around as though her house might be bugged, and dropped his voice. "Top secret. You'd be on a need-to-know basis."

He could have been 007 himself the way she was

staring at him with rapt attention. "What do I need to know?"

"We're watching an import-export company. We believe they're a link in a worldwide drug smuggling operation, but we've had no luck putting an agent in place inside. One of their accountants recently left the firm, then hopped a plane to Hong Kong before we could get to him." Jake experienced again the frustration he'd felt when Harrison had slipped through their fingers. "So I know there's a vacancy in the accounting department."

Some of the sparkle had dimmed from her eyes. "You're asking me to be an accountant? That doesn't sound very exciting."

"Ninety percent of undercover work is mundane," he told her truthfully. "But you'll be able to see things, hear things. You'll be on the inside."

He'd had no luck at all infiltrating the shipping and receiving end of the company, where he was certain the action was. But they sure as hell wouldn't be expecting a plant in the front-office staff. And when they checked Cynthia Baxter out, they'd discover just what he had. She was an experienced accountant with no links to any kind of law enforcement. Lived alone, nice quiet life on the surface. No criminal activities that could bring attention to her. Her bedroom was a fun-house with a revolving door. With any luck, she'd take Neville Percivald for a ride and get him talking. She was perfect.

Her job would be dull, dull, dull. But, Jake thought, salving his conscience, it couldn't be any more dull than her current job with the cement company.

"When the action heats up, you'll be there, right in the thick of things." In a pig's ear. Long before they made a move, he'd get her out. She'd be safely at home playing hide the salami with some beefcake if and when they had cause to move in on Oceanic.

"Will it be dangerous?"

His gut hadn't led him astray. She was falling hook, line and sinker. Her eyes shone with expectation.

Her new job would be about as dangerous as night watchman in a nursing home. "Very dangerous."

Her breathing quickened, sounding like a woman becoming sexually aroused. His body responded to her even as his mind told him to keep his mind on work. No way was he going to get a thing going with the neighborhood nympho. He just wished his brain and his johnson had the same taste in women.

"What do I have to do?"

3

"BE YOURSELF." If ever she'd received a worthless piece of advice, Jake's parting words were it. "Herself" was a dull woman with mousy hair and no life, who'd been balancing the books at a cement company for nine years.

The woman walking toward Oceanic Import-Export was the artificial creation of Michael at the hair salon, the woman at the funky clothing store and the optometrist who'd fitted her with contacts.

Cynthia was wearing the most conservative suit in her new wardrobe, a tight-fitting short black wool jacket and knee-length skirt with a pair of black leather boots. Though nobody knew it but her, the boots were lined with faux leopard skin, which boosted her confidence. The jacket had a faux fur collar, but she'd removed it before the interview, not wanting to appear too stylish.

As she clacked along the pavement in her snazzy new boots, she rehearsed what she'd say at the job interview.

Jake had laughed at her when she'd tried to practice on him. "You're not pretending to be somebody else, you know. Just tell the truth."

Hah. Little did he know. She was living a huge lie, pretending to be fashionable and exciting.

She smelled the smog of a million cars, mixed in with the briny scent of the harbor. The downtown noises hammered at her senses: a bus wheezing as it pulled away from the curb, the honk of an impatient motorist, some kind of generator, and hammering and male voices from a construction site.

A long, appreciative wolf whistle rolled over her, and she glanced around, then realized she was the only one in front of the construction site. Startled, she glanced up. "Lookin' good, babe!" yelled a burly man in a plaid shirt and hard hat.

"Thank you," she said politely, smiling back with real gratitude. The butterflies in her stomach settled. Why shouldn't she get this job or any other job she wanted? She was the new, improved, better than ever Cynthia—make that Cyn—Baxter, full-time CPA, part-time spy.

All she had to do was land a job she could do with her eyes closed.

The den of iniquity, as she'd taken to calling it in her head, had wide double glass doors and a welcoming foyer in marble and granite. Behind the imposing front entrance, the statuesque receptionist led Cynthia down a carpeted corridor to a small boardroom. Cynthia blinked twice at the woman. She looked like one of the models in *Raunch,* from the "Erotically Advanced" section.

On the short journey, Cynthia glanced right and left, but instead of seeing swarthy, pockmarked faces, arsenals of weapons and hastily secured bags of white powder, she saw the same kind of people she'd seen at her last job. They worked on computers, talked on phones, made notes. Nothing remotely sinister.

Unaccountably disappointed, she entered the boardroom.

In it were three men. The middle one smiled politely and rose to extend his hand. Somewhere in his early forties, he had the kind of face that made her relax and smile back. He reminded her of an anchorman she'd seen on a Canadian TV station. Balding, blue-eyed, with the sincere look that suggested he cared about every one of the people injured in the train wreck he'd just described—only he was too much of a professional to let tears well in his eyes.

His handshake was firm and businesslike. No drug-induced tremors, no red haze in the clear blue eyes.

"I'm Neville Percivald," he informed her in an accent that was half-British, with the vowels rounded as though he'd lived for some time on this side of the Atlantic. "These are my associates, Doug Ormond and Lester Dart."

The flunkies gave her hope. They looked awfully muscular for desk jockeys. Doug Ormond had hairy knuckles, she noted when he gripped her hand and grunted a greeting, and Lester Dart deserved the slammer on the grounds of his cologne.

She smiled politely and sat in the chair indicated.

They interviewed her extensively about her previous job. Most of the questions were routine, but every once in a while they threw in an odd one. They even asked if she knew a couple of people who'd never worked at Goring Cement.

Still, she remained polite, privately thinking they didn't have enough brains to run a successful criminal organization. She wondered how the legitimate one was doing, then reminded herself it didn't matter. Once she'd completed her undercover espionage, she could move on. The important thing was she'd made a break from her dull career and her dull life.

In fact, as soon as she wrapped this case up, she was

taking a vacation. She was going to buy a ticket for the first place that caught her fancy, and keep on going.

"Thank you, Miss Baxter. We'll be in touch," the TV anchorman type said. And his eyes telegraphed to her the message that no matter what happened, she'd be the one he'd have chosen if it were up to him.

"I CAN DO THIS. I am Cyn the Bold." But her hands had a death grip on the long roller. She couldn't quite make the move that would put the paint on the wall.

It looked so dark in the tin, a big purple puddle. And the antique white walls looked so... "Dull. You're dull, dull, dull," she muttered. A quick glance at the magazine picture she'd taped to the wall gave her courage. The color was claret, not purple.

The purple was already on the ceiling. When she looked up she felt like she was standing inside a gigantic grape.

Resolutely, she tore her gaze away, reminding herself she'd loved the magazine layout she was copying. Still, she let out a quiet shriek when the first slash of color hit the wall, looking like a blade had knifed the pale wall, making it bleed.

"I can always paint over it," she reminded herself as she gritted her teeth and kept rolling.

"Going for the grape Kool-Aid look?" a deep masculine voice taunted from behind her.

"Aaah!" Her nerveless hands dropped the roller, and it streaked downward until a dark shape hurtled past her. Jake Wheeler grabbed the roller and only a few dark drops hit the tarp that covered the floor.

"It's not grape Kool-Aid, it's claret. How did you get in?"

"Door was open."

"You could have knocked." She glanced at Jake and her mouth went dry. At a guess she'd say he'd been jogging. His navy T-shirt clung damply to the fascinating furrows and ridges of his chest and waist. Baggy running shorts showed off muscular thighs, knobby knees that made her smile, and a butt that made her put her hands in her pockets to keep them from temptation as he turned and bent forward to roll more paint onto the wall.

"I didn't want you to have to stop whatever you were doing to answer the door."

"How considerate." She had a couple of cutting remarks on the tip of her tongue, but the way he put paint on a wall was pure poetry. She stifled her snarkiness, rolled aching shoulders and let him get on with it. "Do you think it's too dark?"

"Too dark for what?"

She let her breath out in an exaggerated huff. "The paint. Do you think the paint's too dark?" She snapped the magazine photo off the wall and stuck it in front of his face. "This is what I want."

He stared at the photo for a minute, at the burgundy walls, aubergine ceiling and gold moldings. "Kind of 'old English pub meets Middle Eastern harem'?"

"Oh, never mind. Do you want some lemonade?"

"Sure."

While she dropped ice into tall glasses and poured lemonade, he yelled, "You know the ceiling doesn't match the walls."

She did a silent *Duh* and rolled her eyes. "It's supposed to be stylish."

"Whatever." Even without seeing him she'd bet he was rolling his own eyes.

"You're just the hired help," she said as she carried the drinks out.

"What's my wage again?" He placed the roller back in the tray and accepted the frosty glass. He gulped the drink back, and she took a moment to enjoy the way the strong muscles in his throat worked as he swallowed.

"In-for-mation." She let all the smugness she felt ooze into the single word.

That got his attention, all right. Ice rattled as he yanked the glass away from his mouth to stare at her. "You got the job?"

She allowed the smugness to come right out, and grinned at him. "Couple of hours ago."

In two strides he was right there in front of her. Even as her senses and nerves went haywire, trying to process the fact that he was invading her personal space, bringing the smell and look and feel of him, everything went into overload.

His mouth came down on hers so swiftly her lips parted on a gasp. She froze in shock, vaguely aware of chilled, lemon-flavored lips that hinted at the hot wet mouth beneath.

Her hands grasped his arms, whether to hold herself up or push him away, she couldn't have said. Under her fingers she felt the heated swell of muscle under a T-shirt still damp from his run. He smelled so... physical. Like sweat and whatever soap he'd showered with that morning, like paint and lemon. Like sex...

On the last thought, her body edged nearer, waiting for more. Wanting more.

But just as she leaned in, he broke the connection

with a shaky laugh. He lifted her and spun her dizzily around. "We're in!"

He set her down and took a gigantic step backward. If she didn't know better, she'd have sworn she made him nervous. If only.

He made *her* something, though. Not nervous, but excited. He might scare the pants off her from time to time, but ever since he'd come on the scene, her boring life seemed to have flipped on its head.

In the last week, she'd been made over top-to-toe, construction workers had ogled her and a man she barely knew had just kissed her. Not only had she changed her appearance, but she'd started changing her house and was about to change her job, plunging into the world of black ops, spies and danger.

A shiver slithered down her spine at the thought of danger. "Will I need a gun?"

He stopped, midway through a rollerful of paint, and shot a comic-terrified glance over his shoulder. "Just slap my face. I promise it won't happen again."

"I meant for the job." He was promising he wouldn't kiss her anymore. After just one little peck. Her self-confidence took a sudden nosedive. It looked as if she hadn't changed much after all.

That little peck had been the most exciting thing she'd ever experienced, and he was promising never to do it again.

She didn't want him to keep that promise. She really, really wanted him to kiss her again.

That and more.

"Have you ever used a gun?" he asked.

"Does an air rifle in Girl Scouts count?"

"Nope." He didn't pause, just kept that smooth rolling motion going. The paint slid onto her walls like rich satin sheets onto a white mattress.

"Everybody who goes undercover in books and movies carries a gun," she argued. She pictured hers now, a ladylike revolver that would fit nicely into her purse, preferably something with a pearl handle.

"No. Everybody does not. If they find a gun on you you're toast." He glanced back over his shoulder at her. "Don't pout. You have much deadlier weapons."

"Like what? My fingernails are soft, I could never stab someone with the office scissors and my karate skills are nonexistent."

He plopped the roller back into the tray and turned to her, pointing to her head. "Your intelligence is your greatest asset."

"Oh, that's exciting. We're going to have crossword puzzle contests to see who wins?" She put on a TV announcer voice and said, "Ooh, sorry. You missed 14 across, the eight-letter word for bad guy, beginning with the letter *C*. That makes the FBI this week's winner in the drug wars!"

Amusement danced in his eyes. "I meant mental agility, thinking fast on your feet." The amusement faded and his eyes took on a smoky hue that made her swallow. "If that fails you can always use your strongest weapon."

"And that is?"

"Sex." The way the man said the simple, three-letter word made it sound like a caress.

"Sex?" *Yes please.*

The sultry claret paint seemed to be raising the temperature of the room, or was all that heat coming from the way his gaze teased her senses? "You might have to seduce the bad guys to get information."

"Seducing bad guys. Is that covered in the FBI employee manual?"

He laughed. "There is nothing official about your involvement in this. As I explained, you've volunteered to pass on anything interesting you see in the course of a normal business day." His face sobered. "And while I don't condone your sexual escapades, it's pretty obvious you're the swinging type. If you do happen to get hot and sweaty between the sheets with a suspect, and they happen to mention anything that might be helpful to our investigation..."

"You mean..."

He winked. "What you do on your own time is your business. Just don't forget to use a condom."

4

SOMETHING WAS WRONG Jake realized, as he watched a blush mount Cynthia's cheeks. The minute she heard the word *condom* her face took on a neon hue. A woman of her experience ought to be accustomed to discussing prophylactics, and she sure as hell better be using them. An unwelcome suspicion crossed his mind.

"You do use condoms, don't you? Every single time?" It was one thing to be wild and carefree, but if she was going around unprotected…

He felt like he'd just said a four-letter word to his aged aunt. Cynthia's bright red face sort of puckered and her lips tightened into a prissy line. "I really don't think that's any of your—"

"You can be damn sure it's my business. If there's any possibility at all that you're carrying something—"

She gave a funny kind of choking sound. "No. Of—of course not."

His eyes narrowed on her face. If she was clean as a whistle, why did she look so odd? "I've got a good mind to make you take a physical before this goes any further."

She seemed to pull herself together. Her color was still high, but the prissy lip line softened. "Agent Wheeler, I am completely healthy. I've never had… never put myself…never conducted… I've been fully protected."

The more her tongue tangled itself up, the more Jake's gut instinct started clamoring for his attention. He couldn't understand why she was getting all worked up about something so simple. While he watched her turn away and busy herself checking that the tarp was taped to the exact edge of the floor, he began to wonder.

And as he did, a second piece of startling information occurred to him.

She kissed like a virgin.

Sure, she'd been surprised when he'd grabbed her and kissed her; he'd been surprised himself. But it was only a quick celebration smacker, nothing that should have raised anybody's blood pressure.

The way she'd responded, first stiff with shock, then warm and yearning, increased his unease. He'd taken umpteen courses and seminars on reading people—body language, facial expression, blah blah blah. He also had a well-developed gut instinct. Right now, all that training and instinct pointed out the obvious—that her reaction to his kiss didn't jive with what he knew about her.

Correction. With what he'd *assumed* about her.

Of course, it was possible he'd just startled her, and if she'd seen him coming she'd have cleaned his tonsils with her tongue. But he owed his life seven times over to listening to his instincts, and right now they were telling him that the sophisticated sexpot was a fake.

What if the evidence of his eyes had deceived him and she was no more a wild woman than old Mrs. Lawrence next door? It was just a theory, probably false, but one worthy of further investigation.

Naturally, there was only one way to find out whether she was the sweet innocent her eyes portrayed or the kinky sex toy he'd first thought her.

He'd have to kiss her again—in the service of his country.

The way his own body had jolted as she swayed, warm and willing, against him, was not something he wanted to analyze. Whatever she was, nothing but trouble could arise from getting involved with her. He couldn't afford to make any mistakes on this investigation. He was out so far on a limb on this one, he might never get back. If this weren't his last shot at avenging Hank's death, he wouldn't have grabbed at straws this way, hoping an untrained volunteer could pick up some leads just by doing her job and listening to office gossip.

It was only a kiss, damn it. Then he'd know. If she was the woman he believed her to be, she'd enjoy a deep wet kiss just for the fun of it. If not…

He went back to the paint roller, determined to begin testing her. Making sure to brush by her at every opportunity, he watched her reactions, and they disturbed him. She was as jumpy as a new recruit in a combat zone. He kept her close, through a variety of ruses, just to invade her space. He had her climb her stepladder with a brush in hand and paint the very top of the walls where the roller couldn't reach. Once she was perched up high, he "accidentally" knocked into the ladder just to grab hold of her waist and steady her.

She quivered beneath his hands, her waist soft and female. He held on just a few seconds longer than necessary, and the way the flesh beneath her tank top went rigid beneath his hands, he knew she was holding her breath.

Did that mean she was nervous or merely waiting for his next move?

When she came down for more paint, he moved

nearer, trapping her against the stepladder. She was close enough that he could see the delicate nutmeg-sprinkle of freckles across the bridge of her nose, tawny against the smooth cream of her skin. Where her hair caught the light it gleamed, in some places old copper, in others the same rich wine of the walls—the exact same shade in one particular spot. He grinned and reached forward to tweak a paint-stiffened tuft. "Are you part of the decorating project?"

He kept his voice casual, but his eyes were alert, watching the pulse in her throat kick up a notch, noting the way her eyes, green as a glacial lake, widened slightly, and that her tongue licked her lips in a nervous gesture—or was that a subtle come-on?

"Excuse me," she said into the thick silence, and he backed off to let her pass. Still he watched her.

The skimpy top did him a favor, letting him see just how he affected her. From her jerky breaths to her pebbling nipples, she was aware of him, all right. He couldn't decide about the nerves, but there was some heavy animal attraction happening under the grape ceiling.

It would have been darkly humorous if he didn't have some major pebbles of his own demanding attention.

"Balls."

Her head jerked as the word echoed loudly off the wet walls. "Pardon?"

Carefully, he put the roller back once again. He had to know.

She was a pace away from him, fiddling with an unwrapped paintbrush.

"Come here."

She hesitated for a moment, looking so absurdly vulnerable he wanted to tell her to forget the whole thing.

Then a sparkle of determination lit her eyes and her chin came up. She took two steps until they were only inches apart. "What do you want with me this time, Agent Wheeler?" she purred.

Now if that wasn't a come-on, he'd never heard one. It wasn't just the words, it was the provocative tone and the challenge in her eyes. Damn if he could figure this woman out.

Since his brain didn't seem able to analyze her correctly, he went with his baser skills. "This," he said softly, and bending his head, he covered her lips with his own.

This time she didn't freeze in shock. She merely trembled. Her lips quivered, then opened tremulously beneath his. Her body quaked when he wrapped his arms around her to pull her close. Even her breath shuddered as she sighed into his mouth.

And at that moment he knew for certain this was not a woman with a ticket booth outside her bedroom door.

It was his last conscious thought before his senses swamped his intellect. He couldn't think anymore, he could only feel. Soft. She was so soft. Her lips were satin, her tongue velvet as he stroked it.

Beneath his hands, her flesh was warm and giving.

He was mindless with need even as he recognized dimly that she wasn't keeping up. Where he wanted to drag off their clothes and play any wild game she could think up, she was behaving like sweet sixteen on her first date.

Her tongue touched his shyly, her forays into his mouth like hit-and-run ops. And, contrary to having any wild games in mind, she seemed to leave everything to him. Although she clung to him, her hands tracing little circles on his back, she was pretty much staying in the area just below his shoulder blades.

Ashley, his ex, would have had them both naked and twisted like pretzels by now.

He couldn't explain how, but he knew this wasn't an act. Cynthia responded to his kiss with tight-closed eyes, sweetly parted lips and not much of a clue about what to do next.

Damn it all to hell. He'd been conned.

He pulled away and she sighed dreamily. He would have been amused at her naive reaction to a single kiss if he weren't so furious with himself for jumping to conclusions. Okay, it had been an obvious conclusion given the circumstances of their first meeting—but he hadn't done the most basic research to confirm his findings.

Now that he stopped to think about it, everything else about her was at odds with the wild lifestyle. Her driver's license photo; her decor, until this Aladdin's cave painting scheme—even her word choices were prim.

She was a bit young for a midlife crisis, but all the signs were there. And the worst of it was she'd already accepted the job at Oceanic. If she were tough, streetwise and a sexual dynamo, she could be very useful to him. If she were a sheltered innocent, she could get them all in trouble.

He was tempted to pull the plug. If she were a special agent picked as part of his team, he'd do it without a second thought. But she wasn't an agent. She was a volunteer. He couldn't force her to quit; he had to make her want to do it on her own.

He'd have to backtrack. Take back all that bunk he'd

told her about the place being dangerous, and give her the truth.

"You know," he said, drawing back from her sweet, warm body, "I'm probably wrong about Oceanic. We've tried every way to find anything suspicious and we're coming up blank. You're basically going in on a fishing expedition."

Her eyes fluttered open and she blinked like a gopher coming up into sunlight. "Fishing...?" Her voice had a dreamy quality and her lips were moist and pouty from his kisses.

He wanted nothing more than to pick up where he'd left off. But he couldn't, not until he'd convinced his volunteer recruit to un-volunteer. "There's probably nothing going on at Oceanic. It's most likely just another boring accounting job."

She laughed softly, a sleepy, sexy sound that had him fisting his hands to keep from reaching for her again. "For nine years I've been an accountant in a cement factory. Goring Cement. We called it Boring Cement for good reason."

"I thought you wanted excitement?"

"I do. And I think there's something pretty fishy going on at Oceanic."

If it wasn't a serious matter of drug running, he'd find her earnestness kind of cute. "You were there about five minutes."

"I have good instincts about people. The two men who were with the president were definitely suspicious-looking characters."

"That's not—"

"And besides," she interrupted, "I really needed a change. If this doesn't turn out to be exciting, I'll quit and find something more interesting. The important thing is that I took charge of my life.''

''What if I tell you I've changed my mind? I don't think you should do it?''

She regarded him for a moment. ''I'd say you were too late.''

She was so blind, so completely pigheaded, that he snapped. ''Don't come crying to me if the job bores you into a coma.''

She stared at him speculatively, a secret little smile curving her lips. ''Don't worry,'' she said in a soft voice. ''I'll come to you for excitement.''

A woman rarely rendered him speechless, but this one just had. She'd conned him and twisted his reasoning until he couldn't think of anything useful except escaping from her as quickly as possible, before he gave her more excitement than either of them needed right now.

''I'll see myself out,'' he snarled as he stomped to the door.

''Don't be a stranger,'' she called softly behind him, and damn if he didn't hear a smile in her voice.

''CHOPSTICKS.''

''Chopsticks?'' Cynthia tried not to let disappointment creep into her tone. Neville Percivald was giving her a tour of his company himself. Not only was she flattered that he was taking the time from what must be a busy schedule, she was determined to use every opportunity to pursue her secret agenda—gathering information that could be valuable to the FBI. ''All those crates contain chopsticks?''

He chuckled without opening his lips, in a terribly refined, British sort of way. ''Not all of them. No. But we do import chopsticks used in many of the Oriental restaurants in the Pacific Northwest."

She gazed at the rows of stacked crates on the cement loading dock. "That's a lot of chow mein." She smiled up into Neville Percivald's guileless blue eyes, reminding herself she was Cyn, undercover agent to the drug and possibly chopstick trade. For all she knew those boxes didn't contain chopsticks at all. They could be loaded with little packets of white powder. She pictured herself sneaking down with a crowbar, cranking open a crate, slitting a packet of white powder and tasting it. Then her fantasy abruptly dissolved. What did drugs taste like, anyway? Would she get intoxicated from tasting them? And who knew what kind of germs they harbored; she very much doubted there were health inspectors at drug packaging plants.

"Is something wrong, Miss Baxter?"

"No, no," she assured him as inspiration struck. "I'm just not looking forward to counting all those chopsticks." And checking all the packaging, searching for false bottoms in the crates, accidentally cracking one open to see if it was hollow.

He did that closed-mouth chuckling thing again. "Don't worry, Miss Baxter. You won't get your hands dirty. You merely reconcile the shipping tallies with the packing slips."

He was looking at her like she was a bit dim for a CPA, which was just fine by her. Among her professional colleagues there were several bean counters who were missing a few beans of their own. If Neville Percivald and his colleagues thought she was one of those, all the better.

The more the top mucky-mucks at Oceanic discounted her, the more they'd let slip, and she definitely planned to be picking up every dropped clue that came her way. Accounting had a pretty bad rap in the excitement department, but it had its moments. She reminded herself that it was accountants who'd brought Al Capone down.

When you followed the trail of money, you could find out a lot about a person and an organization. If Oceanic had any dirty little secrets in the financial department, she'd find them.

Maybe she was a late bloomer, as a woman and a spy, but she was determined to make up for lost time, in both departments.

While she'd been plotting his downfall in her head, Neville Percivald had let his gaze stray, and he was checking out her body in a manner that struck her as immensely foolish in the age of sexual harassment charges. Ooh. This was good. If her boss thought his new bean counter was a bean-brain and a bit of a floozy, he'd soon be putty in her hands.

She swept him a look under her lashes that said, *If this was a singles bar, and not the loading dock of your company, you might get somewhere.* At least, she hoped that was the message she was telegraphing. She'd never actually tried to communicate such a thing before, with or without words.

He was getting some kind of message from her, in any event. His chest puffed out under his navy, double-breasted blazer, and he sent her a smile that didn't seem particularly professional.

He conducted the rest of the tour walking a little closer than was absolutely necessary, and she reveled in her success even as she tried not to get creeped out that a possible drug smuggler might have the hots for her.

Nobody in her life had had so much as the lukewarms for her. Now she had two men giving her smoldering glances. Well, Neville Percivald was too refined to smolder, but his gaze certainly seemed warm when it rested on her.

Now Jake was a man who smoldered. And it wasn't just his glances. His kiss had darn near melted her on the spot. Mmm. She felt warm just thinking about it. For some reason, he'd no sooner convinced her to take this job than he'd started trying to talk her out of it.

Fat chance. He'd recruited her for this spy mission at a time when she was desperate for some excitement in her life. There wasn't an argument he could make that would convince her to give up the most fun thing she'd ever done—before she'd even done it.

She'd love to discover valuable information on her first day, simply for the pleasure of making him eat his words.

By the time Neville Percivald left her at what he euphemistically termed the "accounting department," she'd met most of the staff and toured the entire building. Everything seemed perfectly legitimate and innocent. She tried not to feel discouraged, knowing her sleuthing talents would best be used here in accounting. It was a very small department; there were only two of them. Herself and Agnes Beecham, the bookkeeper.

Agnes terrified Cynthia. She was of an indeterminate age somewhere between fifty and retirement. Colorless from the washed-out gray hair coiled neatly on the top of her head to her sallow face and tired eyes, right down to the flesh-colored support hose and beige walking shoes.

To Cynthia, she was right out of Dickens. Cynthia's own personal Ghost of Things to Come. This woman was herself if she'd stayed on the path she'd been traveling; she was certain of it.

In her soft, monotonous voice, Agnes explained the systems they used and showed Cynthia the files she'd need.

"It's all computerized now, of course. I've never become accustomed to that."

"Have you worked here long?"

Agnes sighed, sadly. "Thirty years."

With a pang of cold horror, Cynthia recalled her nine years at Goring Cement, which could so easily have stretched to thirty.

Then a thought struck. "You've been here thirty years?"

"Yes," said Agnes. "Thirty-one next March."

"But surely Mr. Percivald's too young to have been here that long?"

Even the woman's laugh was colorless. And mirthless. "I started working for his stepfather, George Percivald. He founded the company, importing fine china from England." She sighed softly. "A very genteel man."

And now the son had ditched the teapots for chopsticks. A tingle of excitement swirled in Cynthia's middle. Obviously, they weren't exporting drugs from Stoke on Trent. Mr. Percivald junior had switched the operation to South America, for obvious reasons. Did Jake know about this?

"Here's your office." Agnes ushered her into a smallish box, Spartan, but fully equipped. "You'll want to redecorate, I'm sure."

"I doubt I'll—" She'd been about to say she doubted she'd be here that long. Cynthia would have to watch herself if she didn't want to blow her cover the very first day. "I doubt I'll bother changing it for a while. I'll be too busy getting up to speed on all your systems."

She glanced around. The walls were beige and, apart from a big road-racing poster, a wall calendar from a real-estate agent and a poor quality print of swimming mallards, there was no decor. But the desk was spacious, the chair had lumbar support and the computer equipment was up-to-date. It would do.

Agnes stood in the doorway, her drabness matching the office. "I'll leave you to get settled, then. If you want to know anything at all, please don't hesitate to ask."

"Thanks." Cynthia sent her a vivid smile. "I'm sure you'll be sorry you offered." She wondered what else Agnes could tell her that would help her investigation. The woman had been there thirty years; she must know all kinds of secrets. "Since we'll be working together, perhaps we could have lunch one day soon."

Her suggestion was greeted with a shy but grateful smile. Instantly, Cyn felt like a miserable sneak, although she hadn't suggested lunch just to pick Agnes's brains; the truth was she'd felt an immediate kinship with the older woman.

The minute Agnes left the room, Cynthia booted up the computer and searched it as thoroughly as she knew how. Jake had told her that the former accountant had skipped town before the FBI could contact him. They had no idea whether he knew anything about Oceanic that could be useful, or even if he might be involved in drug smuggling or money laundering. She'd heard the frustration in Jake's voice, and knew it irked him that the former Oceanic accountant had left the country before the FBI had had a chance to interview him.

If there was any money laundering going on here, Cynthia bet there'd be a way for a smart accountant to figure it out. Maybe her predecessor had left her some clues.

But her search yielded nothing. All traces of Harrison had been expunged. She had been assigned an e-mail address, but her predecessor's was gone, as were any messages he might have left behind.

She couldn't locate a single personal file, though she easily found the software programs, the company books and the files for the pension plan, which it was her responsibility to administer. She'd crack the books at the first opportunity, but common sense told her they wouldn't be right there in front of her nose if they weren't clean.

While pretending to stock the empty desk with items from the supply cupboard, she surreptitiously ran her fingers into every crevice. At the back of the second drawer in the bank of three, her searching fingers hit an obstacle and her heart began to hammer. She tugged and wiggled the object, snapping a freshly manicured nail in the process, only to find her hidden treasure was nothing but a paperclip that had wedged itself into a corner.

She stared at the twisted metal clip while she sucked her sore finger, wondering how much of the spy business was this frustrating.

THE GATE CREAKED as Cynthia entered Mrs. Jorgensen's front garden—which didn't belong to Mrs. Jorgensen any longer, of course, but to FBI Agent Jake Wheeler. An early fall nip was in the air, taking its toll on the profusion of late summer flowers already sagging with neglect. Cynthia hoped Jake was a better agent than gardener; Mrs. Jorgensen would cry if she could see the state of the roses.

As she walked up the path she'd trod so many times to visit the older woman, Cynthia felt a flicker of apprehension. It wouldn't be Mrs. Jorgensen greeting her when she knocked on the sturdy oak door, it would be Jake Wheeler.

She wanted to give him a report on her impressions of Oceanic after one day on the job. She could fill him in on the personalities she'd met, the unfortunate lack of evidence in Harrison's computer and desk, and her suspicions about the "chopstick" shipment from Colombia. Colombia had one major export she knew about, apart from coffee and bananas, and it wasn't chopsticks. She wished she had some concrete evidence to support her theory that those crates contained cocaine, but not even Jake Wheeler could expect her to crack the case in one day.

Now that she was here, in his front garden, she hesitated. Her steps slowed and she paused to snap a few dead heads off the chrysanthemums while she debated continuing up to the door or bolting for home.

On the one hand, she ought to report her progress from her first day on the job.

On the other hand, he carried a gun for a living and scared the pants off her.

While she tried to make up her mind, she busied herself picking off shriveled orange and purple flowers until she had a neat little pile ready for the compost.

She never did make up her mind whether to go to his door or not.

While she was lost in her mental arguments, a strong arm came round her shoulders and hustled her to the house. That clinched it. She made up her mind on the spot. She didn't want to stay here; she wanted to go home. But even as she tried to pull away, Jake frog-marched her to his front door and shoved her inside.

She was standing in his front hall before she'd had a chance to do more than squeak. And he was staring grimly out from behind the living-room drapes.

"What the hell do you think you're doing?" His voice bounced from the other room.

She gulped. "I just stopped to..." Her gaze dropped to the dead petals crushed in her hand. What was she going to say? She'd dropped by to do some gardening?

Get a grip! You are Cyn! Cyn wouldn't apologize for visiting a single man uninvited. Cyn would probably have him half-naked and begging by now.

She straightened her shoulders and gazed at the hard line of his back. Tension radiated off him. There were certain men Cyn could probably have half-naked and begging in no time. This was not one of those men. This was not one of those times.

He swung round and his face was tightly controlled, but anger sizzled through his pores. "What are you doing?" This time his tone was soft, but far more scary than if he'd yelled the words.

5

THE HECK WITH GETTING HIM naked; she just wanted to get out of here in one piece. "I was reporting in. But I obviously picked a bad time." Her gaze faltered under the hard assault of those eyes. She bunched the petals more tightly in her fist. "I'll get going now."

"You don't come here," he said in that same soft, fierce tone.

Her pulse hammered under that merciless gaze.

"You never come here. They could be watching you."

"But—"

"No buts. That's an order. I can't believe you were stupid enough to come waltzing up my front path."

"You can't order me—"

"Yes I can. Or I'll yank you out of Oceanic so fast your hair will change color. Again."

He was scaring her, but also she was getting the feeling that maybe he didn't think her job was going to be such a waste of time, after all. "I'm a volunteer. You can't fire me."

"I can arrest you."

Her jaw gaped. "You'd arrest me?"

"If you don't cooperate, you could jeopardize an operation we've been working on for months. If I have to go in and haul your ass out of there, you're damn right I'll arrest you."

"But—"

His finger shot up and pointed at her heart, reminding her uncomfortably of that horrible gun. "Don't push it, Cyn."

She felt a little light-headed and sank to the bottom stair. "I was only going to tell you about my first day." Her voice sounded like a little kid's, which infuriated her.

His face softened slightly, along with his voice. "I know you're new to this stuff, but it's not a game. You're working at Oceanic as an accountant. That's it. If it were me, or another agent, it would be a cover. But the beauty of this whole thing is that *you really are an accountant working at Oceanic.*" He glanced down at her. "Do you see where I'm going with this?"

She nodded miserably.

"If I need information, I'll find a way to contact you." He let out a breath and it seemed like he made a conscious effort to cool down. "Want a beer?"

"I thought you were throwing me out." She didn't move from the bottom of the stairs, where she could keep the front door in plain view in case she needed to bolt for safety. She couldn't process that he'd gone from Mr. Fury to Mr. Hospitality in under two minutes.

He shrugged. "Now you're in, you'll have to stay until after dark. And in future, don't come sashaying up my front path any time you feel like it. I'll give you a number for emergencies. Otherwise, don't phone me or visit my house."

"Don't you want me to report in?"

He regarded her calmly. "I'll find a way to stay in touch. Don't come near me unless it's an emergency. Got it?"

She nodded. "I think I will have a beer." She followed him to the kitchen, noting the changes he'd already made in the house. He'd kept a lot of the furniture, but still the house looked different. Mostly it was less cluttered. Mrs. Jorgensen hadn't ever forgotten her Danish and Dutch heritage, and had married the two enthusiastically, filling her house with teak furniture and covering every surface with starched linens and Delft pottery.

Jake walked to the fridge, and Cynthia took a seat at the small rectangular teak table that looked so different without the hand-embroidered blue-and-white cloth on it and the little Dutch boy and girl salt and pepper shakers in the middle. His salt and pepper was a tubular contraption that could have been designed by NASA.

"You cook," she noted in surprise, eyeing the pans hanging from a wall, copper bottoms blackened from use, the well-stocked fridge she'd glimpsed when he got the beer, and the hefty selection of cookbooks on the shelf.

Passing her a bottle of beer and a glass, he raised his eyebrows and half grinned. "Men cook. Got another news flash for you. The earth's round."

"I didn't mean—"

"If a man today looks twice at a woman rebuilding a car engine, or reroofing her own house, he's a chauvinist. But women still like to think a man in the kitchen is like..."

"A fish without a bicycle?" she offered sweetly.

He poked a finger in her direction. "That's exactly what I'm talking about, that feminist superiority complex you women pull. There's a few things you gals still need us men for..." his gaze intensified on hers and the pause grew heavy "...and I'm not talking about cooking."

How did he do that? One minute he scared the pants off her, the next he was sending glances her way that made her knees weak. Well, she wasn't falling for it. Or him. "I admit we'd need a few gallons of cryogenically frozen sperm and some turkey basters. After that, you men'd be history."

She almost gasped as she realized she'd said the words aloud. Usually she kept those kind of comments to herself, but ever since her makeover her whole personality seemed to have changed to match the faux fur and funky hair. Maybe some of the hair dye had seeped into her brain and scrambled her neurons. She thought about that for a second and decided she really didn't care. She liked the fact that her flip comment had wiped the sparkle out of Wheeler's eye.

She liked it until she realized he'd replaced it with a purposeful gleam as he crossed the kitchen in two strides. "I won't demean my sex with the obvious advantages we offer over a turkey baster. I'll just remind you that there's one thing science will never replace."

"The male ego?"

"The kiss."

She dropped her gaze, flustered at the way those two words had her blood heating as memories of their brief kisses crowded her mind.

He tipped back the bottle and drank, then said, "You want to give my talents a try?"

"Pardon?" Her gaze snapped back to his. Had he read her mind?

A disturbing tilt to his lips made her think he could see right inside her thoughts. "My cooking. How about I make us some dinner, since you're stuck here for a few hours."

"Dinner!" Right, the talent he referred to was *cooking*. "Yes, thank you. I'd love to stay."

He put water on to boil, started pulling vegetables out of the crisper and took a small brown-paper-wrapped package out of the meat keeper. "You're lucky, I spent a couple of hours at Pike Place Market this morning. You like scallops?"

"Mmm-hmm. When I cook them they always go rubbery."

"You're cooking them too long."

She blinked bemused eyes and rose. "What can I do to help?"

"Chop the cilantro."

"Fresh herbs," she said weakly.

"Like I said, you're lucky I went marketing today." He donned a striped denim apron that made him look like a very sexy head chef in some trendy bistro.

"Where did you learn to cook?"

"My mom went back to work full-time when we started school. She taught us all how to cook, and we had to take turns cooking for the family. Best thing she could have done."

They continued to chat while Cynthia cut, chopped or peeled what he put in front of her, according to his instructions. "What did your mother do?"

"She's a lawyer. Well, she's semiretired now."

"And your father?"

"He's a lawyer, too. In private practice. Mom worked for the D.A.'s office. Conversation around our dinner table could get...pretty interesting."

"I can imagine." Cynthia smiled, picturing noisy, argumentative meals in the Wheeler household. She bet they were a lot more stimulating than those in her house, where the no-controversy rule stifled dinner-table conversation. "How about your siblings? You said 'we.'"

"There are four of us. Molly's an environmental lawyer, Clay's a trial lawyer and Pete's undecided. He's still in law school."

Cynthia's knife stilled in the middle of slicing a lemon. "Your entire family are lawyers?"

He grinned at her across a sizzling skillet. "All but me. I'm the black sheep."

"Did you ever want to be a lawyer?"

He tossed onion and garlic into the skillet and began to stir. The aroma made her mouth water. "For the first two years of law school I thought so, but it wasn't my thing. I hate all that sitting around arguing. I like action."

That sounded like an understatement. "Were your parents disappointed?"

"They got over it."

JAKE SMILED TO HIMSELF as he opened a bottle of Washington Sauvignon Blanc he'd bought today on impulse. Cyn was seated at the table gazing at the steaming plate in front of her while he opened the wine. Had his family ever got over his defection! There wasn't one who hadn't picked his brains shamelessly on some point of investigative procedure. Of course, he drew just as shamelessly on the combined legal expertise of his family, especially when he was skating close to the edge of the law.

The cork emerged with a quiet sigh. It wasn't an oversight that he hadn't asked his siblings or his parents for an opinion on his latest stunt. They'd all yell at once if they found out he was on his own. He doubted he could make them understand. But then, no one in his family had ever caused a friend's death.

"This is fantastic," Cyn told him, licking her lips.

He gazed across the table at her. What was he thinking? He wasn't completely on his own. He had an untrained volunteer, a kinky wannabe sexpot, as a sidekick. That would help his family sleep at night.

"Tell me about your first day," he said to Cyn. Although the dumb-assed way she'd wandered down his front path in daylight still rankled, he was interested in what she had to say. He'd had every intention of getting her first impressions, but he'd planned on visiting her after dark.

Her eyes lit up at his question. "Guess what came in a new shipment last night?"

"I couldn't begin to guess."

"Chopsticks!"

He faked amazement. "No!"

"It gets better."

"I hope so."

"Guess where they were from?"

"China?"

She leaned forward and whispered, "Colombia."

He kept his face impassive, but he was interested, all right. If it was coffee or fish meal he'd have been more intrigued—it was common practice among smugglers to hide coke inside strong-smelling commodities to put the dogs off. Chopsticks would be a new one on him. "Interesting."

"So, what do you think is in those crates?"

"I'm guessing chopsticks."

"Don't you think it might be drugs?"

"Everything coming into port gets checked. Dogs, random customs checks...you don't just pack a bunch of drugs in a box and ship it to the U.S. Especially if you're shipping from Colombia."

"Darn. I hadn't thought of that."

He topped up her wineglass.

They ate at the kitchen table, but even so the atmosphere was intimate. Jake cursed himself for opening wine. This was looking far too much like a date, rather than a debriefing. He'd wanted her relaxed and open, he just didn't want anybody getting the wrong idea here.

"Tell me about your co-workers."

She listed names and physical descriptions until he was convinced she must have a photographic memory. More names and snatches of boring office conversation bombarded him until he lost track and just let her talk while he once more tried to figure out a way to get her to back off from the amateur spy shtick.

She hadn't told him anything he didn't know, except that, for some inexplicable reason, Oceanic was importing chopsticks from Colombia. "I thought they made chopsticks around here, from scrap wood chips or something," he said, as soon as there was a pause.

"Neville says it's part of a new trade program to try and reduce the country's dependence on drug income. South America's climate grows trees much faster than ours. Did you know that cocaine is Colombia's biggest export? Almost twice as big as coffee? That's the largest legitimate export."

"Yeah. I knew that." He swirled wine in his glass, thinking. "And Percivald told you all this?"

"Yes."

Why would the pantywaist tell her that? It was the sort of thing an innocent businessman would say. Or a very devious one. Jake scowled. "What else did he tell you?"

"Lots of things. Neville gave me a tour personally." Jake heard the tiny note of pride in her voice.

"Congratulations. Did he try anything?"

Her color heightened. "Not exactly."

His gut tightened. She wasn't in Percivald's league. If she got involved with that pervert, she could end up hurt, or psychologically damaged. "What do you mean, not exactly?"

"He...well, he flirted with me, I guess."

Jake let his tightened belly muscles relax. If a little flirting over the coffee machine had her this flustered, an all-out pass would have her racing home faster than her stiletto heels could carry her.

Of course. The obvious strategy to getting her out of Oceanic hit him like a bullet.

"How do you feel about...*you know*...with Neville Percivald to get more information?"

Her forehead wrinkled. "You don't mean..."

"I mean, have sex with the guy and pump him for information."

In an instant her face went from flushed to whiter than his marble rolling pin. "I don't think so." She fiddled with the stem of her wineglass. "He's really not my type."

Yes. Jake's strategy was working. He pushed harder, knowing in his gut he had to get her out of Oceanic, wishing he'd never been fool enough to involve an innocent woman in his personal vendetta. Unfortunately, his common sense had returned a little late. If he couldn't persuade her to back away from Oceanic, he'd have to trick her into doing it. Deliberately, he hardened his voice. "This isn't a game, you know. It's a serious investigation. You're either in or you're out. And if you're in, I do mean *all the way.*"

He waited for her to throw the wine in his face and storm out. With luck he'd get a chance to explain his behavior when this thing was all over, maybe even pursue this tantalizing attraction between them. But for right now, he'd risk her good opinion to get her safely out of Oceanic.

Instead of throwing the wine or a tantrum, she rose with a polite smile. "I should have brought that welcome-to-the-neighborhood Bundt cake, then we'd have had dessert."

"Look, Cyn—"

"It's dark now, Agent Wheeler. May I go home?"

The sky was dark, all right, but not nearly as dark as his mood as he skulked with her down the back alley.

Before she slipped into her house, she gripped his arm. "I am not a quitter," she whispered.

Somehow, he'd have to find a way to make her become one. If Neville Percivald couldn't stop her, Jake would have to find a way to do it himself.

A WEEK LATER, he was still trying to figure out a way to get Cynthia Baxter to un-volunteer. He'd stubbornly refused to contact her all week, and despite the fact that he'd kept his cell phone turned on and near him all week, day and night, he hadn't heard a peep from her.

He hated stubborn women.

He'd have been worried sick if he hadn't joined the rest of the neighborhood curtain-twitching squad and taken to monitoring her movements in the most low-tech way of all. He peered out his window at her when she left for work in the morning, and he'd become so finely tuned to the sound of her car motor that he was back at his post each evening when she returned, driving past his house with her nose pointed straight ahead and her chin in the air in a little *up yours* posture that kept his blood perpetually on low simmer.

He had to do something. She was getting in the way of his work. He had to schedule all his appointments, do all his digging, after she'd left for work in the morning, then be home again in time to watch for her safe arrival.

It was all her fault for pretending to be someone she wasn't. He never would have asked her to be his informal spy if he hadn't believed she was tough, street smart and kinkier than the Marquis de Sade.

He felt like a chump. And the worst part was she had him thinking about her at night, too—remembering how she'd looked naked, her naturally slender body gently rounded in all the right places. Then there was the way she'd felt in his arms. Like she belonged there.

Thinking about her made him irritable and edgy as he hovered by the window like a damned den mother, checking his watch and straining his ears for her engine. It was six-thirty. She was always home by six.

He checked the battery on his cell phone, started to pace. His blood pressure rose as he pictured Cynthia in danger. Being forced onto a fishing boat...

"No!" he said aloud, shoving the ugly vision away.

He heard a car turn onto Rodonda Drive, but his ears told him immediately it wasn't Cyn's. He twitched his curtain and saw a yellow taxi pull up outside Mrs. Lawrence's place. He grabbed his keys and wallet, pulled on a jacket and sprinted for his front door.

His elderly neighbor was just starting up her front path.

"Nice evening," he said by way of greeting.

She smiled at him. "Yes." Good, she had her hearing aid turned on.

He sauntered to the fence. "I've been helping Cynthia with some painting."

"Yes, I know," Mrs. Lawrence said, not even blushing at being such a nosy neighbor.

"I said I'd help her tonight, but she's not home yet."

"Oh, well. It's Tuesday, isn't it?"

"Ye-es."

She smiled, like she'd just won at bingo. "Deep water aerobics. She'll be home by half past seven."

Relief washed through him, while the nagging fear turned to annoyance. That woman had wasted enough of his time and mental energy. He was going to make certain she quit Oceanic once and for all. Tonight.

He didn't let any of his emotions show on his face, just said, "Well, she gave me a key to her house." He waved his own key at the elderly woman. "Might as well get started."

Mrs. Lawrence beamed. "She certainly is a lucky girl."

Guilt smote him. An old lady would need his help a lot more than a young one. "If there's anything you want done around the house, Mrs. Lawrence, give me a shout."

"Why, thank you, dear. I'll remember that. Good night."

"'Night."

He sauntered to Cyn's door in full view of the neighborhood, knowing he'd just been stamped with the Rodonda Drive Seal of Approval. If he'd learned nothing else this week, he'd confirmed that nobody sinister was watching Cynthia's house—just him and the rest of the neighbors.

Five minutes later, he was inside. With a good forty-five minutes until she returned home, he marshaled his arguments and settled down to wait.

He snapped on a lamp, and had to admit he kind of liked the color of the walls, Grape Kool-Aid or Chateauneuf du Pape, or whatever the hell color she called it. The room was an intriguing mixture of old and new. Some of the stuff he remembered from before—fancy antique-store knickknacks and so on—but she'd added some new, ultramodern looking cushions, an abstract picture on the wall and some kind of chunk of rock on the mantel. Maybe it was supposed to be a sculpture. He shrugged. Looked like a hunk of rock to him.

Also new were a few additions to the library. An "inside the FBI" exposé, and a book about money laundering. Great. All he needed was her thinking she was an expert because she'd read a book about the bureau by some guy he'd never heard of, and an academic study on money laundering.

With a groan of frustration, he flopped to the couch and picked up a magazine from the stack on the floor. Her accounting association magazine. He made it through three pages and his eyes started to drift shut.

He flicked through the pile looking for *Gourmet* or *Bon Appétit.* Found *Accounting Boring Monthly, Time, Newsweek, Raunch...*

Raunch?

He flopped back on the couch, taking the magazine with him. First thing he noted was this magazine was a lot more thumbed through than her accounting periodical. The second thing he noticed was that the saucy dominatrix on the front cover had breasts like twin *Hindenburgs.* You could hang on to her ankles and float to Australia.

Raunch's annual fantasy issue pretty much ran the

gamut, he noted, from the traditional to the, well, out there. He'd never found space aliens attractive, himself, but then, he was definitely more of a down-to-earth kind of guy.

Boudoir Beginners? He snorted. Who wrote this stuff?

Somebody, no doubt Cyn, had highlighted a few of the fantasies in yellow marker. Pretty much all of them were in the beginner section.

He paused to read one highlighted passage, then rolled his eyes. What was it with women and sheiks? No way he'd stick a damn towel on his head and dress up his bedroom like a silk tent. Jeez.

He flipped the page to the next fantasy. Not only was this one highlighted, it was starred—triple starred, actually. "Helpless Virgin Ravaged by a Dark Dangerous Stranger." His mind flipped to the way he'd found her. So that's what that was all about! She'd been enacting a magazine fantasy. The joke was on her, though. She must have just about had a heart attack when a gun-wielding stranger crashed her private party. She'd got her fantasy, all right—well, he hadn't ravished her, of course, but to Cyn he must have looked mighty dangerous. She'd appeared terrified, not a bit turned on by the whole situation. Which just showed why fantasies should remain fantasies.

Wait a minute. He snapped his fingers. That was the answer, staring him right in the face. He knew just what Cyn would do if a dangerous stranger tried to ravish her. She'd run a mile, that's what she'd do.

He read the setup more carefully, a slow smile forming.

WITH A SIGH Cynthia stepped into the hallway in her stocking feet and froze, dropping the canvas bag with her swimsuit and towel on the floor. There was a light on in the living room. One she certainly hadn't left on this morning. Another furtive step forward revealed a lean and dangerous man sprawled on her new floral tapestry couch—one who also hadn't been there this morning.

"What are you doing here, Jake?"

"Waiting for you." Those doll-blue eyes with the fringe of impossibly dark, curly lashes set in a face of stone gave her the usual shiver of apprehension, and the same unwanted tug of attraction.

"My security system is supposed to be foolproof." The way her pulse went all jumpy when he was around annoyed her as much as his casual entry past her defenses.

"But I'm no fool," he said, both arrogance and amusement dancing in his eyes. He replaced the accounting magazine he'd been reading on the stack on her mahogany coffee table.

With a start of pure horror she recalled that *Raunch Magazine* was somewhere in that pile. Too embarrassed to put it in recycling, in case any of her neighbors peeked, she'd planned to burn the thing, but with her new duties as the most boring spy in the world, she hadn't had time.

The pile of magazines looked undisturbed, and she figured Jake would have chosen *Raunch* over *Accounting Today* if he'd come across it.

"What do you want?"

"A status report."

"It's a short report," she said, choosing a wing chair opposite him and giving her ridiculously short red leather skirt a yank. "No progress. The only accounting discrepancy I can find is eight cents that won't balance. And another load of chopsticks arrives in the morning. Who knew Chinese food was so popular?"

He crossed his arms and lounged back, a gesture that made his biceps bulge and her heart skitter. He was so impossibly male, with an aura of danger that drew her even as it repelled her. His chest was broad and taut with muscle, his belly flat under the navy polo shirt. Her eyes slipped lower, and with a start she jerked her gaze to the colorful arrangement of tulips centered on the coffee table.

"Heard anything interesting around the water cooler?"

"Since we spoke last week? Let's see..." She'd better not tell him she'd searched Neville's computer files as well as Lester Dart's and Doug Ormond's one afternoon when they'd all gone to a meeting. Jake would have a fit if she told him. Besides, she hadn't found anything suspicious, certainly not a second set of books.

"Well?"

"Marilyn's getting married to her personal trainer in September. She's the front office receptionist. We're throwing her a shower in two weeks. Eddie from the loading dock's seeing Suze, Neville's secretary, on the side. It's supposed to be a secret, but everybody knows—except Suze's husband, I hope. And as for Delores—"

His hands jerked up in surrender. "Okay, okay. It was just a thought."

"That the staff would chitchat about a drug money laundering operation at the water cooler." Cynthia let the sarcasm drip from her tongue. "I can see why they put you in charge of the operation."

Her insult didn't appear to annoy him nearly as much

as she'd hoped, but he did sit up straighter, with a gleam in his eye that made her wish she'd kept her mouth shut. "You'd be amazed what people let slip when they get relaxed." His blue, blue eyes shot her a glance of pure innocence she'd learned to distrust.

"Really."

"Seduced anybody yet, Cyn?"

"Seduced anybody..." Her voice sounded high and funny. The thought of seducing any of her co-workers made her feel ill. In fact the only man who caused erotic scenarios in her head was sitting right across from her. "Well, no. I..."

Jake's gaze slid slowly down her red leather suit, making her feel like it was shrink-wrapped to her flesh. "You're advertising—" his voice taunted her "—but are you selling?"

A flush heated her cheeks. It had been fun pretending, but there was no way she could continue this charade. She wasn't the sexy siren Mata Hari he believed her. She was boring accountant Cynthia Baxter. "Of course I'm not selling," she snapped.

"Why not?" Lazy flames seemed to curl the edges of his words.

"Because I'm not—I mean, I'm..." But she couldn't find the words to tell him she was a complete dud in bed, and that even the most risqué fantasy in *Raunch Magazine* couldn't save her last relationship. She could not look into those dangerous, hot blue eyes and humiliate herself. "I, uh, don't usually do the seducing," she finally managed to say, trying desperately to look worldly and slightly bored.

Jake's mouth quirked up at that, softening his tough-guy face and etching wonderful little crinkles around his baby doll eyes. "Then I guess you'd better start practicing."

"Practice what?"

"Seducing men. You can start with me."

"You want *me* to seduce *you?*" She was so far out of her league, they weren't even in the same stadium.

He was openly grinning now, and what that grin did to her heartbeat could be dangerous to her health. "Let's call it on-the-job training."

"But I already put in eight hours on the job," she complained, grabbing at straws while she tried to compose herself.

"You'll get paid the overtime rate. Time-and-a-half."

She rose jerkily. Enough was enough. She'd been stupid to volunteer to go undercover. She knew nothing about drugs, or espionage, or money laundering. And she absolutely, definitely knew nothing about seducing men. She'd just show him the door and tell him she was quitting. No more Oceanic. No more FBI. No more Jake Wheeler throwing her pulse into disarray.

"Well?" he taunted.

She gazed at him, opened her mouth to throw him out, and closed it without a word.

Suddenly she knew. It was now or never. Fate had offered her a chance at exploring all that stuff she'd only read about and fantasized about. The man in front of her was every sheik, every pirate, every bad boy of her dreams, and she could have him. All she had to do was step across the room and seduce him.

Walking toward him was the most courageous action she'd ever taken.

He lounged back on the couch and watched her through gleaming eyes as she approached.

Gingerly she sat beside him and glanced nervously at his mouth. Should she kiss him first or would he expect a woman of her experience to begin undressing him right away?

Seconds ticked by.

"If you're worried about a sexual harassment charge, I'm telling you right up front, I'm a willing partner here. If you want me to write that down and sign it, I will."

"No, I... That won't be necessary. I believe you."

"Then go ahead and kiss me."

Thankfully he'd given her her first cue. She took a deep breath and leaned forward, assailed by the all-male scent of him, warm and musky, with a hint of the mints he'd filched from her crystal candy dish. Bracing herself against his chest, she felt hard muscles and the steady thud of a heartbeat under her palms.

She licked dry lips and gazed into his face for a moment. His eyes were fiercely focused on her mouth. The very air crackled between them and suddenly she didn't care if she did everything wrong, she *had* to kiss him.

She pressed her lips against his, and almost moaned at the heat that arced through her body at that slight touch. She let her tongue trail slowly along his bottom lip, and felt him shudder. *Had she done that?* Her own power intoxicated her and made her bold enough to do it again. And again. Finally, she worked up the courage to slip her tongue between his lips, and something inside her exploded as she dipped into that hot, wet mouth. It was as though all the rules of her life ceased to matter. She crushed them with her lips, flouted them with her greedy tongue.

Like a starving woman at a banquet table, she wanted to taste and devour everything before her. Her lips left his and began kissing his jaw, his neck, where a steady pulse thrummed—pretty fast for a guy in such good shape.

Her fingers tugged at his navy polo shirt, clawing at it until she'd released it from his jeans and could run her fingers over his warm, taut flesh. As her hands ascended, the smoothness gave way to rough hair. Mmm. She needed to see it, and that gave her the courage to yank his shirt over his head.

He let her coo and touch and kiss his chest for a few minutes, then complained, "Seems to me you're having all the fun here. How 'bout we both bare our chests?"

A bucket of cold water couldn't have doused her libido faster. "Oh." She glanced down at her chest. "It's really not all that exciting."

His voice teased. "Looks pretty good from here."

"That's a marvel of modern engineering and underwire. Uncomfortable, too."

"Then, as a humanitarian gesture, I think we should release you. I can't enjoy myself knowing you're uncomfortable."

"It's just so bright in here," she whispered.

"Why don't we adjourn to the bedroom?" He kissed the back of her exposed neck, and even that simple little caress shivered along all her sex-starved nerve endings.

"No. Really, I can't—"

"Hey, I'm the one being seduced. Don't I get a say? I'd feel a lot more comfortable in a bed." He shot her a sideways glance. "With the lights off."

Relief scudded through her. "You would?"

"Absolutely. It's more, um…well, I just would."

She didn't really believe him. But there was a telltale bulge in his pants that suggested something was going right in her sex life for a change. "Okay."

"Get ready in the bathroom. I'll meet you in the bedroom."

She nodded agreement and slipped into her en suite bathroom. What exactly had he meant by "get ready?" She was on the Pill, but she'd still expect him to use a condom.

She brushed her teeth. Then flossed. She popped two vitamin B stress tabs to calm her nerves. Was she supposed to get undressed? It would save all that embarrassing fumbling later. Ooh, but what if it wasn't dark when she left the bathroom? She slipped out of her jacket and skirt and the fancy stockings, leaving just her bra and panties on, then took a deep breath, switched off the bathroom light and opened the door.

He hadn't been kidding about liking things dark. Her bedroom was pitch-black. Eerily so. The curtains were drawn, the door closed. She couldn't see a thing.

She knew he was there, though. She could feel him. Sense him through her pores, taste him in the air around her. "Jake?"

From out of the darkness a hand brushed her naked belly, and she sucked in her breath, startled.

He stroked her belly, her side, traced her breasts through the lacy bra, then snapped open the front closure. Everything inside her came alert, each nerve ending vying for his attention. She felt each separate pad of each separate finger as he stroked and caressed her exposed breasts.

Only his fingertips touched her. Nothing else. Not his mouth. Especially not his mouth. And she wanted his mouth on hers so badly she could taste it. Each time she took a step toward where she thought he was, she met empty air. When she raised her arms, he put them back at her sides.

"I thought I was seducing you," she groaned.

"You did." His voice was a husky whisper. "You do."

Those clever fingers stripped her of her bra and panties, and she barely noticed. Taking her by the hand, he led her to the bed, placing her on her back.

And, at last, he kissed her. Taking firm possession of her mouth with his lips and tongue, delving deep until she was mindless with the pleasure of it. He took her wrists in his hands and lifted them over her head. She felt glorious, as though she could fly on those wide-stretched arms.

Somewhere, dimly, she was aware of the cold shock of metal on the heated flesh of her wrists, but he was kissing her so fiercely she couldn't concentrate on this new sensation. Not until she heard the ominous tinny snap did she realize what he'd done.

"No!" she cried, pulling frantically, but she was handcuffed securely to the bed. And bitterly did she know how helpless she was. "Jake! Let me go."

There was no other answer than the shifting of bedsprings as he left the bed.

Next she heard the scrape of a match being lit. She followed the tiny bobbing flame of the match as he lit one candle, then another. She recognized her emergency candle stash, and soon flickering candles added a luminescent glow to the room, and to the man in possession of it—and her.

She glared at him. "You read the magazine."

He bent to light another candle on her bedside table. He glanced at her and she saw twin candle flames like devil lights reflected in his eyes. "Yep. Personally, my favorite fantasy was 'Servant Girl Washing her Master's Plinth.' But you'd highlighted 'Helpless Virgin Ravaged by a Dark Dangerous Stranger' in yellow marker, so I figured it turned your crank."

"You were wrong."

"Are you sure?" His voice sent a shiver over her flesh.

"Yes." She might be helpless, but she'd be damned if she'd be intimidated.

"Well, you're certainly helpless, and since I'm a gentleman, I'm going to assume you're a virgin. But, just so it doesn't get too frightening, I'm going to tell you in advance what I'm going to do, every step of the way."

"Couldn't you just let me go?"

He shook his head. "Not until I've ravished you."

Politically correct this wasn't. But the thrill that shot through her was visceral. He might act the part of the fierce stranger, but she was sure he'd never really hurt or frighten her. Well, pretty sure.

"Now, I've gone easy on you, seeing it's your first time. Your legs aren't shackled. But you give me one little bit of trouble and you'll be spread-eagled. Understand?"

She gulped. "Mmm-hmm."

"First thing I'm going to do is touch those pretty breasts of yours." He moved toward her as he spoke, still dressed in his jeans, bare chest glowing in candlelight. "I'll probably play with the nipples quite a bit, too." At his words, her breasts, and most of all, her nipples, began to throb, longing for his touch, and she felt an echoing throb between her legs.

He put his big, capable hands on her breasts, cupping and kneading the flesh, then pulling on her nipples until she gasped. "I'm going to put my mouth there now," he told her softly. "I'll be using my teeth on those little cherries, so brace yourself."

She moaned. It was as though each caress came twice. When he told her what he was going to do to her, her imagination played it through, while the part of her body he described ached and tingled in anticipation. Then, when he actually touched her, the excitement was almost more than she could bear.

Everything from the palms of her shackled hands to the toes of her feet was subjected to this double caress. Everything except the desperately aching core of her.

She was almost sobbing with need when he stood back, stripped off his jeans and slipped on a condom. The sight of that proudly jutting manhood was too much for her self-control. She whimpered, and the handcuffs rattled against the mahogany four-poster.

He smirked. "Don't be frightened," he soothed, knowing damn well she wasn't scared. "I'll go slowly and try not to hurt you."

"Not slowly, no. Please."

"I understand you want to get this over with. But taking a man into your body can be painful the first time. Now, I want you to spread your legs open for me so I can see if you're ready to take me yet."

And she did it. Lord help her, she parted her legs for him eagerly, and watched as well as felt him settle himself at the bottom of the bed and just *look*.

He was so close his breath stirred the damp curls. She was heavy and swollen with desire, too wired to be embarrassed at the intimate way he stared at her. With his index finger he traced her opening and she hissed in her breath. "I'm going to put just this one finger inside you, to see if you're ready."

She would have kicked him upside the head if she

wasn't certain he'd tease her for hours more if she did. Instead, she watched in agonized frustration as he slipped a finger slowly inside her. Unable to help herself, she cried out and bucked against his hand.

The finger was gone in an instant, and with more phony concern he said, "I'm sorry, honey. I guess I hurt you."

"No. No!"

"Shh. I know I hurt you. I'll kiss it better."

Then he touched his tongue to her. Right on that needy little button of pure sensation.

Her head fell back and she cried out as she began to shudder. She closed her eyes and saw stars. Her very blood seemed to sparkle as he played his tongue over and over her most sensitive part, sending her at long last soaring into the light.

Maybe the game was over, or maybe he'd forgotten the rules, but he didn't tell her what he was going to do this time, just rose above her and plunged. She was still shuddering on the tail end of her climax when he thrust into her, stretching her body and filling her as no one ever had.

"You're so tight, so soft, so sweet," he murmured, holding her head in his hands and staring into her eyes as he began to move inside her, long steady thrusts that built her up again toward that impossibly high peak. With her arms cuffed, she could only use her legs to wrap herself around him, arching up even as he thrust down, and this time when she flew off that mountaintop, she wasn't alone.

Hours later, Jake woke suddenly, his well-developed senses warning him of danger. Instinctively he reached for the Sig 9mm under his pillow, but his hand wouldn't move. He jerked awake to the sounds of metal clinking against wood, and soft, feminine laughter.

This time, he was the one handcuffed to the bed.

"If you're very good, we might get to 'Concubine Washing her Master's Plinth,'" Cynthia promised. "Eventually..."

He groaned. His plan to make Cyn quit her job had backfired. Resoundingly. He'd have to think up a new plan.

But her tongue was drawing patterns on his chest, which made it difficult to plan. Then her mouth traveled lower, until thought was completely out of the question.

6

"WHAT ARE YOU LOOKIN' SO happy about? Get laid last night?" Eddie from the loading dock shuffled past Cynthia in the corridor, a bleary-eyed leer on his face.

"What kind of—" She stopped herself in the middle of a self-righteous rant, remembering Cyn would have those kind of earth-shattering experiences practically every night and not feel a bit embarrassed by her smug morning-after smile. She changed her tone to sultry, and threw in a little laugh. "What kind of girl kisses and tells?" She winked at Eddie and watched his complexion go even ruddier. Really, she was getting pretty good at this sexy stuff.

"Mornin', Mr. Percivald," he said as he shuffled on by.

"Good morning, Eddie." Neville Percivald's voice came from just behind her. She felt herself blush. Darn it, how much had he heard?

"Good morning, Cynthia."

She was forced to turn around, hoping she hadn't shocked him. He didn't seem shocked, though. He looked...interested.

She didn't want Neville interested in her sex life.

Last night, Cynthia Baxter had discovered she could have sex so mind-bogglingly fantastic she giggled every time she thought about it. She wanted to hold that special knowledge to herself, not bring it to the office with her.

She'd had so little sleep last night, she should be exhausted this morning, but instead she felt invigorated. *Empowered* was a favorite word in those self-help books she'd been reading, and that was how she felt this morning. Empowered. She could do anything to-day!

Which reminded her. She had work to do, important undercover work, and following Jake's rules about do-ing nothing but her job hadn't helped her get any closer to discovering whether Oceanic was involved in drug smuggling, and if so, how.

Maybe it was time to use that newfound empower-ment. Take a bit of a risk and see what she could find.

Today she could risk anything, do anything. She was Cyn the Bold! And she'd been bold last night in bed—bold in a way that should have made her blush this morning. Instead she felt a warm, sexy and invigorating glow.

She smiled to herself. Having a man like Jake help-less beneath her and literally begging was the best kind of empowerment a woman could find. She could prob-ably get a Ph.D. on the subject.

Which would involve finding a pretty broad-minded university. Perhaps she'd be better off continuing her research in private, her dissertation fit for nobody's ears but Jake's. Perhaps, instead of the traditional thesis, she could do more of a one-on-one, performance-art kind of thing. She licked her lips as scenarios filled her mind.

She found herself back at her desk, her coffee mug still empty. How had she managed to walk to the coffee room and forget the coffee? Apart from her empty cof-fee mug, there was nothing more exciting on her desk than a routine stack of packing slips. She glanced at the first one. It was for another load of chopsticks.

Oceanic seemed to be bringing in an awful lot of chopsticks, she thought idly, as she flicked through a stack of paper. She stopped and picked up a pencil, tapping the eraser end against her desktop.

According to the documentation, these chopsticks had also come from Colombia. Excitement stirred in her belly. Were the drug cartels eating a lot of chop suey these days?

The same boat had also shipped a large order of coffee. Her eyes widened in excitement. Jake had mentioned the practice of smuggling cocaine inside sacks of coffee, so the overpowering fragrance of coffee beans hid the smell of drugs from the dogs.

She glanced up at the Grand Prix racing poster her predecessor had left behind, knowing she didn't fit in at this company any more than that poster fit in her office. She had to take a more active role in this investigation or she'd be weeping from boredom. She stretched her legs out in front of her and admired the brand-new, strappy black heels. They were the most frivolous and expensive shoes she'd ever owned. She loved them. A woman in shoes like these didn't worry about stepping out of the box.

She rose.

A woman in shoes like these made her own rules.

She walked down the corridor and through the double fire doors into the warehouse. As she'd hoped, the guys were already moving the boxes, sacks and crates from the loading dock into the warehouse. She tripped up to Eddie, who was supervising a grunting, sweating crew, and gave him her best smile. She leaned against the wall of coffee sacks they were building.

''Hey, Cyn,'' Eddie greeted her.

''Eddie, I don't know what to get Marilyn for a shower present. I've seen you two together a few times, so wondered if you might have some ideas?''

''Present for Marilyn. Hmm.'' Eddie leaned beside her, his freckled arms crossed over his massive chest. Damp sweat rings circled his underarms.

While he pondered, and it wasn't a quick process, she began digging and twisting her brand-new, very expensive, pencil-thin heel into a burlap sack, trying to tear a hole big enough for the beans, and whatever else was in the sack, to come spilling out. It broke her heart to damage her brand-new shoes, but she was willing to make the odd personal sacrifice if she was going to help the FBI.

Trouble was, when she'd thought up this maneuver she hadn't taken into account how tough burlap was.

''A tablecloth could be good,'' Eddie said.

''Do you know how big their table is?'' She stabbed her heel harder, trying not to grunt.

''No.'' His attention was caught by the forklift, which held a pallet of coffee sacks poised in midair, one lone sack teetering at the edge. ''Watch what you're doin','' he shouted, just as the sack toppled off and crashed to the ground.

Cynthia beamed with delight as it exploded on contact, sending coffee bouncing and flying until the floor was thick with fragrant black beans.

Eddie and Cyn both rushed forward, but Eddie's feet slipped out from under him as if he were a man walking on ball bearings, and he landed on his butt with an oath.

By planting those thin heels of hers, Cyn managed to reach the burlap sack first. Pretending to stumble, she upended it until the last bean had bounced to the cement. She felt like stamping her stiletto heels in frustration when no incriminating packages tumbled to the floor.

There was nothing there but coffee.

After helping Eddie to his feet, she said, "I guess I picked a bad time to ask about wedding presents. I'll catch you later," and with a cheerful wave she returned to her office. Her mug was still empty, but she'd lost the taste for coffee.

If the drugs weren't in the coffee, they had to be hidden in the crates of chopsticks. As she reconciled invoices and drudged away with columns of numbers, a plan began to form in her head. As Jake was so fond of reminding her, she wasn't a real FBI agent, she was a volunteer. And volunteers didn't have to follow the same rules and regulations as real agents. In fact, as far as she was concerned, they didn't have to follow any rules but their own.

She was going to check out those "chopsticks."

"Are you free for lunch today, Cynthia?" Agnes asked just before noon. The two women had become friendly and Cyn hated to turn her down, but she had no choice.

"I'm sorry, Agnes. I've got some errands to run today."

"I understand," the bookkeeper said in the resigned tone of one who is used to rejection. Guilt smote Cynthia.

"How about tomorrow?"

"All right, I—"

"Oh, no. Wait. I'm getting my hair colored at lunch."

"You're so brave." Agnes sighed enviously. "I wish

I had the courage to color my hair. It's always been mouse-brown, and now it's mouse-gray."

"My true color is mouse, too. Come with me. It'll be fun." Really, Agnes was such a nice lady, it would be a pleasure to get her started in the right direction.

"I couldn't come back to work after lunch with a different color..." She patted her hair, with such a wistful expression on her face, Cyn had to smile.

"Tell you what. I'll change my appointment and we'll go together Saturday morning. Then you'll have the whole weekend to get used to the new you." She thought about suggesting they go clothes shopping afterward, but she was probably pushing it to get Agnes to agree to the hair.

"I don't know. I've never done anything like that." Agnes turned with a half eager, half fearful smile. "Do you think I should?"

"Absolutely. Take my motto—Live a Little."

The older woman sighed. "I wish I could be as bold and adventurous as you, Cynthia. I admire you."

"There's nothing to it. Trust me on this one."

"I'll think about it."

Having salved her conscience, and fobbed Agnes off, Cyn left for lunch a few minutes early and headed for the closest hardware store. She bought a crowbar, industrial flashlight, dark gloves and a black woolen sailor's hat. She glanced at her watch and saw she'd been almost an hour.

Drat. She'd hoped to have a filling lunch, but there wasn't time. On her way back to the office, she passed a shoe and handbag store with a nifty looking black leather knapsack in the window. Perfect! It would match her black leather miniskirt and she could stuff her purchases in it. While she was there she also bought a pair of black trainers, more suitable for after-dark snooping than the strappy heels.

Then she ran all the way back to work, pausing at a newsstand to grab two chocolate bars. Hardly a nutritious lunch. Good thing she'd remembered her multivitamin this morning. She promised herself an extra serving of veggies when she got home.

She arrived back at work breathless, but feeling awfully pleased with herself. She unwrapped one of the candy bars and ate it at her desk while she tried to concentrate on work.

Was Jake thinking about her? Was he reliving last night as often as she was? She touched a finger to a tender spot on her wrist. *Raunch Magazine* hadn't let her down. She'd written her own "orgasmic drama of legendary proportions." Now she was ready for the curtain to go up again. And again.

Now that they'd broken the ice, and he knew about the magazine, she wondered if they could explore some of the ideas in Intimate Intermediates. There was that one with ice cream....

"Cynthia. Cynthia!"

"Hmm?" She turned, and her vision melted like the ice cream would on Jake's— "Sorry, Agnes, I was miles away." She shot the older woman a sheepish grin, straightened her spine and yanked her skirt down a bit. "What did you say?"

"I've decided to take you up on your kind offer." Agnes stood there in her doorway like a Crusader about to start off for the Holy Land. "I'm ready to get my hair colored."

"That's great! I'll make the appointments right now." Before Agnes could change her mind, which she looked in imminent danger of doing, Cyn dug Michael's card out of her purse and made appointments for the two of them for Saturday morning.

As the afternoon dragged on and boredom threatened to set in, she nudged her lumpy backpack with her foot, just to remind herself of the adventure she'd promised herself later.

Frequent peeks at the office clock didn't speed the afternoon at all.

Finally, the clock showed it was just a few minutes before five. The office staff were starting to pack up, ready to go home. Cynthia turned off her computer, straightened her desk and picked up the backpack, slipping her purse inside. "I'm just going to visit the washroom, then I'm leaving for the day," she said breezily to Agnes as she headed out of the accounting department and into the main office.

She didn't mention that the washroom she'd be visiting was located in the warehouse. She saw Eddie and a couple of casual workers on the far side as she entered. A quick glance revealed where they'd stacked a shipment of chopsticks. The crates appeared untouched. Excellent.

Casually, just in case anyone was watching, she sauntered to the ladies' room. She'd never seen a woman working in this area of the company, so she imagined the women's bathroom was a tip of the hat to equal opportunity. An easier step than actually hiring a woman on the shipping crew.

Not that such behavior was evidence that the bigwigs in Oceanic were drug smugglers, but it didn't help their case that they were antifeminists—didn't help it at all, in Cynthia's eyes.

She was grateful that the men were too macho to enter a door with a silhouette of a woman on it. The tiny bathroom was spotless, and smelled faintly of disinfectant.

Using the light from the open door, she did a quick reconnoiter—very quick; it was a pretty small bathroom—and in seconds had the layout memorized. One stall, a single white sink with a small mirror stuck to the wall above it. A paper towel dispenser, empty trash can. Lino floor that looked pretty clean. No window.

Swiftly she closed the door behind her, not turning on the light just in case it showed under the door.

Her heart began to pound. For the first time since she'd started the job, she was going against Jake's specific instructions to stick to her regular job and do nothing out of the ordinary. If he found out she was actively snooping he'd kill her. Of course, if there were drugs in this warehouse and she got caught hiding in a pitch-dark bathroom with a knapsack full of tools, somebody might do the job for him.

The darkness started to close in on her and she felt mildly panicked. It wasn't too late to change her mind. She could still waltz out of this tiny bathroom, say goodbye to the guys and saunter on home. No one would know about her botched undercover spying attempt. She gnawed on her thumb and listened to her heart pound.

She took a step backward and halted. She had to stop being a coward. Jake had offered her danger and excitement, and she'd been thrilled. Now she had a chance to grab some of that excitement by doing a little sleuthing, and she wanted to wimp out.

Well, forget it. She was doing this. And not just for her own personal satisfaction.

She kept up with the news; she knew the devastation caused by drugs. Families were torn apart. Teens became addicted and ruined their lives. And the senseless violence of drug wars made Cynthia sick. If there was any chance she could play the smallest role in helping to keep illegal drugs out of the country, she'd do it.

Considering her options, she decided to sit on the floor rather than the toilet. She'd be here awhile. She sank down, wishing she'd chosen to wear her black leather pants this morning instead of the miniskirt. At least her black wool jacket was warm.

She wished she had a way to pass the hours. She also wished she'd had time for lunch. She was already hungry. She ate the second chocolate bar in tiny bits, making it last as long as possible.

After an eternity had gone by, she realized she had no idea what time it was. If she was going for a career in the spy business, she should invest in one of those fancy watches with a luminescent dial that were good to thirty feet underwater. Then she spent a long time fantasizing about doing naughty things with Jake thirty feet underwater.

Which naturally led to memories of the night before and the way he'd made her feel: sexy and wanton. Powerless and yet powerful enough to make a man like Jake whimper. She smiled smugly at that. He'd moaned, too. But best of all was when she'd made him beg.

She was starting to feel very warm all of a sudden. He'd been gone when she'd woken this morning, which was to be expected, given his paranoia about secrecy. She'd swallowed her disappointment and searched eagerly for a note. There hadn't been one, but then again, if the bad guys broke into her house, he wouldn't want them finding a note. It was so sweet of him to worry about her.

Over coffee and granola it had occurred to her that

if the bad guys broke into her house, she'd have more to worry about than a note. Her euphoria dipped sharply and all her old insecurities rushed back. Maybe he hadn't had such a good time, after all. Maybe he thought it was a huge mistake.

With a heavy heart, she'd prepared for work, defiantly putting on the black miniskirt and black panty hose even though she felt more of a fraud than usual in her sexy getup.

She'd grabbed her purse with a sniff, set the alarm—vowing to upgrade to a top-of-the-line, state-of-the-art, unbreakable system—and hauled out her keys to lock the door. On her key ring was a small silver key she didn't recognize. Puzzled, she stared at it for a moment—then felt a rush of delicious joy.

It was the key to the handcuffs.

That was better than any old note, or dozens of red roses. What he was telling her, she was certain, was that he'd had a great time—and why put the key on her chain unless he was thinking she'd be needing it on a regular basis? The silver key tinkled merrily against the sturdier house and car keys.

If she wasn't scared of making a noise, she'd take her keys out now, just for the comfort of holding the little key that reminded her of her connection to Jake.

Her backside went numb and she reviewed sections of the Tax Code in her head to stay awake. She knew the shipping and receiving guys worked until eight. She'd planned to wait until somewhere around midnight to make her move. Trouble was, she'd forgotten she wouldn't be able to read her watch. She'd have to risk using the flashlight she'd purchased. Slowly, and as quietly as possible, she eased the big flashlight out of her bag and flicked it on.

Nothing happened.

She flicked the switch a few more times in increasing agitation. Still nothing. She should have tested it before she purchased it. Was it broken? She shook it.

Then she ground her teeth. *Batteries.* She'd forgotten all about batteries.

It must be hours and hours she'd sat here. If she wasn't careful, they'd find her sound asleep on the bathroom floor in the morning, and that would not look good at all. She slipped out of her heels and donned the black trainers she'd purchased earlier.

Slowly, she stood. She rested her ear against the door and listened.

Silence.

Feeling for the door handle in the dark, she eased the door open a crack. A faint glow from emergency lights illuminated the warehouse, but it was very different from daytime. The dim lighting cast horror-movie shadows and turned the crates and boxes into sinister masses.

But at least she was alone. No gang of cutthroat drug dealers had come to collect their booty, which had been her greatest fear.

Still, she fought an impulse to dive back into the bathroom and curl up into a ball. *I am Cyn the Bold!* she reminded herself over and over as she crept slowly out of the bathroom, closing the door soundlessly behind her.

Now what?

Deciding to get her nosing around over as quickly as possible so she could get out of there, she crept toward a heap of crates stacked on a wooden pallet.

She tiptoed along the cement, searching ahead for a path. She skirted trollies and a hydraulic lift. She passed boxes fresh from England and Ireland, thanks to Mr. Percivald senior.

At last she reached the chopstick crates. They were stacked in front of the coffee, with an aisle width between.

She stared at the heaped coffee sacks. The one she'd seen break had contained nothing but coffee, but wasn't it possible some of the sacks contained drugs? She gnawed her thumb in indecision, then decided to stick with her original plan of action. She could always investigate the rest of the coffee later if she had time.

She put her packsack on the ground beside her and dug inside it for the crowbar. She'd bought the smallest one she could find, for obvious reasons, but when she tried to pry the lid off the first wooden crate, she wished she'd gone for jumbo.

Although she was happy to be the first person opening the crate, she cursed at how difficult it was. And noisy. Sweat prickled her forehead and neck as she worked the crowbar up and down, trying to ease the lid off as quietly as possible.

She paused and her heart pounded double time. Had she heard something? Her eyes tried to penetrate the murky corners of the warehouse, but all she saw were menacing shadows. The crowbar grew slick in her hands.

She remained rigid, all senses alert, for a minute or so, then decided she'd imagined the noise, and went back to the crowbar. Her arms began to ache from the strain, but slowly the lid started to rise. With a final loud squeal, it came free.

Like a kid on Christmas morning, she leaned forward to peer inside the crate.

What made her lift her head? Another sound? The sense she wasn't alone?

She turned just in time to see a black shape hurtling toward her. Even as she opened her mouth to scream, it was too late. A black-gloved hand closed over her mouth and she was hauled backward, her body shoved hard against the pile of coffee sacks. She still had the crowbar in her hand, but as she tried to wield it, she realized that her attacker was holding it, along with her hand, in an unbreakable grip.

His other hand still covered her mouth and half her face. Through a fog of terror, she smelled the leather of his glove, felt the rigid strength of his hand. She worked her jaw, trying to bite him, but the hand clamped so hard she couldn't even move her tongue.

Frantically, she twisted her body, trying to get a good shot at kneeing him in the groin. Blood was ringing in her ears, and if it was possible to pant through her nose, she was doing it.

"Stay still. I'm not going to kill you till later," a fierce voice hissed in her ear.

Her body stilled and sank bonelessly against the burlap bags. After a moment the hand eased from her mouth.

"Jake!" she whispered, relief making her feel faint.

"Don't sound so happy to see me. I'm serious. You're dead meat."

"What are you doing here?"

"Same as you."

"Chopsticks?"

"Chopsticks." He cocked his head, listening. "Since you're here, you can hold the flashlight."

For a second she pondered arguing, then she remembered how glad she was to see him, and what hard work it had been just getting the lid off one crate. "Did you remember the batteries?"

"What?"

"For your flashlight."

A quiet sound she could have sworn was a chuckle erupted from his general direction. "Don't tell me Mata Hari forgot batteries for her flashlight?" His teeth gleamed white for a second, while she decided it was more dignified not to answer. She didn't care for him laughing at her, but at least his anger had cooled.

She held the flashlight he handed her, and got her first glimpse inside the crate. Rows and rows of chopsticks met her gaze. "Could be a ruse. Maybe the drugs are underneath," she whispered.

He shot her a glance that, even in the dim lighting, she had no trouble interpreting. *Shut up.*

She did. And watched as Jake lifted layer after layer of chopsticks out of the box, each layer buffered by transparent packing material. Patiently, he removed each layer from the crate and laid the chopsticks on the cement. Then he got right in the box, taking the flashlight from her and doing a minute inspection of the wooden crate.

He shook his head as he emerged. Then turned his attention to the chopsticks themselves. Slipping a set from its paper sleeve, he broke them apart, then snapped one in pieces, sniffing it, then touching it to his tongue. He grimaced and wiped his tongue on his gloved hand.

"Drugs?" she cried hopefully.

"Sliver."

"Ouch."

He wrapped the chopstick pieces in a bit of the packaging and slipped the small bundle into his pocket. He made a close inspection of each layer as he returned it to the crate, careful to preserve the same order.

Suddenly he cocked his head, listening.

She heard it, too. A deep male voice, muffled, but growing louder. Even as her eyes widened and her heart pounded in panic, she watched Jake shove the last few layers of chopsticks back into the crate.

The flashlight beam wavered all over the place as her hand started shaking.

He slid the lid back on top of the crate, then grabbed the flashlight, flicked it off and took her hand in his. He hauled her back behind the last of the crates, against the sacks.

They crouched there, and he lifted a black sleeve to reveal a watch with a luminescent dial, which had to be good to at least thirty feet underwater. *Figured.* Cynthia hoped it also had some kind of secret agent contraption to get them the hell out of there before they were discovered. The glowing numbers showed it was just after midnight.

Jake leaned toward her and put his lips to her ear. "Night watchman," he whispered.

She turned to him, startled. She didn't remember seeing any night watchman on the payroll. But, of course, they employed a security firm. The night watchman—or men—must be part of the security contract.

The sound she'd been listening for, and dreading, came. She heard the heavy door to the warehouse open. She peered cautiously over the top of a crate and saw two uniformed security guards. They were armed and burly, which was not good, but they also carried lunch boxes and thermoses, which made them somehow less frightening.

They headed straight for the scarred table where the

guys played cards on their lunch breaks. They put their stuff down, and one said to the other, "I'll take a turn round the main offices, you do a walk around in here." He gestured broadly, and Cynthia felt her already tight nerves crank another notch.

Agent Wheeler, who obviously didn't have any nerves, put a finger to his lips and flipped the flashlight so the handle faced out. She was puzzled until she recalled how heavy it had felt when she was holding it. Presumably it doubled as some kind of a weapon. He reached beneath his jacket with his free hand and withdrew his gun.

Jake angled his body so it blocked hers from sight, and she stared at the dark outline of his back until it started to blur. Her senses were superheightened as she crouched there, feeling as though she were caught in a nightmare. She heard the slow footfalls of the guard against the cement. He was overweight and wheezed slightly as he walked. The coffee beans smelled as potent as a triple espresso. She heard her own swallow, and tasted a hint of the chocolate bar she'd eaten earlier.

Closer and closer the slow, plodding footsteps came. She felt Jake's muscles tense in readiness. Her own fight or flight response was on full alert, adrenaline pumping through her system. She reached for the crowbar, knowing it wasn't much, but it was heavy and she could whack the guard with it if she had to.

Had the man seen them? He seemed to be heading straight for their hiding spot, not checking the other areas of the warehouse. But if he'd seen them, why hadn't he called his partner? She licked dry lips and tried to think up some plausible explanation as to why she, an office accountant, might be crouching among the crates in the dark.

Nothing plausible occurred to her.

"I know you're back there! Come on out," the guard said suddenly, in the voice a father might use with a child acting up. She didn't need Jake's signal to stay where she was. She was paralyzed by fear.

"Come on. I've got something for you." The voice came again, closer now.

Jake was poised on the balls of his feet, ready to spring.

Something hairy brushed her hand and she squeaked in alarm before biting off her own cry of horror. She jerked her hand back and watched a big dark shape scuttle by. It had a long snaking tail.

Oh, God. A rat.

"Hey, Wally. How are you, buddy?" the guard crooned, just as she heard the heavy door open once again.

"You gotta stop feedin' that rodent, it's disgusting," a grumpy older man's voice complained.

"Don't hurt his feelings, Harry. He's a very smart rat. Look how he knows I got Oreos in here." The voice sounded fainter, and she heard the boots heading away, then the clicking of a lunch box.

"He's vermin. I got rat poison in here."

"Aw, you wouldn't. Wally's like family, ain't you, little buddy?"

"I have to leave now," Cynthia whispered urgently to Jake, rubbing her hand frantically against her jacket. "They have rats here. Rats carry diseases like the bubonic plague, and are generally revolting."

Jake shot her a warning look and put a finger to his lips.

Okay. She was losing it. In some recess of her mind where a smidgen of sanity remained, she recognized that she was losing it, but her only coherent thought was to get out of this horrible rat-infested nightmare as quickly as possible.

Like yesterday.

"I really have to leave," she whispered.

"How are you going to get out?" he whispered back.

"I'll crawl past them. They're playing cards or something."

"The rat's up there." Was it her imagination or was he laughing at her?

It was the last straw. She'd had a miserable evening, learned absolutely squat, forgotten to buy batteries, and her last meal on earth could turn out to be a candy bar. Not only that, but Jake, her brand-new lover, hadn't even bothered to tell her he'd be dropping by. To top it all off, a rat had run over her hand. And Jake thought it was funny?

"Excuse me," she said furiously, and tried to shove her way past him.

Next thing she knew, he had his blasted hand clamped over her mouth again, the other just under her breasts, and he was hauling her backward. When he'd finished manhandling her, he bumped her down onto his lap, and she found herself leaning against his chest, while he leaned against the sacks. The smell of coffee, pungent and unattainable, made her stomach growl.

Jake held her still and began whispering soothingly into her ear. "Relax. They'll probably do rounds every couple of hours. Next time they do, we'll leave. Understand?"

She shuddered, but sanity had returned. Her panic was already ebbing as he cradled her, his words warm and reassuring in her ear. Somehow she felt nothing too terrible could happen to her now that Jake was holding her. In her head she knew how stupid that was, but he felt solid and warm beneath her.

"Just try to relax."

She felt his chest rise and fall as he whispered, imagined she could hear the steady pounding of his heart against her shoulder. His whispered breath sent shivers down her neck, and unbidden, images of him naked in her bed last night flashed before her eyes like a particularly luscious film.

His hand rested just under her breasts as though it belonged there, and suddenly she didn't want to go anywhere.

She heard the slap of cards and the low rumble of the guards' voices, not fifty feet away. She should be cowering in terror, but instead, a warm, powerful urge pervaded her body. It was as though all the fear and tension, all the adrenaline that had coursed through her body moments ago, had settled, hot and insistent, between her legs.

Relax? Not a chance.

She shifted her hips, doing her own private version of a fully clothed lap dance, and all thoughts of rodents fled. Maybe it wasn't the smartest thing she could be doing under the circumstances, but she was unable to control the raw need that gripped her.

The hand under her breasts tightened, grabbing her ribs as though to stop her movements, but it would have taken a full body cast to prevent the instinctive gyrations of her woman's body urging her mate to fill her. She heard a muttered oath, then felt Agent Wheeler's breathing change, as did the topography of his lap.

"What's on your mind, Cyn?" No longer soothing, his whisper was as ragged as a torn curtain, revealing his own urges.

Since he didn't move his hand from her mouth, her only way of answering him was with body language. She wiggled, as suggestively as she knew how, against the bulge pressing against her backside.

He nipped her earlobe, then traced its shape with his tongue, hot and wet in the cool, dank atmosphere of the warehouse. "I guess we don't have anything else to do for the next couple of hours." He still didn't move his hand from her mouth, but the other hand slipped inside her jacket and began to trace the contours of her breasts, while his lips trailed over the back of her neck, making her shiver all over.

She arched against him, rubbing her hands on the outside of his thighs, up to his waist as far as she could reach. All her fear had sublimated itself into an arousal so fierce she burned with it.

Helplessly her movements changed from the controlled gyrations she'd started with. She began squirming on his lap.

"Can you keep quiet?" he whispered.

She debated with herself for a moment. Could she? His left hand was doing such delicious things to her nipple that she felt a moan building in her throat. With two hands on her flesh, he could have her crying aloud in no time. And his right hand was such a talented hand. Clapped over her mouth the way it was, it just wasn't living up to its potential. There were areas of her body that needed that hand much more than her mouth did. Figuring the presence of the guards would act as a pretty efficient gag, she jerked her head up and down. *Yes.*

His hand released her mouth and reached down between her legs as if he'd read her mind. She pulled them open, as though she were doing a frog kick, and sighed softly as he cupped her heat.

"I hate panty hose," he whispered in frustration, pausing to fumble something out of his pocket.

Glancing down, she saw a knife and swallowed sharply. "What are you—?"

His other hand left her breast. She closed her eyes and held her breath, and next thing she knew, cool air fanned her intimate parts through the gaping hole in the crotch of her panty hose.

Maybe the air was cool, but she wasn't. She'd never felt like this before. Feverish with want. Shameless and wanton with the urge to take and be taken. Deep inside herself she recognized that part of the feverish excitement was caused by the fact that the guards were only several yards away and that this game she and Jake were playing was a dangerous one.

She bit her lip to stop herself from crying out as his fingers reached for her again.

"Now this, I like," he whispered, slipping his hand beneath the silk thong she'd donned that morning in a fit of bravado. She felt her own slickness as his fingers slid over her, seeking and finding her throbbing clit.

He shocked her by clamping a hand once more over her mouth. Before she had time to wonder why, he plunged two fingers inside her, deep and hard. Once.

And again.

And again.

She gripped the hard muscles of his thighs, trying to anchor herself as her body bucked helplessly against him. But there was no anchor that could hold her. He wouldn't allow it, forcing her to the brink, then flinging her over. The climax rocketed through her, urgent and explosive, while his hand silenced her cries.

But it wasn't enough. It wasn't nearly enough. All

he'd done was whet her appetite, only reminding her of the depth of her hunger.

As quietly as she could, given the raging need inside her, she turned and straddled him, feeling the cold shock of cement against her knees, startling against the heat in the rest of her body.

Her trembling hands fumbled a little as she found the zipper of his pants and drew it down slowly and oh, so quietly. His eyes were gleaming slits, mesmerizing her as she released him, warm and solid, into her hand. She took a moment to stroke him, loving the feel of him.

Her body ached, wanting him deep inside her. "I don't suppose you—"

"In my pocket."

Even in the dim light her surprise must have registered, for he continued, "I was planning to come by your place later."

Feeling wonderfully smug, she waited until he'd sheathed himself, then, lifting her hips, she guided him through the ragged tear in her panty hose, and pushing her thong to one side, nudged him against the still-throbbing entrance to her body.

She gazed at his face for a moment. It was rigid with suppressed tension, the jaw clamped, eyes half-shut. Very deliberately, she placed a hand over his mouth and brought his up to cover hers once more. Then she lowered herself slowly, feeling the delicious stretch, taking him deep.

She set the pace, and she kept it slow, partly to keep the noise to a minimum, but partly, she had to acknowledge, to watch the helpless need build in his eyes as he thrust up against her. Sweat began to bead on his forehead. His nostrils distended as his breathing thickened, sending puffs of warm breath against her knuckles.

Her own breathing was just as thick, her need just as potent. As she struggled to drag air into her lungs, she smelled coffee beans, dust and cement, leather and sweat. With each slide of her body against his, she felt the connection between them deepen, until she couldn't hold back any longer. Her hand squeezed hard against his mouth in warning, and he responded, pressing his palm more firmly over her lips.

Their gazes locked, saying all the things they couldn't say with their covered mouths. Unable to keep to her slow pace, she thrust her hips faster, pushing them both beyond control. As her body spasmed around him, squeezed by wave after wave of pleasure, his hand stopped her cries. She kept her gaze on his, watching his eyes widen and darken, until the moment when he also broke. She felt the rigid control slip as he bucked up inside her, once, twice, three times as she felt the glorious rush of his passion.

She slumped forward, amazed their noisy breathing alone hadn't been enough to summon the guards. But after listening for a tense moment, she heard a hoarse cry of triumph. "Full house beats your straight."

"Jeez. You got all the luck tonight," the rat-lover grumbled good-naturedly.

Jake kissed her palm as she started to remove it from his mouth. "He's wrong," he murmured. "I got all the luck."

She wanted to touch him and hug him, snuggle under the duvet and swap secrets in sleepy lovers' voices. Under the circumstances, she contented herself with leaning forward and kissing him, slowly and thoroughly.

Jake went along with it all right, but she could tell his heart wasn't in it.

"What the matter?" she whispered in her sleepy lover's voice into his ear.

"I don't want to get caught bare-assed by the guards," he muttered, shifting her off his lap.

"Oh. Right."

They fumbled their clothing back into place, although it was awfully breezy where her nylons had been sliced open. She reached for Jake's hand while they settled back to wait. They overheard the muffled sounds of another hand of poker in progress, and she tried not to wonder about the whereabouts of the rat. And whether or not it lived alone. Jake glanced at his watch from time to time, but otherwise sat as still as the unopened crates.

Now that the fun was over, boredom set in. They hadn't found anything but chopsticks. The floor was cold and hard, she was tired, she wanted to go home.

Maybe he read her mood, for Jake put an arm around her and pulled her toward him, dropping a light kiss on her hair.

She felt a wash of tenderness for this strong, scary man who made her life so exciting. She snuggled against him and rested her head on his chest. For a while she listened to his heart beat, slow and regular. It was odd to feel so languorous, hiding in a warehouse with two guards, at least one rat and possibly an illegal shipment of cocaine. She thought about how happy she was that Jake had showed up. She thought about what they'd just done, and how much she wanted to do it again, at home in bed. Then she just drifted....

She jerked awake. Someone was shaking her.

"Time to go," Jake said, his voice soft but no longer a whisper.

She blinked and stretched as she tried to get her bearings. With a shock, it all came back to her. She gazed around, wondering if she'd just had the strangest nightmare/wet dream combo of her life, but the cold cement and hunger were real, as was Jake urging her to her feet. "I can't believe I fell asleep," she grumbled on a yawn.

"Good thing you don't snore."

The card game was obviously over; she couldn't hear the guards. "Are they gone?" she mumbled sleepily.

"Doing their rounds. Come on."

He grabbed her hand and they skulked around the crates, past the trucking bays, over to the corner of the warehouse, where a door was set into the wall. Jake kept his back between her and the security panel so she couldn't see what he was doing, but the next thing she knew, he'd opened the door—and no alarms sounded, no lights flashed. She remembered how easily he'd slipped past her own alarm system the night before, and wasn't at all surprised.

Belatedly she realized she hadn't thought to provide herself with an escape route. If Jake hadn't been there, she'd have had to spend the entire night at Oceanic, either cowering among the crates with the rats or holed up in that teeny tiny washroom, then somehow pretend to arrive at work the next morning. In yesterday's clothes.

She shuddered at the thought.

"Boy, am I glad that's over."

As they walked out into the chilly night, Cyn really thought it *was* over.

Until she saw the fence.

7

"JAKE. I'm scared of heights," she hissed frantically.

The receiving area was completely fenced in, the gate heavily padlocked. But he led her away from the gate, to a shadowy corner. As they got closer, the fence appeared to grow higher. It had to be eight feet at least. "After you," he said.

Where was her bravado now? Nothing in those empowerment books had mentioned climbing eight-foot fences in a skirt. "I can't climb up there. I just told you, I'm scared of heights."

"How else do you plan to get out of here?"

"I, uh—"

He gestured impatiently with his thumb. "Up."

"I'm wearing a skirt, for God's sake. Panty hose—"

"They're already ripped. Go."

She raised her foot, then had a thought. "It's not an electric fence, is it?"

"Not at the moment. Up." His hands cupped her butt and lifted her, not exactly gently, off the ground, so she had no choice but to find what foothold she could in the fencing and start climbing.

She'd never been any good at this stuff as a kid, and age hadn't increased her agility or her courage. The cold metal fencing dug into the fleshy parts of her fingers, scraped her knees and barely gave purchase to her trainers. She'd have given up and taken her chances hiding on the property till morning, but Jake didn't offer her a choice. He was right behind her, urging her on—close enough that she'd fall on him if she slipped.

"Don't look down. Just keep climbing. You're doing great."

Cold air wafted around her legs and reminded her again of the rip in her panty hose. As she hoisted herself almost to the top, she glanced down and forgot to be scared at how high up she was perched. Jake was looking up her skirt.

"What are you doing?" she whispered furiously.

"Enjoying the view."

"You'll be enjoying it for a while. I'm stuck." And she was. The barbed wire stared her in the face and she had no idea how to get over it.

She heard a muttered curse, then scuffling below her. Jake handed his black leather jacket up to her. "Put that over the barbed wire. Try not to rip it."

She hated letting go even with one hand. But it was the only way she was going to get down. Luckily, it was dark enough that she couldn't see the ground all that clearly. Refusing to even think about that, she gingerly took the jacket, still warm from his body, and laid it over the spiky wire. "Now what?"

"Climb up, get one leg over, find a foothold and pull the other leg over. Don't think about it. And don't look down."

Her teeth were starting to chatter. She gulped and got one leg over. And froze.

"You can do it." His voice was so calm and reasonable, some of the rigid fear seeped out. He clung like some kind of superhero to the wire fence, urging her on.

Keeping her eyes on him, she muttered a prayer and

scrambled over the top. Then she half climbed, half slid to the ground as fast as possible. She hit the dirt with a thud. Once she knew she was on solid ground again she thought she was going to throw up. She bent forward, hugging her aching arms and gasping.

A dark shape plopped down at her side.

"You're okay. Hang on," he said, and put his jacket around her shoulders. "Let's get you home."

"DON'T YOU EVER, EVER do anything so stupid again!" Jake raged. "You could have blown the whole operation. Destroyed months of work. You could have been killed."

"So could you," she reminded him. Now that they were safe and the night's adventure over, she had time to savor her first night as a kick-ass investigator. She'd searched for drugs, evaded guards, climbed a sky-high fence. And that didn't even include the sex. No wonder she was high from her evening's adventures.

And Jake with his yelling wasn't going to spoil her mood.

She drank hot tea seriously doctored with rum while Jake stalked up and down. It was three in the morning, but sleep was out of the question.

In fact, the more he ranted, the more she started to feel her own anger bubble, until she snapped, "What's the point in me working there if you won't let me do anything but reconcile invoices?"

"You're supposed to study the books, find discrepancies in the accounting. You—"

"The books are clean, Jake. I've told you that. There has to be another set somewhere. But I don't know where. If we found drugs we could—"

"*We* don't search for drugs." His face burned a deep

red as he stomped forward and brought it mere inches from her own. Only stubborn pride stopped her from jerking backward. "*I* search for drugs. *You* stay in the office and keep your nose clean." Only the sound of true worry in his tone stopped her from blasting off at him.

Her attention also snagged on something else that bothered her. What was wrong with this picture? Something niggled in the back of her brain, something that had hovered at the edge of her consciousness for weeks. Suddenly it hit her. He always talked in the singular, and she'd never seen any other FBI personnel in his vicinity. Something was very odd here.

Watching him intently, she said, "I thought the FBI always worked in teams."

"What are you talking about?"

"You. You said '*I* search for drugs, *I* do this job.' On TV agents always work in pairs, or teams."

His complexion deepened a shade and he glanced away. "Don't believe everything you see on TV."

She might be an amateur, but she wasn't stupid. She could tell he was hiding something. "So, you work all by yourself?"

He was out of her face in a heartbeat, taking a sudden interest in a spot on his thumb. "That's classified."

She let a second or two tick by. "Maybe I should phone the FBI and ask to speak to your boss. She could tell me."

"He," Jake answered automatically, then his head shot up. "Don't you even think about calling."

"Why not?"

"Because it's none of your business."

"I'm a taxpayer. Of course it's my business."

He grimaced. "Let it go, Cyn."

She shook her head. "Not a chance."

There was a long silence. "Who are you going to talk to at three in the morning?"

"I'll leave a message." She rose and went to the kitchen to fetch her telephone book. Returning, she made a show of flipping it open to the *F*s. She shot a glance at Jake under her lashes to make certain she had his attention.

He glared at her.

"Let's see, Farnsworth, Finkleman...oops, too far..."

He made a sound like a man goaded to the end of his sanity. "I'm on holiday."

She stared at Finkleman's phone number while the quiet words sank in.

The book crashed to the floor. "What?"

She'd never seen Jake Wheeler lose control in the slightest—well, except in bed, which was not something she wanted to think about at the moment. Right now, he looked like a man losing control of a situation he thought he'd had nailed. He paced, dragging a hand through his hair till it stood out in charcoal tufts. "Sort of a holiday."

"*Holiday* means playing golf, fishing, scuba diving. Lazing in a hammock composing your memoirs. *Holiday* does not mean working on a case. I don't believe you." She bent down, hauled the bulky telephone book back up and plopped herself on the couch, letting him see she meant business.

He walked slowly over and sank down beside her. "Okay, it's not a holiday, exactly. I'm on stress leave."

"Stress leave?" Oh, man, could she pick 'em. First Walter, the tightwad with no sex drive; now Jake, who had a sex overdrive, but was either a rogue agent or a

lunatic. She dropped her head into her hands. "Why me?" she moaned to no one in particular.

He rested a hand, warm and heavy, on her ankle, where it lay beside him on the couch. Even as mad as she was, that connection reminded her that whatever kind of nutcase he was, at least he was a great lover. And she trusted him.

It shocked her as the thought occurred, but it was true. She did trust him. Enough to abandon a long-term job and throw her future into jeopardy, although she was beginning to wonder how much jeopardy there really was. Maybe he'd hallucinated the whole smuggling thing. Maybe she wasn't the only one with a rich fantasy life.

Still, even if he was crazy, he'd made the past few weeks more fun and exciting than any she'd ever known. She still tingled when she thought about the awful, terrifying climb up and over that fence. She tingled even more when she remembered the blazing heat that had consumed them both as they made love in the warehouse, not fifty feet from armed guards. In fact, she was getting warm all over again just thinking about it.

She turned to gaze into his smoky-blue eyes and felt even hotter. They'd been in danger tonight. They could have been caught. She was as nutty as he was, she knew, but the very thought of danger had her wanting to strip that sexy FBI agent naked and have her way with him.

"I guess I'd better explain," he said in a voice that sounded like he'd rather chew broken glass.

"All right." She didn't really want talk, not when she was feeling like this, but she could see he wanted to tell her something, and since he wasn't normally a big communicator, she decided she'd better listen.

"One of our agents was killed," he said at last, his words dousing her heat like a jug of ice water.

"Killed?"

"He'd crewed on to a fishing boat we suspected was smuggling cocaine." Jake drew in a deep breath and let it out slowly, while she stared at him. "Hank and I started out together at Quantico. He was a good guy."

"What happened?"

He jerked to his feet and stalked across the room. "They found him tangled in a fishing net, drowned. Looked like an accident."

Anger and disbelief were written all over his face. "You don't think it was an accident."

"He wasn't that stupid or that careless. He was murdered."

A chill skittered across her chest. "What's Oceanic got to do with your friend?"

"Maybe nothing." He shrugged. "Accidents happen, even to guys in my line of work. But when I checked his apartment, I knew it was no accident."

"The place had been trashed?" She pictured how it would look: clothes strewn, belongings broken, the dead man's home desecrated.

"No. It was neat."

"Neat?" Oh, God. He really was a lunatic. Her love life was going to land her on one of those talk shows. *Women who lust after psychos.* That, or the comedy network.

He walked across the room and straightened the Picasso print she'd hung on the claret-colored walls. She loved the vibrant drama of the skewed lines and the woman's lopsided features, but she didn't think Jake even noticed what was in the frame he'd mechanically straightened. "Too neat. Hank was a slob. But this place was clean. So clean the back of my neck prickled."

She was experiencing the same feeling on her own neck. "Maybe he had a neatnik girlfriend?"

Jake nudged the right side of the print slightly. "I double-checked. He was single. No girlfriends, no cleaning service."

"I still don't see how—"

"I went back through his things one more time. That's when I found the Oceanic business card."

This whole clandestine operation was being waged over a lone business card? "I have a purse full of Oceanic business cards. So what?"

He abandoned the picture and resumed pacing. "You work there. But why would Hank have one? I found it in the lining of his duffel bag. And the bag was all neat and tidy, too." He shot that statement at her as though she'd argued with him. "Socks rolled, everything in his wallet in perfect order. I'm telling you, somebody went through his stuff. But they missed the card because they didn't want to arouse suspicion by tearing the duffel bag to bits like I did."

Her stomach felt strange, as if she'd eaten a carton of jumping beans. "Was anything written on the card?"

He shook his head. "He was a professional—he wouldn't carry anything that couldn't be explained away if he was caught. There could be a million reasons he'd have that card in his bag. Most of them innocent."

"But you don't think it was innocent?"

"I don't know." And she heard how much he hated the not knowing. "That business card is the only clue we've got. Officially, Hank's death is being treated as an accident. We had some leads into a drug operation, but they've all dried up. My boss agrees with you that one business card isn't grounds for an investigation into Oceanic." Jake turned to her, his face grim. "Officially, I don't have any support on this."

"And unofficially?"

He gave a wry grin. "My stress leave could end at any time. We all want these guys, Cyn. If I can find hard evidence, Oceanic won't know what hit them."

"That's where I come in." She felt in her bones that he was telling the truth; he *was* an agent, and there was a possibility she was the key to unlocking the entire drug-ring conspiracy. One man had already been killed. This wasn't a game. It was dangerous work. Incredibly dangerous. And Jake had chosen her to help him. Even though it was the middle of the night, she'd never felt more awake. Or more alive.

"Look, I think we should talk about that...." He turned to gaze at her, two lines of worry etched between his brows.

She jumped up, knowing now that he was all alone in this investigation. He might not want to admit it, but he needed her. "Don't fire me, Jake. I'm the only team you've got—and I'm on your side." She was, too. They were a great team, both professionally and personally; he just hadn't figured it out yet.

He rubbed a hand over his face, and the pain he tried to hide almost broke her heart. "I was the one who recruited Hank for this job. I got him killed. I don't want the same thing to happen to you."

"Of course you didn't get him killed. He made his own choices, just like I did. And nothing's going to happen to me. I won't snoop anymore. I promise." She went to him, reached out a hand to touch his arm.

He pulled away. "It's late. Get some sleep. I'll call you tomorrow." He started walking toward the door.

"Don't go." Her heart ached for the grief she felt emanating from him. Grief he wouldn't, or couldn't, share. Even though he halted, he didn't come back to her. "I'm sorry about your friend," she said softly, going to him once more. She wrapped her arms around his torso.

He remained stiff and rigid in her arms. "I have to go."

"No, you don't." She cupped his cheek with her palm, rubbing the abrasive, shadowy stubble; his jaw was like iron, but as her thumb passed below it she felt a pulse jump in his neck.

He needed her, and damn it, she needed him. That knowledge gave her the courage to rise on tiptoe and feather her lips over his. It felt like kissing a stone statue. "Stay with me tonight," she whispered against his rigid lips.

"No."

"Yes," she said softly, and ran her tongue along his lower lip. It trembled. The stone beginning to crack. Tenderness washed over her as she felt his need for comfort breaking through the rigid control. How had she ever let this man frighten her? He was strong and noble, fighting for what was good in the world.

"Stop it!"

There was no bloody way Jake was going to let her do this to him. The fact that they'd found nothing suspicious tonight only added to the fury that had churned within him from the moment he heard about Hank. If he didn't find some hard evidence soon, Hank's death would stay unsolved, his killers free. Miss Fun and Games wasn't turning this into *Raunch* scenario number fifty-three.

"I can't be some friggin' magazine fantasy for you

tonight. I'll hurt you." He grabbed her shoulders, knowing he should push her away, but loving the feel of her warm flesh in his hands.

"No, you won't."

He stared down at her. Her big green eyes were so wide and trusting. Her cheeks were flushed and her breathing rapid—she was still high on the adrenaline reaction. But she didn't know what he was capable of—that as much as he'd like to give her what she wanted, he might hurt her in the mood he was in.

There was some powerful stuff sizzling in the atmosphere between them: anger, lust, guilt, need. He should go home and grab a cold shower while he still could. He made a move to pull away, but even as he tried to sever the warm connection, he found he couldn't.

He made a sound between a growl and an oath, and yanked her, not away from him, but toward him.

His lips slammed down on hers like prison doors, trapping her in the angry passion that consumed him. He ravaged her mouth with need rather than tenderness, nipping at her lips, invading her mouth with his tongue, plundering her sweetness. Doing his best to warn her off, he grabbed her hips and ground himself against her so she could feel the strength of his arousal.

And if she wanted to call a halt she'd better do it fast.

Instead of pulling away from him, she seemed to match his mood, holding him tight and rubbing herself intimately against his erection.

Now that he'd let himself go, he literally ached for her. "I need you," he admitted on a groan.

"Yes."

He didn't bother with any more talk, just picked her up bodily and carried her into the bedroom, where he tossed her on the bed, then went to work unbuckling his belt. Once more he warned her, "I can't be a gentleman tonight."

"I know." The emotions running in him were explosive, and he needed to bury himself in her soft heat as much as he needed to drag in the next ragged breath.

He watched her, his innocent vixen, as her trembling fingers reached for the buttons of her blouse.

"Forget it. Get your panties off."

He thought she might refuse, tell him to go to hell. Instead she whimpered, deep in her throat. Her eyes held his gaze as she reached under her skirt, raised her hips and dragged the torn panty hose and thong off in one bone-meltingly sexy motion.

His black denims flew across the room and then he was on top of her. "You make me crazy," he muttered, grabbing her knees and pushing them up against her chest, so her skirt caught between her hips and waist. Then he plunged into her and couldn't think anymore. He could only feel.

It was like diving into molten honey. Slick, hot and tight. He thrust savagely into her, as though he could drive his demons out where they'd perish in her sweetness.

He kissed her, a deep, devastating kiss that left him longing for more. He couldn't get close enough, thrust deep enough....

Beneath him, her body was going crazy, rocking up against him to take him even deeper, getting hotter and slicker by the second.

She offered up everything she had. Giving him comfort in her body, kissing his hurts better every time their mouths met, stroking, touching him everywhere as they pushed each other higher.

She cried out, her body arching against him, her head thrashing on the pillow, and he was gone, swirling into the black current that sucked him into its depths.

And something amazing happened. As his release flowed into her body, as he stared down at her heaving chest, still clothed because he'd been in too much of a hurry to undress her, he felt some of his anger dissipate. Gently, he kissed her lips in gratitude, and a feeling of tenderness washed through him. She seemed so fragile, but she wasn't. She was strong and gutsy and incredibly generous.

He wanted to say "thank you" as he collapsed at her side, damp and breathing raggedly. He wanted to tell her...but before he could finish the thought or form words, he was asleep.

8

JAKE WOKE SUDDENLY and completely, a loud and unfamiliar noise jarring him out of a deep, dreamless sleep. He blinked and shook his head, confused. Then he heard a groan and an arm flapped across his body, the spread-fingered hand banging futilely in the direction of the buzzing alarm clock.

It occurred to him that Cyn was not a morning person. She looked like a woodland animal coming out of hibernation and deciding it was too early for spring. Her eyes stayed shut as her hand flailed away.

Taking pity, he punched the snooze button for her, then grinned, watching her burrow back down in the covers. She wiggled until she found the right spot, then curled into herself.

He breathed deeply. He felt easier than he had in months, and he knew he had Cyn to thank for that. He hadn't wanted to talk about Hank, and the guilt he'd always carry. The best therapy Jake could imagine for getting over his grief would be to catch the bastards who'd killed his friend. But Cyn had given him comfort, too. More than comfort, a deep sense of peace.

He wished he could let her sleep longer—she'd had three hours at the most—but she shouldn't draw attention to herself if she was going back to Oceanic. So long as she kept her promise to stay away from snooping, she'd be safe, and he'd still have eyes and ears inside the company.

They hadn't found a thing last night, so chances were the place was clean, anyway. He couldn't keep this one-man operation going much longer. He knew that. Adam had given him more time than he'd expected, but it couldn't last much longer. He'd have to acknowledge defeat.

Maybe it was time to accept that Hank was gone.

A mutter drew his attention to the warm, naked woman beside him. He kissed her awake. "Sorry, babe, but you slept through your alarm."

Her eyes opened, blank and sleepy. Then she focused on him and her smile lit his world. "Morning."

He kissed her again, taking his time, filling his hands with her sleep-warmed skin while his body suggested all sorts of great ideas for starting the day off right. "I can never get enough of you," he mumbled against her lips.

"Good," she replied, wrapping her arms around him and rubbing up against him.

The snooze alarm made another attempt, and with a cry of horror, Cyn pushed herself up to a sitting position.

She batted his hands off her breasts and jumped to her feet. "Stop it. I'm going to be late."

He had the indefinable pleasure of watching Cyn race through her morning routine, still with the sleepy, half-dazed expression on her face. She ran into the shower, raced back out, naked and damp, and he wanted her again.

Sex was obviously the last thing on her mind as she scrambled around drying her hair and doing her makeup at the same time, tossing panties and bra on the bed.

"Where are my stockings?" She gave a cry of triumph and picked up a pair of black panty hose off the floor, then glared at him.

"What?"

She stuck her fist through where the crotch used to be. Their eyes met, and damn if the air didn't sizzle. If he stood there, staring at her, while they both thought about last night, he was either going to catch fire or make her really, really late for work.

"I'll get the coffee started," he said abruptly, and escaped before he got them both in trouble.

"MMM," SHE SAID DREAMILY as she took her first sip of coffee, her eyes closed and a blissful expression on her face. "You have a standing invitation to make my morning coffee."

He loved the way she could make drinking coffee seem so special. In fact, he loved a lot of things about this woman. "I may take you up on that offer—if I get a night like last night thrown into the bargain."

Her eyes stayed closed, but a dimple peeped in her cheek. "Deal." She opened her eyes and popped two pieces of grainy bread into the toaster. "What are you going to do today?"

Before he could answer, his cell phone rang.

"Wheeler."

"Jake, it's Adam."

Jake's good morning mood evaporated along with the fragrant steam from the coffee. If the special agent in charge was calling, it probably wasn't to wish him a good morning.

"Any progress on the Oceanic investigation?" Adam asked.

Jake closed his eyes and leaned against the kitchen

counter, knowing he was about to lie to a man he respected. "I've found something, yeah." He fished the chopstick pieces out of his pocket. In the daylight they looked even less exciting than they had last night. "I'm sending a sample into the lab today for analysis." That would buy him several days of extra time, and he sure as hell better come up with something by then.

Or he'd be bombarded with lame jokes involving Chinese food when he returned to the bureau.

"What is—"

"Look, I can't say right now."

"Somebody there?"

"Yeah."

His boss sighed grumpily. "She better be good-looking."

"Oh, yeah, she's good-looking," Jake said, winking at Cyn and watching her blush.

His grin went south at Adam's next words. "I need you back at work, Jake. I'm stretching things as it is. You've got one more week."

"Yeah, okay." As he ended the call, he tried to feel angry, but he'd have done the same thing in Adam's place. And when the man discovered the evidence he'd uncovered was a broken chopstick…well, it had bought him a week. He'd better make the most of those seven days.

"A broken chopstick is the new development?" Cyn had obviously gone back to thinking he was insane. Rightly so.

Jake blew out a breath, wondering if he should just chuck the chopstick in the trash and admit defeat. But he was stubborn. One week could be all he needed. "You'd be amazed how much the crime labs will get from this." He stared at the uninspiring piece of evidence. "What kind of tree wood, possibly a location where the chopsticks were made." He shrugged irritably. The utter frustration he felt made him wish he had a punching bag handy. "Damn it. I wish we'd found something."

Her brow creased in ready sympathy. "You've got another week. There must be something else you can try. Old ground you can revisit."

"Harrison's the key. I know it. I can't believe the little weasel split the country so fast."

"Could he be back from vacation?"

Jake shook his head. "If his passport's used anywhere, we'll be notified right away. Interpol and the cops in Hong Kong are keeping an eye out for him. But he's disappeared." And Jake had a bad feeling about that. If Harrison had cut and run, Hong Kong was the perfect place to get a new passport, a new identity. Hell, with enough money, he could have had so much cosmetic surgery his own mother wouldn't recognize him. He could be anywhere in the world right now.

"What about his home?"

"I went there right after he left town. Looked like he was coming back. There was fresh milk in the fridge, his stuff all around. Phone still hooked up."

She tapped her coffee mug, a black-and-white affair with zigzagging patterns on it. "Does he rent or own?"

"Rents an apartment downtown. Look, I appreciate your help but—"

"It's the second of the month," she said, glancing at her wall calendar to confirm the date.

"I told you we'd be notified if he comes—"

"What about his rent? It would have been due yesterday. Did he wire money to pay it? Contact the landlord? That might help us track him down."

For a second Jake just stared at her, wondering how he could have been so stupid as to have missed something so obvious. Then he leaned forward, grabbed her head in his hands and kissed her. "You are not only beautiful, you're brilliant."

Her eyes shone. "You really think I'm beautiful?"

"Gorgeous. Now get going or you'll be late for work." As if on cue, the toast popped up, and so did Cyn.

"I'm coming with you," she said, grabbing health-food-store peanut butter and slapping it on both pieces of toast.

"Too dangerous," he replied, and immediately regretted the words. Danger was her drug of choice; he had to remember that. "Dangerously boring," he amended hastily.

She handed him a piece of toast. "Who's going with you?"

"Nobody."

"What if Harrison's there?"

"I'll ask him some questions. That's it."

"He might—"

"He won't. Now get."

She sent him a look that promised retribution, then grabbed her coat and bag and headed for the door.

"Hey!" He halted her in the doorway. "About last night."

A wary expression entered her green eyes. She was obviously expecting him to lecture her again about keeping out of trouble. But that wasn't what was on his mind. He was remembering how she'd wrapped her arms around him when he most needed comfort, how she'd held him and loved him when his mood was black with pain and grief.

He wanted to kiss her, but her mouth was busy chewing toast, so he raised her hand and kissed the palm. "Thanks."

Once he'd returned to his place long enough for a quick shower and change of clothes, he headed to Harrison's apartment building. On the way, he called the bureau from his car.

"What?" a voice snarled.

Even though his buddy Carl couldn't see him, Jake grinned. "You been taking more of those public relations courses?"

"Wheeler! You better be calling to tell me you're hauling your ass back in here."

"Soon, Carl. I need you to confirm that Harrison, the former Oceanic accountant, hasn't returned to the States."

There was a huffy blasphemy. "I got a terrorist plot that looks like a hoax, but I gotta check it out, two bank robberies with the same M.O. as a string of heists in Texas, a murdered drug dealer and an ulcer. And you want me keeping tabs on some clerk who's taking a holiday." Jake heard papers scrabbling; Carl's chair squealed as he rolled it to his file drawer. "Seems like everybody's on holiday," he grumbled. "Hold on."

The line clicked and Jake waited.

Ahead of him a van with a pile of kids in it pulled into his lane. Some kind of field trip, he imagined. Or maybe a day care; they didn't look old enough to his inexperienced eye to be in school. The mom, or teacher, appeared pretty perky for a woman with a vanful of kids. She had short red hair, but it didn't have the attitude Cyn's hair did. And just like that he pictured Cyn with kids.

He felt as if he'd just been punched. The kids he'd

imagined were *his* kids. His and Cynthia's. Which just made him agree with Carl that he'd been on holiday too long. Jake needed a good dose of reality.

The line clicked and he took a right turn, losing sight of the toddler van. "Nope. No sign of Harrison. If he's reentered the States he used a different passport."

"Thanks, buddy."

"No sweat. Hey, come by for dinner one night next week. Susan's got a friend she wants you to meet."

Jake's expletive was met with a coarse chuckle. He figured they were both recalling the women Carl's wife had already set him up with: a belly dancer who'd just dumped her fourth husband and a dog groomer who'd rubbed his thigh and made sexual innuendos about his "gun" all through dinner. He mostly went along with it for the entertainment value, and because he liked Carl and his wife. "Who is it this time?"

"A medium."

There was a second of silence. "As in, talks to dead people?"

"Yep." Carl gave a snort of ill-disguised merriment.

Jake shook his head. "Doesn't Susan have any friends who are sane?"

"Not that she'd let you get near."

He tapped his fingers against the steering wheel while he waited for the light to go green. "Tell Susan thanks, but I'm seeing someone."

"No kidding. Is she hot?"

Jake thought about Cyn and a reluctant grin kicked up one side of his mouth. The light turned green and he put his foot on the gas. "Oh, yeah. She's hot."

"Bring her for dinner. We'd love to meet her. You pick the day."

"I'll ask her." He didn't know what Carl would

make of the new woman in his life, but he had a feeling Susan and Cyn would get on like a house on fire. They were equally nuts, and he was crazy about both of them.

JAKE'S CELL PHONE RANG. Thinking it was Carl calling back, he stuck the earpiece back in his ear and spoke in the direction of the microphone once more. "Wheeler."

"That's not a very friendly greeting. It could be a girl calling." Just hearing Cyn's deliberately provocative purr made him jerk the wheel.

A low laugh traveled through his earpiece as intimately as though she had her lips pressed against him. "Careful, you don't want to run off the road."

"Where are you?" But he already knew. He gritted his teeth and glared into the rearview mirror. She wasn't hard to spot. She was right behind him, following in her sensible blue compact, sending him a cheery little wave. The car didn't suit her at all; she should be driving a bad-girl black speed machine, suitable for driving a man insane. "Why aren't you at work?"

"I am. I'm helping you. Don't fuss. I can't let you go alone to a suspect's apartment without backup."

He was touched as well as mildly amused that she thought he needed her to protect him. "So, you're my backup."

"That's right." Something in her tone told him to leave it, so he did. "I told Agnes I had a dentist appointment. I'll go in later."

He could argue, he could rant, he could order her to turn around. But he knew it wouldn't do a damn bit of good. "I could lose you in less than five minutes." He eyed the next exit off the I-5 and his gas-pedal foot started to itch. She might think she was protecting him by tagging along, but in fact he'd just lose his concentration if she were around.

"You wouldn't be such a spoilsport."

No. Unfortunately for him, he wouldn't. He owed her too much. Something had changed between them last night and he didn't think he could ever treat her quite the same. Besides, she was already late for work. Another hour wouldn't change anything.

Thoughts of Cyn, him and an hour naturally led him in a certain direction. He hesitated a moment. His line was secure; so was hers. Traffic was slow, and they were both over twenty-one. He glanced back and she blew him a kiss. "What exactly are you going to do as my backup?"

That laugh of hers channeled right to his *cojones,* inspiring all kinds of lustful ideas. She seemed to catch right on to his mood. "What will I do? It seems to me—but you're the expert, so put me straight if you need to—it seems to me that I'm here as your sidekick, to help and aid you in any way whatsoever."

"And in return? What do you expect of me, your...partner?"

He tilted the rearview mirror so he could watch her as she settled back and shot him a provocative glance that scorched even through her front windscreen and his rear one. "I want another night like last night. In fact, I want lots of them."

Why was he not surprised the woman even used a telephone as a sex toy? "Great. Nightly stud service. Anything else?"

"Then there's the daytime...." Her lustful sigh surprised a chuckle out of him.

The traffic was brought to a standstill for road construction, so he settled back in his seat to play her game for a few minutes. "What about the daytime?"

"I have wants…needs. They aren't always governed by the clock."

He could swear he saw her chest rising and falling as her breathing quickened. He shifted in his seat, struggling to control his own breathing. "Ms. Baxter. Is it possible you're trying to have phone sex with a federal agent?"

"I'm not sure…I never thought about it." Her lips tilted. "Yes."

"It's only fair to warn you, we're not supposed to have phone sex on the job."

"Ignoring the fact that you're on stress leave, don't you get a coffee break?"

"I suppose I could relax for a few minutes," he admitted, thoroughly enjoying himself. He glanced at Cyn again and wondered if she had any idea just how unrelaxed he was at this moment.

"Now, let's see…."

There was a pause during which he imagined all kinds of wicked and wacky scenarios she might come up with, while nothing but silence came from the phone. "Still there?" he asked at last.

"Yes." She sounded hesitant. "It's just that I've never had phone sex before. I'm not sure how to begin."

Damn, there she went again. One minute sexy vixen, next the innocent act. He just wished he could determine which one *was* the act. "Well, you're doing something right."

"What do you mean?"

"If you were with me, you'd understand."

"You mean you're, um…?"

"I've got a boner with your name on it, if that's what you're trying to ask."

She sighed as though he'd just whispered love words in her ear. Some innocent. She wanted dirty talk, he'd give it to her. "Do you know what I'm going to do with this boner?"

In the rearview mirror he watched her shake her head before he heard her whispered, "No."

"I'll tell you just exactly what I'm going to do." And in the time it took for the gal holding the Stop-Slow sign to finish a cigarette, he did, using explicit language and coming up with a few scenarios he wasn't sure a man could pull off without bionic limbs.

"Oh, stop it." Cyn laughed, but there was a breathless, turned-on edge to it. "You can't do that on a hang glider. You'd die trying."

"I'd die with a smile on my face."

"Me, too," she whispered. Their gazes connected and held, and he was surprised the two car windows separating them didn't melt.

The traffic had started moving and he was able to take the next turnoff. She followed. And kept on following until he pulled into a parking spot and cut the engine. She parked beside him and got out, looking around with a puzzled expression. He rolled down the window and she leaned in. "This is a shopping mall."

"It is? You got me so turned inside out I couldn't remember where I was going." He grinned at her raised eyebrows. "Hop in. No sense taking two cars."

Her eyes narrowed and she stared at him for a moment as though debating whether she should trust him. Smart lady. He leaned over and opened the passenger side, and she swung in beside him.

"So, where are we—"

She never finished the sentence. He had his arms around her and his lips on hers so fast she didn't even have time to shut her eyes. He didn't shut his, either, just watched as her eyes gave away what her body was feeling. From wide-eyed and stiff, she went to dilated pupils and a soft, yielding form. She smelled good, she felt good, she tasted good. And he forgot himself as his teasing taste of her turned into a serious feast.

The honk of a horn brought him to his senses. This was a suburban shopping mall in midmorning, not the bridal suite at a fancy lodge in the middle of nowhere. And that's where he'd really rather be, he realized, as he pulled back.

"What was that for?" she asked hazily.

"Cover," he croaked.

"Cover?"

Like a sinful thought, a light twinkled deep in her amazing green eyes. "You said you were going to the dentist. Now you can say with perfect truth that you had your mouth thoroughly examined."

"Do I have any cavities?"

"Oh, yeah. One particular cavity I'm going to have to fill later." She snorted with laughter, and he grinned as he settled back into his own seat and started the engine. "I might have to use my drill."

"I don't have time to play dentist."

"Looked to me like that cavity needed urgent attention," he said, letting his finger trail up her thigh.

She slapped his hand away and crossed her legs. Which only made the view better. "I think you'd better unplug that *drill* for a while. It's going to wear out."

"Now who's a spoilsport?"

She was trying to appear prim, but having a hard time

of it. Finally, she gave up and outright grinned at him. "So, where *are* we going?"

"The Buena Vista Garden Apartments. A pricey California-style lowrise recently home to a Mr. Harrison."

"Do you suppose he'll be there?"

"I checked this morning. He definitely didn't reenter the States with his own passport." Jake gritted his teeth just knowing that slimy little bean counter had left the country in the first place, before they'd had a chance to talk to him.

"I know, but his rent was due. Maybe he came back under an assumed name." She was bubbling with excitement at the prospect of interviewing a suspected drug dealer–money launderer.

As they pulled into a visitor's parking spot outside the Buena Vista Garden Apartments, she flipped open a pocket mirror and pulled out a tube of coppery lipstick, probably to replace the stuff he'd kissed off her lips earlier.

Watching her out of the corner of his eye, he did his best to sound bored. "Well—" he sighed heavily "—this'll be a waste of time. Tell you what. You wait here and I'll try to hurry things up, then get you back to the office."

She made kissing noises to herself in the mirror, then snapped the mirror shut before turning to him. "Don't even think about it," she said, and opened the car door.

So much for reverse psychology. He joined her and together they made their way to the front door. "Okay. You can come. But I do all the talking. Understand?"

"Mmm-hmm. I'm just your sidekick."

He rolled his eyes. "Right." He stuck a finger under his tie knot where it bulged against his Adam's apple. "Damn tie. I hate the things."

"Then why are you wearing one?"

"The super's an old guy. Saw action in World War II. It matters to him."

Making sure his badge was attached to his belt buckle and visible, his gun holster adjacent to the badge, he buzzed the super and identified himself.

The man appeared promptly, wiping crumbs off his mouth before straightening to attention when he saw who it was.

"Sorry to bother you, sir," Jake said. "I was here before about Mr. Harrison in apartment 408."

The man nodded eagerly. "Yes. I remember. Are you looking for his forwarding address?"

"Forwarding address?" His gut clenched, and beside him Cyn shuffled her feet.

"Yes. He's moved out."

Jake took a deep, slow breath and kept his face pleasant with an effort. "As I recall, you promised to phone me if you saw or heard from Mr. Harrison."

"I didn't see him. He sent a couple of his friends, with a letter of instruction signed by him."

The hair started to rise on the back of Jake's neck. He swore silently. One phone call from that super and they might have been able to track down Harrison through his "friends." Yelling at this mental midget wasn't going to help.

He said, with forced calmness, "Do you still have that letter?"

"Of course." The old guy puffed his chest out as if he should get a medal for keeping a letter when he'd allowed live suspects to get away. "Come in."

Jake stood back to let Cyn enter first.

"Are you with the FBI, too?"

"My associate. Miss Smith," he said quickly, before she could state her real name.

"How do you do?" She extended her hand to the superintendent. "And it's *Ms.* Smith." She glared at Jake just long enough to let him know she didn't think much of his imagination. Or his chauvinism.

He turned his attention back to the super. "Did they give you anything else? Their names or proof of identity?"

"No. The letter looked all right, and I checked his signature against the lease. They paid cash in lieu of a month's notice. I've documented the cash transaction and I can show you the deposit slip. Everything's aboveboard."

"I'm sure it is, sir." While the man was still nervous, Jake asked, "Could we take a look at his suite?"

"It's occupied. I just rented it to a nice young couple." And so much for any evidence the *movers* might have left behind. The elevator whirred.

"Did Harrison leave a forwarding address for his mail?"

The man nodded eagerly. "The same post office box in Hong Kong that was on his letter." An elderly woman clutching a gray purse emerged from the elevator, stared at Jake and Cyn curiously as she walked past and greeted the super primly.

Jake nodded slowly. "I'll need that letter. You can take a photocopy for your files, and we'll return the original as soon as we're done with it."

"Of course, of course." The super's nervousness had disappeared and now he just seemed to be enjoying his involvement with an FBI investigation. As they entered his tiny office off the lobby, Jake wondered just who had moved Harrison's stuff. And where they'd taken it.

It could all be perfectly innocent. But then why was his neck still tingling?

The super's pudgy fingers fumbled open an unlocked metal filing cabinet and began leafing through. As Jake watched, a look of alarm crossed the man's face. Once more he flicked through, more slowly, then shook his head sharply. "I don't understand. It should be right here." He glanced up, sweat beading his forehead. "My wife must have moved it. Wait here, I'll ask her."

Jake nodded, knowing damn well the letter wasn't misfiled. It was gone—and with it went any possibility of an innocent explanation.

Minutes later, a tiny plump woman bustled in with the nervous superintendent in her wake. She went through the same process of searching fruitlessly for the missing document. "I can't understand it," she exclaimed at last.

The small, airless office held only two chairs and was suddenly overcrowded. Jake was about to take his leave, and kiss his last lead goodbye, when *Ms. Smith* piped up.

"Perhaps we could go into your apartment and sit down?" she suggested with a reassuring smile.

"Yes. Yes. All right. I'll make some tea," said the wife.

Jake glared at Cyn, but got nothing back but a bland smile. Oh, she was going to hear about this. "What are you doing?" he demanded in a furious undertone as they trooped down the hall to the manager's suite.

"You make them nervous. If they relax, they might remember something."

Save me from amateurs.

THE FOUR OF THEM were sitting on spotless colonial-style furniture drinking tea out of china cups. A neatly arranged plate of shortbread cookies sat on the dark coffee table, but none of them took one. If they got out of here before the next ice age, Ms. Smith was going to get one hell of an earful.

"Now," began Cyn. "Tell us everything you remember about those men."

"Well," said the wife, "they wore suit jackets. They looked like nice businessmen."

"Height?" Jake asked, knowing it was hopeless, but determined to try and get some useful information over the teacups.

The wife shrugged. "Medium. Everything about them was average, really. Oh, I did notice one thing. One of them had hairy knuckles."

That should solve the case. "Thank you for your time." Jake rose, grabbing Cyn's elbow to get her on her feet, as well, and the couple rose with him. "If you think of anything at all, please call me. Day or night." He handed them his card.

"Thank you. The tea was lovely," Cyn said. She smiled at the old couple as if they'd just solved the FBI's top ten crimes.

"You're welcome, dear. It's so nice to see young people with manners. Shall we call you when those men come back for Mr. Harrison's car?"

9

"CAR?"

"Yeah," the super said. "They didn't have any authorization for his car, and they didn't have the keys, so we couldn't release Mr. Harrison's vehicle. They said they'd be back."

Cyn and Jake glanced at each other. "I'll need to see that car."

"Sure. This way."

The super led them through a fire door to a set of cement stairs leading to an unsecured underground parking garage. "Mr. Harrison's car is over there, the gold one."

Jake spotted it immediately. A gold Lexus sedan. He did a double take. A gold Lexus with the driver's door partially open. A sneakered foot rested on the cement floor of the garage and was attached to some little bastard who was hot-wiring Harrison's car.

He hadn't heard them. Jake smiled grimly. Suspect number one was about to be interviewed, whether he wanted to be or not. Jake reached for his Sig, motioned for Cyn to stay back, and moved silently forward.

"Hey," shouted the moronic super before Jake could stop him. "Get away from that car!"

Inside the vehicle, a head jerked their way. A young guy with longish hair.

''FBI, freeze!'' Jake shouted just as he saw the kid's gun.

''Get down!'' he shouted to the old guy, while grabbing Cyn and shoving her to the steps.

Even as he vaulted the cement stair wall he heard the roar of a car engine. He landed, crouched and took aim as the vehicle reversed, tires screeching.

''Jake! Look out!'' Cyn screamed from above him.

''Stay down!'' he yelled back.

He'd already seen what had caused her alarm. The little bugger gunned the engine and headed straight for him.

Jake lunged for one of the cement columns, heard a bullet thud into cement somewhere above him, then jumped out and got one shot off as the Lexus fishtailed its way out of the garage.

He was already running for his own car. ''Stay put,'' he yelled at Cyn, wishing he had time to tie her up in the manager's apartment just to keep her out of trouble.

He sprinted out of the parking garage and headed for his vehicle. Cyn came flying out the front door of the apartment building, shoes clacking on the pavement, skirt riding high on her thighs as she ran.

''No!'' he shouted, but he had no time to stop and argue with the most stubborn woman God ever put on planet earth. They sprinted in a dead heat, but the race was pretty even. He hit the automatic locks and she dragged open the passenger door just as he reached the driver's side.

''He turned right,'' she panted as they screeched out of the visitor's parking.

''You're crazy,'' Jake told her. ''You know that?''

''I can navigate while you drive.''

''Do up your seat belt and hang on.''

"Now he's turning left. Three streets ahead."

He saw the blur of gold metal, heard tires squeal as the vehicle swung around the corner. "Call the cops. Tell them FBI requests backup and give the location and vehicle description. Looks like he's headed for the highway."

While she dug into her purse for her cell phone, he concentrated on driving. A high speed chase in a residential neighborhood was his worst nightmare. His plan was to keep the Lexus in sight without freaking the kid so he did something stupid.

But just keeping the gold bullet in sight had them racing through the quiet streets. A moving truck started to lumber out from a side street, but a long blast from Jake's horn halted it.

After she'd finished the call, it seemed to him Cyn's breathing grew more ragged instead of quieting. He must be scaring the bejesus out of her. "Hang on, babe," he soothed as he rounded a corner, only just staying on all four wheels. He had to catch that kid. Had to find out who was behind Harrison's *move.*

Up ahead the Lexus made another sharp turn. Jake didn't hear any sirens and he wasn't taking any chances. He began closing the distance between the vehicles. The speedometer crept up and so did the rhythm of Cyn's breathing.

He swung around the same turn the Lexus had taken moments before.

"Shit!" he yelled, as he stared ahead.

"Jake, stop!" Cyn shouted at the same time. But he was already slamming on the brakes. His own tires howled as he came to an abrupt halt. Ahead of them a class of schoolchildren was crossing the street. He swore again in frustration as he watched helplessly. The gold Lexus took a sudden turn into an alley.

"Come on, come on!" he urged the last straggler, a little girl in a pink raincoat and matching boots who trailed the rest of the class. He saw a teacher urge her on, which must have flustered Pinkie so much she dropped her lunch bag. By the time the teacher had picked up her lunch and walked her the rest of the way, Jake knew his chase was over.

"Maybe the police will catch him," Cyn said breathlessly, as they turned into the now empty alley.

"Yeah, maybe. Except he's not headed for the highway anymore."

They spent half an hour cruising the area in the hope of seeing the stolen Lexus, but luck wasn't with them. Cyn kept her eyes peeled, looking everywhere, and he knew she wanted that creep driver as badly as he did. But eventually they had to admit defeat. "I'll take you back to your car."

"You should go back and arrest that building superintendent," she said, her voice echoing all the frustration he felt.

"You did okay," he told her.

On the way back to the shopping mall he realized her breathing was still ragged. Maybe she wasn't cut out for this stuff as much as she thought. "Hey. It's okay, it's over now," he soothed her.

"I know," she said. "I can't help it."

He reached out to give her a comforting one-armed hug and felt the heat in her body. A glance at her face showed him flushed cheeks and bright eyes. It was a sight he was beginning to know well.

He let his comforting hand slip between her legs. She was hot, wet and ready. "You're not scared. You're turned on." Even as he cupped her heat she moaned and squirmed beneath him.

"I'm sorry," she gasped. "I can't help it."

"It's the adrenaline. Takes people different ways," he explained. But instead of removing his hand, he increased the pressure. "You're a danger junkie."

"How does it take you?" she whispered.

"Are you talking about right now?"

"Yes."

In answer he took her left hand and placed it in his lap. Although truth to tell, it wasn't the adrenaline, but her excitement that he was responding to. All he could think about was plunging into all that heat.

Her hand found and grasped his erection, and he heard the breath hiss out from between his teeth.

She glanced up at him from beneath her lashes. "I have to go home and shower."

Shower. Warm water cascading down her naked skin, beading on her nipples. A bar of soap in his hands. "Me, too."

"Shame to waste water." Her hand started moving on him, light strokes that burned through his slacks.

"Might as well share. I'll bring the soap." If they made it that far. He cupped her more intimately.

"Isn't it dangerous to drive with only one hand on the wheel?"

"Not as dangerous as driving with no blood in my head. It's all drained down south."

CYNTHIA FELT LIKE a criminal walking in the front entrance of Oceanic later that morning as though she hadn't sneaked over the back fence in the middle of the night.

But everything seemed the same as usual. The receptionist was just as bored, filing her inch-long pink fingernails while flipping through a bridal magazine. Cyn's work was as uninteresting, and Agnes was still gray.

After the excitement of the morning, culminating in a shower unlike any Cynthia had ever had before, month end just wasn't doing it for her. She tried to keep her mind on her task, but just being in Oceanic had her thinking about last night.

Images of her and Jake making love in the warehouse kept intruding until the columns of figures on her screen wavered and she forgot what she was doing. She had this horrible notion that she might somehow have left behind a sign of their passion among the packing crates—a tube of lipstick, a piece of clothing.

As ludicrous as she knew it was, she couldn't rest until she'd checked the area. At last, she made an excuse to go back there, timing her visit for when the men usually took their lunch break. She breezed in, trying not to blush. If those guys only knew what she'd been up to in here last night!

As she'd suspected, they were all sitting at the scarred table chomping sandwiches or slurping soda, and from the laughter she heard as she entered, she guessed someone had been telling a smutty joke.

"Hey, Cyn. Hot sweater." It wasn't hot at all. It was freezing, and she had an uncomfortable suspicion her nipples were sticking out from the cold. The top was made of some kind of thin clingy material and was patterned in bold geometric shapes in black and gray. She'd put it on after she discovered her black nylons were ruined and all she had left in her top drawer was an unopened package of geometrically patterned stockings. She'd found these outlandish geometric earrings at the art gallery. Her skirt was tight, short and black.

"Thanks. Hot baseball cap. I love the John Deere logo."

They all laughed good-naturedly, and she flapped an invoice in the air. "I'm just checking something."

Nobody seemed to care, especially while they were on their break, which was just as she'd hoped. She made her way among the crates, boxes and machinery, making a great show of scanning the odd label and comparing it with the invoice in her hand, until she reached the crate she and Jake had searched last night.

Luckily, it looked completely undisturbed. She took one step farther and slid a glance to where they'd made love—not moving any closer in case the rat was back there.

She let her shoulders relax. There were no stray lipsticks or undergarments. There was nothing on the ground but a sheet of packaging with a corner snipped off.

She felt her eyes widen, and she would have sworn her eyeballs bugged right out of her head. She gasped softly. It was the wrapping Jake had cut to transport the broken chopsticks. If anybody saw it, they'd wonder how it had gotten out of a crate that supposedly had never been opened.

Heat crept up her neck.

There was a garbage can in the corner. Maybe she could bundle the wrapper over to the trash. They were all busy laughing and chatting. No one would notice. She bent down and picked up the wrap. It crinkled and crunched in her hands.

"Why, Cynthia! I'd know those luscious hips anywhere," Neville Percivald's voice boomed from behind her.

Panic made her do the only thing she could think of.

She swayed her hips provocatively in an impromptu bump and grind while she frantically stuffed the packaging under a wooden pallet.

She rose and turned, giving Neville the most dazzling smile she could manage. He gave her his usual bland anchorman smile. "Whatever were you doing down there, my dear—your exercises?" He said it with a kind of gentlemanly leer.

"No," she giggled, and batted her eyes. She was actually getting pretty good at this, judging from his reaction. "I was just fixing my stockings." She did her best imitation of a pretty pout. "My diamonds were crooked."

She walked toward him, putting as much distance as possible between her and the crate she and Jake had opened.

Neville watched her legs the entire way. "Yes, I see what you mean," he said when she arrived in front of him. "Allow me." And before she knew what was happening, he was on one knee before her, running his hands up and down her legs.

She swallowed the impulse to kick him in the chin with her snazzy ankle boots, while she kept the smile stuck to her face—even though it had gone rigid, due to her clenched teeth.

He rose, his cheeks a little flushed. "What brings you back here this morning?"

It was an opportunity for her to finesse details out of him, interrogate him without him even knowing she'd done it. With only one week left before Jake was pulled off the case, she couldn't let any opportunity pass.

She shot Neville a demure little smile. "I just wanted to check that I had the correct number of crates for this packing slip, that's all."

A slight crease formed between Neville's brows. "The boys do that, my dear. You don't have to count crates."

She giggled again. God, she was starting to get on her own nerves. How could men stand women like this? It seemed to be working for Neville, though. His bland smile was back.

"I know I don't *have* to, it just seemed like something was wrong on the computer, but probably it was just me." Would one more giggle be pushing it? She pushed it.

He relaxed against a crate. "It's wonderful to have someone so thorough. And dedicated."

"Well, I try. I'm just so interested." Here was her chance. She'd keep her ears open for any nuance of guilt, any accidentally spilled clue. "I mean, how do you decide to bring in..." she fluttered her hands vaguely "...chopsticks from South America?"

He smiled at her and settled his arms across his chest. "Business strategy. The South Americans grow trees rapidly because of their climate, as you know, and since their currencies are devalued, we get very good prices. We then sell those same chopsticks to our clients all over the U.S. and make a nice profit."

"Oh." She was *so* disappointed. She'd expected him to fidget, at least, but his explanation made perfect sense.

After last night, she wanted to bring Hank's killers to justice almost as much as Jake did. But it was looking more and more like Jake and she were searching in the wrong place. Oceanic just wasn't all that sinister. It had some problems, sure, but nothing criminal.

The company's pension plan, for instance, sucked. They had so many retired employees that the plan was overburdened, and management had to keep topping it up just to stay afloat. She doubted there'd be enough left in the plan to support people like Agnes when their time came. If Cynthia stayed for any length of time, she'd have to do something about helping management improve the longevity of the plan.

It wasn't as exciting as catching criminals, she thought with an inner sigh, but she was awfully good at accounting. She knew she could help them fix the problem. At least then she'd leave Oceanic knowing she hadn't been a complete fraud.

She tried a different tack. "Your ships must go round the world. I find that so thrilling. I've always wanted to travel." That at least was true.

"I imagine you'd have quite a few adventures."

She didn't want to talk about her nonexistent adventures, she wanted information about his ships. Honestly, the man could be so thick. "Do they go all over the world? Your ships?"

"Our ships?" Aha, was it her imagination, or did a shifty expression cross his face? Hard to say; the bland smile was back in a flash. "We don't have our own ships. We contract shipping companies to carry our cargo."

Her brow furrowed. "But I'm sure I saw a ship listed in the company's assets."

"Ah, you have been diligent. You must mean the *Pacific Princess,* a pleasure boat we use to take clients out fishing. You'll get a chance to see it next summer when we have our annual staff trip. Or perhaps, if you're a good girl, I might arrange to take you out myself one of these days."

Oh, gag.

Once again her excitement plummeted. The *Pacific*

Princess obviously wasn't the fishing trawler Jake's friend had been aboard when he was killed.

If she could just find some evidence, anything at all...

She'd witnessed Jake's grief last night, and had come to understand how important this investigation was to him. She wanted to help him bring Hank's killers to justice.

If a part of her was panicked that once she was off the case, Jake wouldn't be part of her life anymore, well, she just wouldn't think about that.

Neville glanced at his watch. Oh, no. She had to come up with something to keep him talking. She'd get him to drop a clue if she had to shake it out of him. "I really want to understand how this company works. I'd just love it if you could explain it all to me," she gushed.

His chest puffed up like a preening seagull. "I'd be happy to. I've got to run to a meeting now, but why don't I answer all your questions when we have more time?"

She hid her chagrin. "That would be wonderful."

"Say over dinner, Saturday night?"

She jerked backward a step, jabbing her hip against the rough corner of a crate. "Dinner?" She cleared her throat. "Saturday night?" Well, she wanted to interrogate him, didn't she? "Uh, sure. Thanks."

As she stumbled numbly back to her desk she mentally kicked herself all the way. Why hadn't she made an excuse? She didn't want to date Neville Percivald on Saturday night. She wanted to date Jake.

However, a few hours of uninterrupted time with Neville Percivald could be a perfect opportunity to try and get information that might help the FBI. She wouldn't seduce Neville, of course, in spite of what

Jake had once proposed. But when her boss was relaxed, maybe having a couple of drinks, he'd be much more likely to reveal secrets.

She wondered what Jake would think about her "date" with Neville. A few weeks ago, she'd have laughed if anyone told her she'd have two men showing interest in her.

She flopped into her desk chair and noticed she had a voice-mail message. She played it and then groaned. It wasn't two men interested in her.

It was three.

Walter had asked her to have dinner with him on Saturday night.

Aargh!

She dropped her head in her hands. "I can't date three men!" she wailed aloud.

"I hope this isn't a bad time, Cynthia." Agnes's apologetic tone interrupted her.

"Not unless you're asking me for a date."

"Oh. The very idea!" Agnes chortled. "Well. I suppose I am, in a way. I'm referring to our hair appointments. Did you make them?"

"Hair. Right! Of course I haven't forgotten. I'll pick you up at ten Saturday morning."

"That would be wonderful. I just feel...oh, never mind."

"Agnes, I thought that was your voice." An older man Cyn didn't recognize stood just outside her door.

As Cynthia watched, Agnes's face transformed. She turned red, then white, and put a trembling hand to her mousy hair before assuming her usual placid, apologetic expression. She turned and said, "Hello, George. We weren't expecting you until next week."

"Had to make sure you hadn't run off with a sailor while I was gone," the hearty voice boomed.

Agnes smiled her sad smile. "Really, George."

So this was Neville's stepfather. Cyn liked the look of the man. He reminded her of a character actor on the British stage, with his snow-white hair and military mustache, the piercing blue eyes—a much deeper blue than those of his stepson—and his weather-beaten countenance. His dress was dapper, his manner jocular. He was as full of personality and verve as Agnes was lacking. And unless Cynthia was very much mistaken, the poor woman harbored a gigantic crush on the older man.

"And who's this?"

Agnes edged back into Cyn's office as Mr. Percivald senior came through the door, his hand held out in greeting.

"I'm Cynthia Baxter," she said, taking his hand automatically and receiving a firm shake. "The new accountant."

"Hmm? Where's Harrison?"

"I believe he's in Hong Kong. I got the job after he left, so I never met him."

"Hong Kong. What on earth for? Met a woman, I expect," he said, answering his own question. "Well, he was a good man, but you're much easier on my old eyes." He twinkled at her and she found herself grinning back. He might be years older, but she liked him better than his bland stepson.

"And where's Percivald the younger?"

Since Agnes was gazing at him and seemed to be in her own world, Cyn answered. "Neville? I think he's in a meeting."

"Ah. Well. I'll just wait for him in his office, then.

Agnes, my dear, might you take pity on a lonely old man and have dinner with me Saturday night?"

"Hmm? Oh, yes. Thank you."

"Right-o. I'm off."

Cynthia could barely contain her excitement until Mr. Percivald senior had moved out of earshot. "Agnes! You've been keeping secrets."

"I don't have any secrets. I wish I did."

"But that Laurence Olivier knockoff just asked you for a date!"

"What? Oh, no." She sighed—a long, heartbroken sound that stirred all Cyn's sympathies. "He usually asks me for dinner when he's in Seattle. I keep him up to date with Oceanic, and—" her voice became brittle "—he usually asks my advice about his current lady friend."

"*Current* lady friend? How many have there been?"

Agnes smiled thinly. "I've lost count."

"But that's so...wrong! You're in love with him. Any fool can see that."

Pink blotches mottled Agnes's skin. "In love with him? That's ridicul—" She flopped into Cynthia's single visitor's chair and burst into tears.

Cynthia shut the door and dug out a pack of tissues.

"He doesn't even see me. All these y-years I've been the one he trusts, discusses things with. I h-helped him pull himself together when his wife d-died. And I waited. I hoped at last..." A sob shook her. "I might as well be a piece of office furniture."

The poor woman was so desperately unhappy, and once again Cyn had the uncomfortable feeling this could have been her, had her life not taken an unexpected turn. Maybe it was too late for Agnes, but then again, maybe it wasn't. "Agnes, it's time you let Mr. Percivald know how you feel about him."

"He'd just think I was a pathetic old woman."

"Desperate times call for desperate measures."

Agnes hiccuped.

"We're pulling out the big guns."

Agnes sniffed.

"It's not just a makeover anymore."

Agnes blew her nose.

"We're bringing in *Raunch Magazine.*"

"I beg your pardon?"

"We have to get Mr. Percivald to notice you, see you as an attractive woman."

"He didn't see me as an attractive woman thirty years ago. How are you going to make him see me as an attractive woman now?"

"Sex." Cynthia ignored the choked outburst from the chair. "It's all about sex."

"But sex is so..." Agnes shuddered delicately, and a picture of Walter popped into Cyn's head.

"Awful? It doesn't have to be. I've just figured that out."

Agnes's eyes popped. "You've just...? But you're so... Well, pardon me for saying this, but you're so...sexy!"

A little chuckle escaped Cynthia. She couldn't help it. "Take a look at this." And she hauled out her driver's license. "Do you know who this is?"

Agnes dabbed her eyes before squinting at the little photo. "Looks like me when I was young."

"It's me."

"Stop making fun of me when I'm miserable."

"I'm serious, Agnes. Look at that picture, and look at the name on the license. I got a makeover and that helped. But I got a new attitude, too.'' Also some mind-blowing sex, but she didn't want to startle her new friend too much all at once. Maybe she'd discover her own "personal orgasmic drama of legendary proportions'' with the elder Mr. Percivald—who looked as if he'd be only too happy to play most of the games in *Raunch*'s fantasy issue—and maybe she wouldn't. The important thing was that she'd gain enough confidence to believe it was possible.

If Jake Wheeler found Cynthia Baxter irresistible, anything was possible.

"Come on, Agnes. Saturday, we're getting you a makeover along with that new hairstyle. After that, I have a...store I want you to see.'' She decided not to let on it was a sex shop, or that they'd be buying a copy of *Raunch*—Agnes could only take so much.

Cyn needed to go there, anyway; she wanted to pick up a couple of things herself.

10

CYNTHIA DROVE SLOWLY past Jake's house, just two doors down from her own. It was dark and quiet, which was odd. His car was always parked in the driveway when she came home. Darn. She needed to see him, to tell him the latest development—that a suspect had asked her out for dinner.

Oh, who did she think she was kidding? She just wanted to see him.

Never for one second did she think the information that she had a date with Neville might make him jealous. But if it did… She grinned slyly. He'd just have to make sure he booked ahead next time he wanted to see her.

Yes, things were definitely looking up in her dull life. Neville had invited her for dinner Saturday, and when she'd returned Walter's call she'd discovered he wanted to take her to a restaurant she'd been dying to visit—also on Saturday night.

Walter, forking out for a pricey restaurant? After she'd picked herself up off the floor, he'd explained he was seeing a woman who believed you had to make peace with your past before you could move on.

It wasn't something Cynthia had thought much about, but in a way it made sense. Perhaps she needed closure on the Walter stage of her life as much as his new girlfriend obviously thought he needed it. Just the fact that he now saw her as a woman to be taken to fancy restaurants, instead of someone to cook for him at his convenience, made Cynthia feel like forgiving him and wishing him happiness. So she'd agreed to dinner on Sunday. Now she had two dates coming up this weekend, with two different men.

Only trouble was, the man she really wanted to date wasn't asking. Come to think of it, Jake had *never* asked her out. Mind-blowing sex in the shower this morning aside, she admitted to feeling a little peeved. Sure, he was a spur-of-the-moment kind of guy, but she might like a little advance notice on when he expected to see her.

At this very moment, for example, he could be waiting in her darkened home for her, planning to surprise her with another sexual fantasy, without even bothering to check with her first. She sniffed a little in indignation, and sped the remaining short distance to her house.

A curtain flicked in Mrs. Lawrence's front window and Cyn waved, knowing her arrival had been duly noted by her neighbor.

Her stomach tightened in anticipation as she opened the door and deactivated the alarm. Where might he be hiding? What delicious wickedness did he have planned? But that excitement faded as a quick search of her house yielded nothing. Jake wasn't there.

Well, good. That was fine. She wasn't a 7-Eleven, open at all hours for his convenience. A quiet night at home was just what she needed. She'd cook herself an omelette, then get to bed early. Maybe she'd even have time for a nice hot soak in the tub.

Perhaps she'd better check her messages before dinner.

There weren't any messages.

A sense of ill usage seeped through her bones. She had important information to divulge to Jake. A key suspect had invited her for a date.

She'd probably have to wear a wire!

Such things must involve advance planning.

She gnawed her thumb for a moment, trying to decide if this counted as a real emergency. Saturday night was an opportunity to listen in on both Percivalds, senior and junior. She'd wear some state-of-the-art recording device and, through skillful questioning, have them dropping hints left, right and center. With time running out, it was the big break this case needed.

Phoning Jake on his emergency number seemed a little extreme. Anyway, she'd rather see him in person. All she needed was a plausible excuse for going over. She thought for a minute and then inspiration struck. Hadn't the man been pestering her for a Bundt cake? She turned to her cookbook shelf. She was a woman in charge of her life, and this time *she* was going to make the first move on Jake, thank you very much.

While the cake was cooking, she made her omelette and ate it, knowing she'd need to keep her strength up for what she had in mind.

Mmm. She couldn't believe she was thinking sexy thoughts again. Parts of her body were still sore from her recent escapades, but all she had to do was imagine Jake touching her there and they began to throb with desire. She felt like someone who'd been starved for so long, she couldn't help but binge every time she saw food.

She was turning into a sex addict.

She shrugged. So what? It wasn't hurting anyone. At least not yet. She knew she was in for a big dose of hurting when the Oceanic case was over and Special Agent Wheeler moved on to his next assignment.

She knew the score, and she wasn't going to complain. In only a few weeks, she'd had more fun and more excitement than in the previous thirty-one years put together. She wasn't going to whine when her joyride was over—she was going to revel in every wild and joyous moment while it lasted. And if she had a broken heart at the end of it, well, it would be worth the pain just for the treasured memories.

Maybe his heart wouldn't be touched by their brief affair, but she was darn well going to make sure he had a few memories that would stay with him, as well.

Tonight felt like a good opportunity for making memories.

She bounded into her bedroom, her body already thrumming in anticipation, and donned some of her new racy underwear. Jake had seemed to like that thong. She wondered how he'd feel about the merry widow, which, until a few weeks ago, she'd thought was strictly an opera.

Then she brushed her teeth, fussed with her hair and applied a little makeup. She spritzed perfume into the air, then walked through the cloud of scented spray. And finally, she put on a short slinky dress that was about as subtle as having Take Me tattooed all over her body.

She was humming as she picked up the Bundt cake, checking the clock to make sure she had her timing right. She wanted to hit Mrs. Lawrence's place close enough to the beginning of *Jeopardy!* that there wouldn't be much time to chat. Not that Cynthia minded chatting with her elderly neighbor; usually she enjoyed it. She just didn't want the older woman examining her plans for the evening too closely.

Her strategy worked like a charm. When, bundled in an overcoat, she knocked on her neighbor's door, Mrs. Lawrence answered immediately, feigning surprise—as though she hadn't watched her approach. "Why, hello, Cynthia."

"Hi, Mrs. Lawrence. I need a favor. I've baked our new neighbor a cake, but he's not home. Do you still have the spare key from when Mrs. Jorgensen lived there?"

"Goodness, I'd forgotten all about that. Yes, dear, I do. Come in. I'll get it."

"Thanks." She stepped in, declining to take off her coat. She didn't want Mrs. Lawrence or Alex Trebec getting an eyeful of her take-me-I'm-yours outfit. That was for Jake's eyes only.

"I thought I'd leave the cake on his kitchen counter for a surprise." Well, she thought, salving her conscience, it was partly true. Only it was a two-part surprise. A cake in the kitchen, Cyn in a merry widow. Jake couldn't have moved into a more welcoming neighborhood.

"I took him some of my famous brownies last week," Mrs. Lawrence said, returning to the front hall with a key. "He is such a nice young man. He cleaned my eaves for me the other day, then we had a chat. He asked quite a lot of questions about you." The old woman's eyes twinkled with delight. "I think he's interested."

"Asked questions about me, did he?" Cyn smiled back, hoping Mrs. Lawrence's hearing aid couldn't pick up the sound of gnashing teeth. "What sort of questions?"

"Mostly, he seemed interested in other men you might have seen in the past. Naturally, I told him I never notice what goes on in the neighborhood."

"Thanks." She gave the woman a quick one-armed hug, balancing the cake in the other. It would have been just awful if her neighbor had told the truth—that no other man but Walter had ever visited her.

A canine whine came from the open doorway to Cyn's right, where Mrs. Lawrence indulged in her two great loves: watching television and watching the goings-on in the neighborhood.

"That's Gruber. He doesn't like watching *Jeopardy!* alone." And sure enough, she heard the opening bars of the familiar theme music.

"I'll be on my way. I'll return the key tomorrow."

She walked the short distance to Jake's house and let herself in the front door, pleased he didn't have a security system to worry about. She was fairly certain he knew nothing about the spare key at Mrs. Lawrence's. She planned to surprise him tonight.

She placed the cake on his kitchen counter, wondering when they'd get around to eating it. She thought about stripping and waiting in his bed, but then he'd miss the effect of her sexy new dress and underwear. Instead, she made herself comfortable on the leather couch in his living room. She debated sitting in the dark to wait for him, but who knew how long he'd be? She drew the drapes, snapped on a light and picked up the newspaper. She hadn't checked her stocks for a while.

Apart from the noise of the rustling paper and the creaky sounds of an old house, it was silent. After checking her stocks, she went back to the news and lost herself in an article about a local drug dealer who'd been found dead. There'd been a time when she would have skipped articles about such unsavory subjects, but lately she'd become fascinated with the drug trade. They'd released the man's name, Dominic Torreo, and she could have sworn it seemed familiar. But why?

She heard something else—the sound of a vehicle turning into Jake's drive. She flicked the lights off and waited, blinded by the sudden darkness. Excitement, and a tiny flutter of nerves, filled her body. How would he react when he saw her? What would he think? Her ears strained, but she heard nothing. It seemed to be taking an awfully long time for Jake to come into the house. Maybe she should go looking for him.

Then she squeaked with alarm. She heard a deadly metallic click and felt the pressure of a cold cylinder on the back of her head.

She jumped about half a mile, another cry escaping her lips. "Jake, it's me."

"Cyn?" The gun was removed from her head.

"Oh, my God. Jake. You scared me."

"I damn near blew your head off. What are you doing here?"

"I baked you a cake."

"So that's what I smell." He flipped on a light and glanced at her, then his eyes focused on her dress. He swallowed, and when he spoke again his voice had grown husky. "Is that your apron?"

She licked her lips in what she hoped was a lusciously sexy way—she was supposed to look like a sultry movie star, not a parched lizard. "No." She rose slowly. "I want to fulfill your fantasies."

His eyes narrowed and he stared at her for a long moment. Her heart began to bump against her ribs—or it could have been the wire stays on the merry widow; they were so fused together it was impossible to tell.

He might stare at her from his face of stone, but she saw a pulse thrumming under his jaw. The only workout he was getting right now was from his libido. And if his pulse was any indication, that had just kicked up.

She did another licking-the-lower-lip thing, this time a lot slower, and very deliberate. Then she allowed her gaze to wander his body from top to toe—and she very much liked what she saw. A second, crucial part of his anatomy had also perked up with interest. "Do you have a fantasy?" she asked again, with feigned confidence. She'd tried to memorize all the fantasies from *Raunch*—even the Erotically Advanced—hoping she'd remember all the choreography.

He took a step toward her and her body started to smoulder. "Oh, yeah," he drawled, his voice as smoky as old whiskey. "I have a fantasy." He reached out and put a hand on each shoulder, where his heat burned through the thin silk of her dress.

"I have this fantasy just about every damn day." His hands slipped down to encircle her wrists, imprisoning them lightly, which made her shiver. Here it comes, she thought, hoping it was a scenario she'd at least heard of.

His voice hardened. "I have this fantasy that one day you'll do what you're told." His hands tightened on her wrists. "I fantasize about you following my orders, like staying away from my house."

Oh, dear. This wasn't going at all the way she'd planned. He put his stern face right close to hers. "And for you to keep your nose clean and quit snooping—that's a freakin' wet dream!"

Her shoulders would have slumped forward in failure if she didn't fear her breasts would be impaled on all that underwire. She must have hooked it up too tight.

Now that her heart was pounding, she could barely breathe.

This time when her tongue came out to wet her lips it was pure nerves. "Something important came up."

His hands tightened on her wrists. "If I hadn't smelled chocolate, I might have hurt you first and asked later. I don't want that to happen, Cyn. Not to you."

"I'm sorry." It was the true worry she saw in his face that made her apologize. He cared about her. She wasn't sure how deep it ran, but on some level she knew he cared. She should have realized he might feel differently about secret callers than she did. Next time she'd definitely phone first.

"What's the emergency?"

Now that it came right down to it, she didn't want to tell him. She should have stayed at Mrs. Lawrence's to watch *Jeopardy!* Stayed home and scrubbed out the garburator. Anything but meet Agent Scary on anything but his own terms. She tried to chew her thumb, then realized her wrists were still caught in his grip. And ooh, it was hot. Kind of like the handcuffs again, only made of molten steel.

"What?" he repeated more sharply.

"Neville Percivald asked me for a date," she blurted, not at all the way she'd planned to tell him.

"You broke into my house to tell me some dweeb asked you out?"

"He's not a dweeb! I mean he's—"

"You blew him off, right?" he interrupted.

"No. Not exactly."

His expression was not happy. "Tell me you turned him down."

"I said yes," she told him defiantly. "He's a suspect. I can wear a wire."

A flicker of amusement twinkled deep in those blue, blue eyes. "And what would you do with a wire?"

Stick it in your eyeball didn't seem like the best response, although it was the first thing that came to mind. "I'd get him relaxed and incriminating himself, then you'd arrest him."

"Right after jumping out of the laundry van conveniently parked out front?"

She stuck her chin up and narrowed her eyes. "That's how they do it in the movies."

The atmosphere began to change. His hands loosened and his fingers caressed her wrists. "If you collect incriminating evidence while wearing a wire, then I'd have to debrief you." He elongated each syllable of "de-brief" and a picture popped into her mind of him slipping off her briefs.

She glanced up to see that the humor had disappeared and a far more disturbing twinkle had replaced it. Her heart was pounding again.

"I'm very good at debriefing my volunteer agents."

"You are?" Her voice was as thin and wispy as a sigh.

"First, I'd need the wire back." He ran a single finger across the lace edging of her bodice, hovering at the shadowy cleft between her breasts.

"I could go to the bathroom and take it off."

He shook his head. "Wouldn't stand up in court. Someone could tamper with the evidence. No, I couldn't let you out of my sight until I had removed the wire, debriefed and strip-searched you."

"Strip-searched?" Her voice bounced.

He nodded again, serious but for that disturbing twinkle that acted like the ignition switch on her sex drive. "They usually don't show that part on TV."

"No." She cleared her throat. "I've never seen it."

"I do a very thorough strip search. I'm a bit of a workaholic that way. Stickler for detail."

"What exactly would you be searching for?"

"Don't know until I find it. That's why it has to be such a thorough search. Best we do a dry run now, so you've still got time to back out."

Dry? Was he kidding? She was wet just thinking about what he might do to her once he had her naked, and from the wicked expression that tilted the corners of his mouth, he knew it.

How had he turned the tables on her again? She determined not to give in too easily. She stuck her chin up once more. "But I'm not wearing a wire."

"You sure?" He ran his index finger beneath her breasts, following the line where the underwire lifted her cleavage.

Her breath sucked in with a little whoosh and her nipples beaded, hard and yearning for his touch.

If she'd learned one thing about this man's lovemaking technique, it was that basically he never gave her what she wanted when she wanted it. True to form, he ignored the breasts that were knocking themselves out to get his attention, and traced his fingers up the buttons on her dress. Oh, he was pushing her buttons, all right. All of them, except the ones on her chest that most wanted to be pushed.

"When you're wearing a wire, it's important not to get too nervous or excited." He flicked open her top button, and she swallowed noisily. "You're not, are you?"

"Hmm?"

"Nervous...or excited?" He settled his hand over her heart, which was beating so hard it almost bounced him off. "A little fast," he murmured with deep amusement. "Maybe you should lie down."

"Oh, yes." That sounded like a very good idea.

Linking her hand with his, he led her up the stairs. The old wooden steps creaked and popped as they made their way up. She wanted him so badly, she felt like sprinting up, ripping her clothes off at the same time. But a kind of shyness stopped her—that, and knowing they were acting out his fantasy. She had to face facts; the man liked to play by his own rules.

Not that she wouldn't do her level best to bend them, maybe even break a few. But whatever game they played, she trusted him to make sure she had a whole lot of fun. And that, after all, was the point of this game—to make sure they both had fun.

The master bedroom still bore Mrs. Jorgensen's Scandinavian influence in the blue walls and bare floorboards, but Jake had taken a rather prim room and made it masculine and very much his. A Viking would have felt right at home here, jumping his lusty Viking wench after months at sea. For one thing, he'd replaced Mrs. Jorgensen's prim double bed.

"That bed is huge," she said. It dominated the room.

"It's a king. I'm a restless sleeper. I move around a lot in bed."

"I've noticed."

The head- and footboards were light pine, not as fancy as her four-poster, but solid enough to tie... Where had her mind spun off to? She forced her attention to the navy-and-white duvet that covered the enormous bed, then to the pine side table, which held a lamp, a pair of reading glasses and a well-thumbed paperback copy of *Hamlet.* She squinted; maybe she needed a stronger prescription for her contact lenses. "Shakespeare?"

"Sure. Nobody gets the women on their backs like old Will."

"Really?" What was he thinking of, *Shakespeare in Love?* "Hamlet is a tragedy."

Jake had snapped on the bedside lamp. Now he shut off the overhead light, dimming the whole room, and stepped forward until he was standing in her space, close enough that she could smell him. He cupped the back of her head with one hand and with the other slipped the straps over her shoulders so he could trace the lacy edge that cupped her breasts. His lips skimmed her mouth, cheek, temple, then buried themselves in her hair.

He whispered, "Oh, that this too, too solid flesh would melt, thaw and resolve itself into a dew...." The damp breath swirled into her ear and seemed to channel right down to the core of her, which was, in fact, thawing and melting.

She loved poetry, but she wasn't a simpleton. She remembered her college Shakespeare course pretty well. "Hamlet refers to suicide in that soliloquy," she told him primly, although the effect was somewhat marred when he rolled her nipple between his fingers and she moaned.

"It's open to interpretation," he insisted, slipping his hand under her skirt and between her legs in a really sneaky ploy to prove his point.

She sucked in her breath as he cupped her, knowing she was as dewy as he could wish, then smiled as his hand stilled and went rigid. "Where are your underpants?"

"I'm not wearing any."

His hand was warm and leather-tough against the soft flesh of her inner thighs where they rose above the garter-snapped silk stockings. This whole ridiculous getup might be uncomfortable for everyday wear, but it was deliciously feminine and sexy in situations like this.

"Proves my point about amateurs."

"Who are you calling an amateur?" She tried to sound indignant, but his hand had started moving and she was losing her train of thought.

"Bureau regulations specify that anyone wearing a wire has to wear underpants. I'm sorry, but I'm going to have to search this whole area thoroughly."

She settled her feet farther apart to give him better access, and whispered, "I promise to cooperate."

"First, a visual inspection."

She fought frustration as he left her wet and throbbing and needy to slide the straps all the way off. He stood back as the dress slipped to the floor in a heap no larger than a silk handkerchief. He let out a low whistle. "I like that thing." He turned her this way and that, insisting on a complete visual inspection.

Then he traced the top of her stockings, where the skin was bare.

"I didn't want another pair of panty hose ruined," she whispered.

"Liar," he said softly, and sank two fingers into her, slow and deliberate. Fortunately his left arm was wrapped around her waist or her trembling legs would have dropped her to the floor at the surprise assault. His fingers thrust in and out in a deliberate tempo while his thumb rubbed in counterpoint.

She wanted to strip his shirt off, but her hands had ceased to obey orders from her brain. She just clung to him, feeling the pressure build and build, hearing her own panting cries from a distance, until her head fell back and she cried out loud as a great wave swamped her. Her legs buckled, and he swung her up high against his chest and carried her to the bed.

He stripped, then snapped off the bedside lamp, leaving the curtains open to let in light from the nearly full moon. He took his time unhooking her from the merry widow, touching and caressing each inch of new flesh he revealed. Everything seemed to glow in the moonlight. Her breasts, his teeth, his biceps as he leaned over her; his beautiful eyes as he stared at her.

Something happened.

Something magical and frightening, as enchanted and ephemeral as the moonlight itself. He stared into her eyes, and she stared back, feeling an acute sense of recognition. *It's you,* she found herself thinking. *It's really you.*

She lifted a hand to his face, tracing his lips with her finger as he settled between her thighs. He entered her slowly, and her body welcomed him. It was as mundane and as magical as a ship pulling into port, a car pulling into the garage.... He was home.

His body belonged inside hers just as they belonged together. Her breath shuddered in on a gasp of amazement as moisture pooled in her eyes.

She loved him.

She couldn't tell him. The feeling was as fragile as it was new and unexpected, so she held the words inside her, but let her feelings out through every other method of expression. With each touch, each lift of her hips to meet his thrusts, with each kiss of her lips to his, each sigh and breath, she told him. *I love you.*

His eyes were dark and serious, their expression unreadable. But there was no teasing in them, none of the joking game-playing of earlier. Did he feel it, too? The knowledge that they were meant to be together? Was all the love in this room coming from her, or was some of it his?

She didn't know and feared breaking the spell by speaking, so she held her peace and loved him with every part of her. She heard the slick slap of sweat-dewed flesh, his husky sighs as her blood began to pound louder and louder in her ears. She clung to his straining arms to anchor her to the earth.

Then, nothing could hold her. She was flying free, glowing with the moon, singing with the planets. In the distance she heard him cry out, then he collapsed on top of her. *I love you,* she mouthed silently.

It was 4:00 a.m. by the luminous dial of his clock when he woke her.

"Whaa...?"

"I want you home before it gets light."

"Worried Oceanic's spying on me?" she mumbled when she finally got her eyes to stay open.

"No. I'm worried the neighbors are spying on *me.*"

She chuckled tiredly. "Course they are. But don't worry, you're not as big an attraction as Meals on Wheels."

"Do me a favor. Cancel dinner."

"I don't get Meals on Wheels."

"Your date with Percivald. Cancel it."

"Don't you want me to wear a wire?"

"You failed the test."

Even though he was joking about the test, she knew he wouldn't let her wear any kind of recording device on her date. She felt unreasonably hurt. He wouldn't let her do the simplest thing to try and crack this case. "Why did you bother recruiting me in the first place?" she grumbled.

"To get you into bed."

"Oh." She felt so pleased she decided to forget about the wire. She didn't need fancy FBI equipment, she had an old tape recorder of her dad's; maybe she could stick that in her purse.

"Are you going to cancel?" His voice sounded stern.

Her chin lifted. She loved him, but she wasn't about to let him push her around. "We volunteers can do what we want on our own time."

"Humor me."

She thought about it for a moment while she dragged on clothes. "Why?"

"Assume I'm jealous."

Then he kissed her gaping lips and hustled her out into the predawn blackness. She knew he wouldn't let her talk in case the KGB were hiding behind the garbage cans, so she had time on the short walk to ponder his last statement. He'd said it in a half-joking kind of way, but...what if he really was jealous?

Just because nothing like that had ever happened in her whole life didn't mean it wasn't possible.

Did it?

"IS SHE FROM MOSCOW, too?" Michael whispered in despair when Cyn ushered Agnes into the salon Saturday morning.

She nodded conspiratorially. "Yes, she is. But don't mention it. She's very sensitive. Especially about her appearance. She's going to ask for something boring and mousy, and if you're any kind of a patriot, you won't listen to her. She's had a long stint undercover."

"You mean she was a—"

She held a finger to her lips in warning. "Shh. It's classified. All I can tell you is that for her next assignment she has to seduce a top British diplomat."

"Honey, I'm not a miracle worker."

"Yes, Michael." She smiled secretly as she recalled how her new look had changed her life. "You are."

He heaved a sigh and then led Agnes to his station. He began fluffing gray hair through his fingers, an expression of helpless resignation on his face.

"Perhaps just a trim." Agnes piped up in her timid way, her doe eyes darting nervously to her cloud of gray hair being pouffed this way and that.

But neither Michael nor Cyn were listening. Cyn watched, holding her breath, as the expression on Michael's face changed from hopeless to excited. "The hair is wonderful. I'm seeing blond. I'm seeing an older Ingrid Bergman."

"You are?"

He didn't answer, just narrowed his eyes and shifted and twisted the hair while he watched it in the mirror.

Agnes seemed too petrified to speak.

"We'll keep most of the length." He patted Agnes's shoulder reassuringly, then gestured to the shampoo girl. "But trust me, when I'm done you won't recognize yourself."

"That's what I'm afraid of," Agnes moaned, and followed meekly behind the girl with electric blue hair.

"And for you, *madame?*" Michael ushered Cyn into the chair.

"I really do just need a trim."

"How's the color working?"

"I love it."

"It's too tame for you. How about we add just a touch of platinum?"

"Maybe next time. Mostly I want you to concentrate on Agnes today."

He shot her a slightly panicked look. "Are there many more of you?"

She smiled at him reassuringly. "No. This should be it."

SHE'D EXPECTED TO SEE an improvement in Agnes's appearance, but she was flabbergasted when, at the end of three hours, she returned for her friend. "Your hair, it's...it's beautiful."

Agnes had all the wonder of Cinderella after the fairy godmother had waved her magic wand. She couldn't stop staring at herself in the mirror, turning this way and that. Her hair, now a soft gold, was pulled back in a chic bun, and the makeup artist had done wonders, bringing out the blue in her eyes, putting some color in her cheeks and adding lipstick to her mouth.

"I can barely believe it!" Agnes's voice was hushed, for once in wonder rather than bashfulness.

"Now all we need is to get you some new clothes and a few, um, other things, and you'll be all set for your date tonight."

"Really, it's not a date."

"Maybe it isn't now. Just wait till tonight. I have a feeling the current lady friend he'll be talking about will be you."

While Agnes had been coiffed and made up, Cyn had dashed to the clothing store where she'd started her makeover. There she got some advice on where to take a fifty-something woman in need of a new look.

She bundled a still-stunned Agnes into her car and drove them to an upscale women's wear shop. Agnes stalled on the doorstep. "Oh, I don't know. It looks awfully expensive in there."

"I don't mean to be rude, but what do you spend your money on?"

"Well, my cat is a fussy eater..." Agnes glanced up and obviously realized that wasn't going to cut it. "I support several charities...and, um..."

"You save most of it, don't you?"

Almost ashamed, Agnes nodded. "My nephew and his family will inherit a nice sum when I die."

"What are you, fifty-five?"

"Fifty-two."

"Your nephew will have to wait. You've got a lot of living to do." Cyn fixed Agnes with a fierce eye. "Starting right now. Come on."

It wasn't hard at all, once Agnes caught the spirit of the adventure. They emerged giggling like teenage girls, six bags between them, and a saleswoman practically bowing them out of the shop.

"How do you feel?" Cynthia asked.

"Stunned. Excited."

"Brave?"

"Brave enough for anything."

"All right. I'm Cyn the Bold. I hereby rename you Agnes the Brave."

"Good."

She refused to tell Agnes where they were going, thinking she'd need her newfound bravery to enter a store where the autumn window display included a blow-up doll reclining on a pile of autumn leaves. As Cyn pulled into a parking spot out front, a customer was just leaving, with quite a bag of goodies.

A customer she recognized.

What was Neville Percivald doing in a sex shop? Here she'd thought he was quiet and sweet, a little on the creepy side, but harmless. How harmless could he be if he was buying a sackful of sex goodies on Saturday morning when she had a date with him Saturday night?

"Are you all right, Cynthia? You're making an awfully funny noise," Agnes stated.

"I'm fine," she gasped. "Fine. I just had a great idea. We're both seeing Percivald men tonight. Why don't we double-date?"

"Double-date? But—"

"It'll be fun. After your appearance knocks him out, I'll make sure Mr. Percivald knows you have an active private life."

"But I don't!"

"You will. I know we're going to La Parisienne for dinner, because Neville asked me if I liked it. All you have to do is tell his stepfather how much you'd like to go there. Our double date will be a surprise."

"Well...I would feel more comfortable if you were there. I feel so odd with my hair like this and my new clothes." Agnes paused. "But will he think I'm being presumptuous?"

"Of course he won't. You're the one who lives here full-time. You ought to know which restaurants are good."

"I only wish I did."

"Trust me on this one. Please?" As much as Cynthia wanted to support Agnes, she also felt more comfortable in a foursome. If they were in a group, she'd make darn sure that Mr. Percivald junior kept his hands—and his sex toys—to himself.

11

CYN SWEPT INTO the chic restaurant on the arm of Neville Percivald. Fingers crossed, she glanced around and was relieved to see that Agnes hadn't let her down. There she was, in a cozy corner with Mr. Percivald senior.

A glance under her lashes showed Neville's face reddening as he took an instinctive step back toward the door. But not quickly enough for the tuxedoed maître'd, who bustled forward with an ingratiating smile. "Ah, Mr. Percivald, such a pleasure." His heavy French accent made music of the three syllables of Neville's last name, and brought his stepfather's head up.

"My boy!" the older man boomed. "What a surprise. Come and join us."

Neville's face darkened even more as every head in the intimate restaurant turned his way. "Bloody man should have been the town crier. Sorry about this."

"It's all right, really," Cynthia murmured. He had no idea how all right it was. He'd shown up in a limo, telling her he didn't want to drink and drive, but in reality she got the feeling he didn't want his hands or eyes otherwise occupied when he had her in a small, private space.

With overt courtesy, he'd fixed her shawl around her shoulders, copping a discreet feel as he did so. Then he grabbed her seat belt before she got to it and practically made full body contact while snapping it home. If this wasn't a top secret FBI mission, she would have belted him with her purse, hefty with the weight of her father's old tape recorder.

But since this was a night for snooping, she'd giggled and batted his hands away as coyly as she knew how.

With barely hidden annoyance, Neville agreed that he'd be delighted to join his stepdad on a double date. As Cyn followed the mître d' to the table, she heard Neville muttering behind her, and snatches came through loud and clear: "Belongs in a Brighton carny...old fart...ruined everything...sod off..."

She bit the inside of her lip to stop herself from smirking, then smiled with real pleasure as Neville's stepfather rose and kissed her cheek, insisting she sit beside him, which put her across the table from her date, who was now stuck beside Agnes.

Neville was so busy being put out that he hadn't even noticed Agnes's new look. His stepdad certainly had, though. He kept staring at her with an expression of confusion and disappointment on his face, as though she'd let him down somehow.

What was that all about? The woman knocked herself out to look terrific, and he was disappointed?

If Cyn had ever in her life thought she understood men, she now knew she'd been completely wrong. Even though she was a woman who'd spent her life totally baffled by the opposite sex, she still found his behavior odd.

And the pitiful look Agnes sent her way just about broke her heart. Cynthia had tried to help and it appeared she'd only made things worse.

An awkward silence fell over the table, broken by the

waiter taking predinner cocktail orders. Both Agnes and her date were already sipping martinis. Neville asked for the same, and even though she wasn't much of a drinker and had never tried a martini, Cyn asked for one, as well. She was too busy trying to work out what was going on between George Percivald and Agnes to worry about drink orders.

She'd talked it over with Jake, and he was certain George Percivald had run a clean, honest business. The drug rumors had started after his stepson took the helm. It would be so nice for Agnes to get her heart's desire, and there might come a day very soon when George would want her support. It couldn't be much fun to discover your stepson was a criminal.

When Cynthia's cocktail arrived, it looked awfully sophisticated, chilly and clear as a diamond, with a bright green olive on a fancy silver stick. Then she sipped the sophisticated drink and wondered if Neville had found out about her and slipped poison into it. The martini burned in her throat and brought tears to her eyes. Grabbing her water glass, she took a huge gulp and tried to get her breath back.

"They're a little dry," Mr. Percivald said.

Dry? The thing was pure liquid alcohol. *Blech.* "I should have had it shaken, not stirred," she joked weakly.

Agnes didn't seem to be having any trouble; she was deeply into her second martini, drawing sad little patterns in the glass with her olive. George was keeping pace.

Neville downed his in a swallow and motioned for another round. Cynthia felt as if she were sharing a table with three escapees from the Betty Ford Clinic.

But it gave her an idea. Tough investigators drank

their investigatees under the table all the time in the movies. If she could figure out a way to pretend to keep pace, while ditching her disgusting drinks, she could pry all kinds of information out of Neville.

Plus, she had to remember Plan B, which was to bolster Agnes's image in front of her "old friend."

Since her companions were a long way from blotto, she decided to proceed with Plan B. "I hear a lot of movie stars come to this place when they're in town," she began brightly. "Which reminds me, Agnes. Did I tell you that Michael told me you look like Ingrid Bergman in *Cactus Flower?* I think maybe he has a crush on you."

"Michael from today?" She wasn't surprised Agnes wanted clarification. Michael was happily cohabitating with a male stripper.

"He sure likes your new look." That part at least was true.

"Hmm," said Mr. P., and took a gulp of martini.

"Hmm-mmm," added Agnes, and took a sip of her own.

Cynthia couldn't stand it. How could the man not notice? And Agnes was in love with him. This was her best chance at making him really see her. "Don't you think Agnes looks beautiful, Mr. Percivald?"

"I think she looked fine before," he said grimly, then forced a smile. "And you must call me George, my dear." He put a hand to Cynthia's knee and gave it a squeeze.

Oh, she was so mad she could spit. He was flirting with *her* while his date just sat there miserable and getting plastered.

Agnes raised her head, two bright spots of color on her cheeks. "He likes his little tootsies to look beautiful.

Old Agnes he just wants plain and dull. Like an old couch with broken springs."

"Now, Agnes, that's not—"

"Did he bring you flowers?" Agnes interrupted, staring at Cyn owlishly and jerking her thumb in Neville's direction.

"Yes. A dozen white roses."

"I got a teapot. See what I mean? Roses for the tootsie, a teapot for the old couch."

"Agnes—" George gazed at her empty glass in alarm "—I think you've had enough—"

"You're darn right I've had enough. I am a woman. I have a woman's needs. And you," she finished grandly, "are an old patoot."

You go, girl. Cyn felt a bit like a female Dr. Frankenstein. Even though George Percivald was staring at Agnes as if she were some horrible creation, Cyn knew she was witnessing the birth of Agnes the woman. At last. She might find that her hopeless infatuation with George was just that: hopeless. Just as Cyn had found Walter was not the man for *her.* But she'd be stronger for the knowledge, and able to start looking around for a real man. The right man.

A man like Jake.

With a pang, Cynthia knew that Jake was the right man for her. And face it, her own infatuation was just as hopeless. The FBI agent was just passing time, playing sex games with her. As soon as the Oceanic investigation was closed, he'd be on his way to another assignment and another…tootsie.

She waited for Agnes to rise and sweep majestically out of the restaurant; in fact, it felt as though all three of them were waiting. But Agnes hadn't progressed that far yet on her journey to female empowerment. She just dropped her head on her hand and ate her olive.

"I brought you a teapot from the new line of Chintzware I picked up this trip," George said feebly, a baffled expression creasing his forehead.

"Do you take teapots to your tootsies?" Agnes demanded.

He rubbed his silver mustache. "No, I—wait just a minute. I don't have any tootsies."

"Hah." Agnes straightened and assumed a hearty British accent. "Hannah's simply become too clingy, Agnes. I don't know what to do. She's talking about children. At my age!" George Percivald's face deepened in hue, and Cyn had to stifle a giggle. Where had Agnes been hiding her talent for mimicry? She sounded just like him. "And as for Sarah, oh my dear, the girl's insatiable. She's wearing me out."

"I'm sure I never spoke to you like that."

"You did. I was only Agnes, the old comfy couch. Recipient of teapots." She stabbed her little martini-olive sword in his direction. "I don't even drink tea. I like coffee."

"Well, I'm sorry. From now on, I'll keep my Chintzware and my..."

"Chintzware?" Agnes suggested softly, helping him out.

A reluctant grin tilted his mustache in a most attractive way. "Touché. I'll keep all my Chintzware, both china and female, out of your life."

"You'd do better to keep it out of your own life. Find someone your own age." Agnes gasped and blushed, looking truly distressed. "I didn't mean—"

"Didn't you?" George said softly, staring at her as if he'd never really seen her before.

"I'm sorry, I didn't expect..." Tears started to her eyes, and what boldness hadn't been able to achieve earlier, embarrassment now did; she rose abruptly from her seat and dashed for the door.

"Agnes, wait!" And with a muttered "excuse me," George Percivald was out of his own chair and dodging tables to run after her.

Well, it hadn't gone exactly the way she'd planned, but Cyn had high hopes for the success of Plan B. Unfortunately, it seemed to have played havoc with Plan A, and worst of all, the abrupt departure of George and Agnes had left her alone with Neville.

She glanced up to find him markedly more cheerful. "I do apologize, my dear. Father's always been... theatrical. I hope it hasn't spoiled your appetite?"

"No. No." *Yes. Yes!*

JAKE STOMPED BACK to his vehicle, fuming. Why the hell couldn't Cyn, just once, just one damn time, do what he asked?

Just say no. That's all she had to do. Refuse a date with *Neville.* But no. He'd watched a limo arrive at her door, and the pantywaist had tripped up to her door with a fancy florist's box. Jake would bet his pension there were roses in there. The guy had no imagination.

Except in his perverted sex life.

Jake should have warned Cyn about old Neville's membership in S and M clubs, but he'd been afraid it would turn her on. She might do a damn good job of playing the innocent, but he was beginning to think his first assessment of her was the correct one. She was a wildcat dressed in kitten's clothing.

He'd been a fool to jump into his car and follow them

to this restaurant. He'd almost left when he peered through the window the first time and saw her with Percivald's stepfather and a date; at least Cynthia had been smart enough to organize a chaperon.

Jake had almost gone home. Good thing he'd decided to hang around awhile. He'd just witnessed the other woman storm out of the restaurant with Father of the Pantywaist trotting behind her. Sensing trouble, Jake had drawn his weapon and exited his vehicle, ready for God knows what.

But before he had crossed the street, the old guy had his arms around the older woman and was kissing the life out of her. Give the old guy credit, he was smooth. The pair of them were inside a silver Jaguar right now, steaming up the windows like a pair of teens.

They were probably a hell of a lot warmer than he was. He took another peek in the window and watched Cyn and the pantywaist chatting over the menu, warm and cozy while he froze his butt off.

He stomped back to his car, picked up a newspaper he'd already read this morning, and tried not to remember he was starving. It should be him sitting across from Cyn making goo-goo eyes. Damn it, he wasn't just worried about her safety. He was jealous. He wanted Cyn to have eyes for no one but him. Dates with no one but him.

He should have stuck a wire on her. If he'd started on it early enough in the day, he could have got authorization. But he hadn't, because he'd believed she'd cancel her date. It wasn't like he hadn't been clear. He'd as good as ordered her to cancel.

If she were a rogue agent she could be dealt with, but what did you do with a rogue volunteer? *He had had it.*

He was sorely tempted to go in there right now and drag her ass out of that restaurant. But years of training and discipline kicked in. He wouldn't compromise this investigation—not even for Cyn. He'd just wring her neck when he got her alone, then he'd pull her out of Oceanic.

And in the meantime, what was he supposed to do? She was safe enough in the restaurant, but when Percivald had her in the back of a limo, who knew what he might try? He was possibly a dangerous criminal and Cyn wasn't trained to handle any kind of situation he might put her in. What if he took her to one of his pervs-only clubs? Jake would have a hell of a time getting her out. If she was fool enough to go back to the panty-waist's place, she could be in worse danger.

He tapped the frigid steering wheel in frustration. Damn. He had to get her out of there now. He reached for his phone.

Cynthia had just finished ordering a meal she didn't want when the maître d' appeared at her side. "Excuse me, *madame,* but are you Cynthia Baxter?" At her puzzled nod, he said, "There is a telephone call for you."

"Telephone call?" She stared blankly. *Agnes.* Her friend was probably sobbing in a phone booth, in need of rescue. Cyn excused herself to Neville, who once again appeared annoyed, and followed the Frenchman. A phone was tucked discreetly at the end of the bar, and when she said "Hello," a familiar voice answered her.

"You need to go home right now."

She was outraged. It wasn't a distraught Agnes, it was Jake, sounding furious. "I do not," she whispered back. "How dare you follow me?"

"There's a B and E at your place. The alarm's disturbing the whole neighborhood."

"What? When did this happen?"

"About five minutes from now. Go."

"Don't you even—" He hung up before she finished the sentence.

For a moment she just stood there, staring at the colorful array of bottles behind the bar. What if she ignored Jake? How long would it take till he gave up and turned off her alarm? Which she was certain he could do.

But she knew the answer. He'd let that thing blare out into the quiet neighborhood for as long as it took. The police would come, she'd have to deal with the security company, her neighbors would be upset. Her jaw ached and she realized she was clenching her teeth. After this case was over, she had a feeling she'd need dental surgery.

She had no choice. Jake had bullied her into bailing out of her date. It didn't matter that five minutes ago she'd been racking her brain for an excuse to leave early. The only thing that mattered was Special Agent Jake Wheeler was a high-handed jerk.

If he thought he was going to get away with this, he was about to find out he had made a very significant error in judgment.

She stalked back to the table, fury propelling her like a hand at her back. "I'm sorry, Neville," she said through gritted teeth, "I have to go. My house alarm's been set off."

"Oh, no. A false alarm, I hope."

"So do I."

"Is there no one else who could—"

"No. It's a new system and I didn't want to burden my neighbors." Especially since one of her neighbors had set the thing off in the first place. "Please don't get up." She held up a hand as he rose. "I'll catch a cab."

"Nonsense, my dear. Of course I'll see you home."

"All right. I'm so sorry I ruined your evening."

"Not at all," he said politely, as he called for the bill.

During the limo ride back to her house, she apologized again. "You didn't even get any dinner."

"That's all right. I'll stop off, um, somewhere on my way home for a little nibble. I'll have to take you there sometime. I think a girl of your...appetites, might find it, um, invigorating."

Appetites? What did he mean? *Drugs?* If she could find out more about his illicit drug hangouts, that could be a big help in cracking this case.

"What sort of appetites?" she asked softly, trying to look eager, even though Neville was sitting so close to her she felt claustrophobic.

"Shall I tell you?" The pale blue eyes held a peculiar light. "Sometimes people go there when they've been very, very naughty." He traced a finger along her shoulder. "Are you ever naughty, Cynthia? So naughty you have to be spanked?"

"Is that what they do at this club? Spank people?" she said faintly. There'd been something along those lines in "Erotically Advanced," but those red cheeks in the pictures had looked uncomfortable rather than erotic.

"That's for beginners." *Beginners?* She crossed her legs and edged closer to the door. "For the more sophisticated, there are certain...refinements. There are special rooms where we play games. Intimate games. I'd love to take you there." His voice was getting husky.

IF SHE'D HAD ANY DOUBTS about whether Jake really would break into her house, they were put to rest as the limo turned onto her street. The blaring noise of the alarm put her teeth on edge. As the limo drove along, all the curtains on her block looked as if they had Tourette's syndrome.

A squad car sat outside her house, its lights flashing. Jake, naturally, had his head stuck in the window, talking to the driver.

"Well, here I am. Home," she said brightly, reaching for the door handle.

Neville grabbed her and plastered his wet, fishy lips to hers. She opened her mouth to cry out with shock and disgust, and he stuffed his tongue in her mouth. She grabbed his shoulders to shove him off her, wedged her knee between his to try and flatten his family jewels.

The door swung open and she stared up into Jake's rigid face.

With a mighty shove against Neville's shoulders, she managed to break the suction cup hold he had on her as she dragged herself out of the limo.

Completely disgusted with every human being ever born with a penis, she stalked past the squad car, unlocked her door and disabled the alarm. In the sudden silence, she heard the echo of the shrill siren. Her neighbors would be complaining for weeks—just another grudge she could hold against her newest, and most loathsome, neighbor.

A uniformed officer appeared at her side. "I did a walk around the outside, ma'am, and it looks like you left an upstairs window open. A breeze probably set off a sensor."

She knew darned well there hadn't been an open window upstairs when she left the house, but she thanked him anyway.

"Don't thank me. You'll be getting a bill. We had to start charging for false alarms."

Behind the young officer's shoulder, she saw Jake shrug his shoulders infinitesimally. She hoped he'd be as blasé when she presented him with the bill. Still, she was relieved he'd made it look like her carelessness had set off the alarm, rather than letting her geriatric neighbors worry about a B and E in their safe neighborhood.

"I'll walk through the interior of the house with you, ma'am, just to make sure everything's all right."

"Thank you, Officer." She turned to Neville, who had joined the throng on her doorstep. "I'm so sorry, Neville." She extended her hand and he had no choice but to shake it. "I'll see you at the office Monday."

"Are you sure you wouldn't like me to—"

"Perfectly sure. Thank you again. I'm sorry our evening was spoiled." She refused to look in Jake's direction.

And surprise, surprise. No burglars lay in wait in her home. Nothing had been stolen, broken or otherwise disturbed except her upstairs window and her temper. The latter was shredded.

She wasn't a bit surprised that Jake tagged along on the house tour, or that the young officer accepted him as though he had every right to be there.

Jake seemed to be in as towering a temper as she was herself. Which just made her madder.

They waited until the nice young officer left, apologizing that he'd have to send a bill, then she slammed the door.

Her finger was raised and her mouth was open to start

shouting when she turned and found Jake in the identical posture.

"You're off the case."

"How dare you interfere— *What?*" she shrieked, interrupting herself as his words hit home.

"I said," his voice was not raised, but all the more menacing as he repeated, "you're off the case."

"Don't push me, mister. I have a legitimate job. You can't take it away."

"Yes," he said simply. "I can."

"Don't you threaten me. This isn't about work, it's about power. You're a megalomaniac—you can't stand it if you're not in control of every little thing I do. Well, forget it. I'm my own woman."

"You're anybody's woman!"

A cold, sick feeling swamped her stomach. "Excuse me?"

"Don't play the innocent. Last night it was me, tonight you're slobbering all over that prissy piece of work in the limo and tomorrow night some other poor bastard will be getting tied into knots."

"What are you talking about?"

"Check your calendar. You've got a date at some Italian place."

He must be referring to her date with Walter. "But that's just—"

"Save it!" Jake held up his hands. "I don't care who it is. I'm taking my ball and bat and going home. My first impression of you was right. You're so wild you need a cage, and I'm sick of playing lion tamer. Go knock yourself out with your Nevilles and your Walters and whoever the hell else you're stringing along. As of this moment you and I are through, and the FBI thanks you for your efforts, but they are no longer necessary. Goodbye, Cyn."

She heard the front door bang, and just stood there, stunned. She grabbed the banister and sank down on the second stair, then slowly dropped her head to her knees.

He'd dumped her.

Jake had just dumped her.

And unless she was mistaken, he'd dumped her for being a slut. He was the second man she'd ever slept with, and in her fantasy world she'd dreamed that he'd be the last, that he might actually return her love. That they had a shot at a long and happy future together.

Sure didn't look like that was going to happen.

In her mind, she replayed his bitter words. He'd sounded so angry, so hurt. So *jealous.* Was it possible? Could he be jealous? Her eyes filled with tears.

She'd finally found everything she ever wanted in life. An exciting career, a man she loved. Best of all, she'd found herself—the woman who'd been hiding all those years. Now it looked as if she'd lost the first two in one miserable evening.

12

"WHAT?" Jake snarled into the phone.

"Hey, man. What's got up your nose?" Carl boomed, way too cheerful for a Monday morning.

Cynthia Baxter, that's what. "Nothing. I'm pulling the plug on the Oceanic investigation. Adam wants me back on regular staff, and he's right. Oceanic's clean. There's nothing there." Certainly nothing left between him and one sexy accountant with a wandering eye. When was he going to stop letting himself get fooled like this? First Ashley, now Cyn. Jake was beginning to believe that whole innocent act of hers had been just that—an act designed to drive a normal red-blooded man insane.

What they'd shared had seemed so real. But it had turned out to be about as real as his suspicions about Oceanic.

"You think there's nothing there, huh?"

"Quit rubbing it in. I'll be back in the office tomorrow. I'll see you then."

"Might want to hear what I have to say." Only now did the suppressed excitement in Carl's voice register.

"Why?" Or it could be a practical joke, and he wasn't in the mood.

"Lab results came back this morning on the chopstick."

"What showed up?"

"Mostly tree wood."

"Amazing." In spite of this unhelpful beginning, Jake sensed this wasn't a practical joke. Excitement pulled his belly muscles taut. "Anything else?"

"Yeah. There was a residue on the sticks. They'd come in contact with cocaine."

"I'm listening."

There was a pause on the other end; Jake knew Carl was building up for a payoff. "Then the lab tested the packaging it was wrapped in and hit the freakin' jack-pot."

"The packaging?"

"Yep. It's a pretty new process, but the lab guys have seen it before. Coke converted into bricks, acetate sheets, and now packaging material. Dogs can't sniff it out, it fools the naked eye, it can easily go undetected. Unless a certain stubborn FBI wiseass just won't give up. I'm mentioning no names here, but you might get an inkling of who I'm talking about."

"Sneaky bastards." Jake took a moment to savor the knowledge that Hank's death would finally be vindicated. And if they were very careful, and very lucky, they'd get the network, not just one company—and maybe catch Hank's murderer.

"Adam's called a meeting this afternoon. He's bringing in DEA, customs and the local cops." Jake didn't care. They could call in the Girl Scouts if it would help bust the network. "I'm on my way in. I don't want just Oceanic, I want the whole damn network."

On the other end of the phone, he heard papers rustle. "Want me to start the paperwork for wiretaps?"

"Yeah. Thanks."

"Hey, don't you have somebody inside?"

"Not anymore. I gotta go."

Jake didn't waste time on the phone, but sprinted to Cyn's front door and started banging. She was just stubborn enough to go to work in spite of his orders. He had to stop her.

"Looking for Cynthia?"

No, the tooth fairy. "Yes," he answered Mr. Edgar, the old guy who lived across the street. He was just straightening with his morning paper in hand.

"She left about half an hour ago. Earlier than usual."

"Thanks. It wasn't important." Jake raised a hand in a casual salute, then sauntered back to his place, while inside his gut twisted. He was going to wring her goddamn neck.

If he was worried sick about her safety, he refused to acknowledge it.

IN A DEFIANT MOOD on Monday, Cyn wore extra makeup and her red leather suit. As she walked slowly past reception, she realized her wardrobe choice was a bad idea. She couldn't wear this suit without remembering that she'd worn it the first evening she and Jake had made love.

"Morning, Marilyn."

Cyn had done her best to find out what was going on at Oceanic when Jake had given her no support, nothing to help her in her quest. Quite the opposite, in fact. He'd given her grief for trying to investigate what was in those boxes, and he'd yanked her off her date with Neville before she had a chance to get any information out of him.

He'd also broken her heart and stomped all over it, but she wasn't going there. Not this morning. She decided she'd cried all the tears she was ever going to cry over Jake Wheeler.

At the thought of never seeing him again, of the unfairness of his accusations, her lids started to prickle and she blinked hard. No tears. *No. No. No!*

As she headed toward her office with misery on her mind, she stopped dead in her tracks. The staid accounting department looked like a bridal bower. Dozens and dozens of roses…hundreds, possibly thousands of roses surrounded the place. Red ones, pink ones, yellow, white—in vases, bouquets and scattered on the floor and desk.

The perfume was dizzying.

And in the midst of it all was Agnes, looking harassed but ecstatic as she crammed roses into a coffee mug. Plan A from Saturday night may have been a total disaster, but Plan B, by all indications, had been an outrageous success.

"From George?" Cynthia asked.

A blushing Agnes just nodded her head. With her glow of happiness, she looked even better than she had right after the makeover. Surrounded by hothouse blooms, Agnes reminded Cyn of a rose herself—a neglected back-garden rose bush that had been watered, fertilized and tended to bring it back to its full beauty. "We haven't been apart since Saturday night," she whispered, and blushed some more.

Cyn gazed around at all the roses and a slow smile formed. "I'm guessing you both had a good time."

Agnes giggled. It was a sound Cyn had never heard her make. "This one's my favorite," she said, pointing to a Chintzware teapot that was the base for a florist's arrangement of roses and baby's breath. There was a card attached.

"Forgive me, my darling," it said.

"You've got to give the man credit," Cyn said, gazing around her. "When he apologizes, he apologizes." A thought crossed her mind. "What about the, um…"

"Tootsies?" Agnes asked with a slow smile. "They're history. We talked for hours yesterday and he finally admitted he was tired of dating all those silly girls." She sighed blissfully.

"That's great, Agnes."

The older woman held a pink rosebud to her cheek. "He asked me to marry him."

Tears pricked Cynthia's eyes. "Oh, Agnes. I'm so happy for you." She crossed the room and hugged her.

"I don't know how to thank you. I think deep down he always cared for me. We've been good friends for years, but until I took charge of my life and showed a little backbone, he could keep me as his friend and still see those silly girls."

Cyn nodded. She understood better than anybody how that could happen. "It wasn't the hair dye, or the new clothes, it was the attitude behind them. The one that said 'Look at me, look at who I really am.'"

"Yes." Agnes leaned forward and buried her nose in the roses stuffed into the coffee mug, and Cyn would have bet money she was reminiscing about some particularly juicy moment from the weekend. "I'm sorry I abandoned you the other night. How did the rest of your date go?"

"Dismally. My house alarm went off so I had to go home." Cyn shrugged. "Then Neville left."

Impulsively, Agnes touched her arm, "Don't look so downcast, dear. Things will work out."

"No. It's too late." She sighed sadly, then raised her head to stare at her co-worker. How could Agnes possibly know about Jake? Then she realized Agnes must think she was breaking her heart over the creepy Neville. "I mean, it's not..."

How could she possibly explain? It wasn't Neville she'd cried over. It wasn't Neville she yearned for, body and soul. It wasn't Neville she loved so much her teeth ached when she thought about him.

And it wasn't Neville who'd dumped her on her leather-clad butt.

She forced a cheery smile and congratulated Agnes again. "I'd better get some work done."

WITH A SIGH, she pulled up her month-end files. She started with the pension files. As she was scanning the monthly payouts, she gasped as a very familiar name caught her eye.

Dominic Torreo. That was the name of one of the pensioners. It was also the name of the murdered drug dealer she'd read about in the newspaper.

While her heart pounded and excitement flooded her brain, Cynthia forced herself not to jump to any conclusions. There could be more than one Dominic Torreo, after all. The retired Oceanic employee could be one hundred and five and living in a Florida trailer park for all she knew.

She clicked on the pension file titled *Service Record* and a prickle skipped down her spine. The file was password protected. She thought she'd opened all the files, but she must have missed this one. It was the first she'd come across that required a password. It was a sizable file, too. She'd assumed it held nothing more interesting than vital stats on the company's retired employees. But perhaps the title was just camouflage.

Was this the hidden stash of secrets?

Or was the file password-protected simply because it

contained sensitive information? But she had lots of sensitive information on her computer, none of which was elaborately secured. Why add an extra layer of security to just one file?

"Take some flowers." Agnes entered her office and broke into Cynthia's reverie. "I need to make some room on my desk."

Cyn chuckled, accepting the vase of yellow roses. She buried her nose in the butter-colored blooms. "Mmm. They smell wonderful."

"That foolish man. This must have cost him a small fortune." Agnes tut-tutted, but she couldn't keep the delighted grin off her face.

"And you are worth every petal," Cyn reminded her sternly. "Don't forget it." She placed the roses on her desk and then said, "Um, Agnes, I'm trying to get some information on a retired employee, but my file seems to be corrupted. You have a duplicate set, don't you?"

"Yes. On my computer. Shall I—"

"That's all right. I'll come and have a look."

"Who is it?" Agnes asked as she pulled up the pension files.

"His name is Dominic Torreo."

Agnes shook her head. "I don't recognize the name, but Neville bought out a company a few years ago and, good-hearted man that he is, provided full pensions for all their retirees."

Good-hearted wasn't the epithet that was springing to Cynthia's mind at the moment. Still, she wouldn't jump to conclusions. "That's the one." Cyn pointed to *Service Record.* "I think it's possible Mr. Torreo's being overcompensated. I want to check his record. Don't mention anything to George or Neville, will you? I wouldn't want to make trouble for anyone until I'm certain of my facts.''

''Of course not. I'm just glad you're so diligent. In my opinion you're a much better accountant than your predecessor.''

''Thanks.'' Cyn printed off the entire file, noting as she did so that it was much smaller than the file with the same name on her own computer. And it wasn't password-protected.

Back in her office, she read through the file. Dominic Torreo was listed as sixty-seven years old. His pension checks were deposited directly into a bank account here in Seattle. Scanning through the files, Cyn was amazed at the number of pensioners who also had their monthly checks deposited automatically to accounts in the same bank. Delighted with her own cleverness, she spun in her chair. Things were looking up in the spy business.

Until she tried getting into Harrison's secret file. Then her espionage skills began to seem as feeble as ever. But she was determined to crack the code, today.

She'd evaded Jake this morning, with some vague idea of taking one final inspection of Oceanic, as though there was some vital clue she'd overlooked. She had, too. She'd overlooked the secrets in the pension files. Now at least she had something to give Jake—evidence that might just help track down the drug network that had been responsible for his friend's death.

If she could crack Harrison's password and unearth the second set of books, she'd know she'd struck her own blow against the illegal drug trade.

If it did nothing else for her, trying to crack Harrison's password took her mind off the utter wreck that was her love life. After grabbing a gigantic cup of coffee, Cyn sat at her desk, pulled the keyboard toward her and got to work. All her skills and training came into play as she attempted to outsmart another accountant. It was like being inside a giant sneaky, snaky maze. Dead end after dead end slapped her in the face as she tried to find the entrance to Harrison's secret file.

Of course, the file might turn out to be nothing more interesting than a backup of his home accounts. That was the sort of prudent thing any accountant might do, and it would be perfectly understandable that Harrison would hide the files. But somehow, she didn't think this file was innocent.

She pulled out a notebook and recorded every password combination she tried. She pulled up old payroll records and gleaned his birth date, middle name, address and phone number. Nothing. She let her mind drift. If she were Harrison, what would she do?

She stared at the colorful blooms on her desk, a faint replica of Agnes's smile on her own lips. Whatever happened, she knew she'd carry away the knowledge that she'd helped two people find love. It wasn't the job she'd been sent to Oceanic to do, but at least it was something good.

She sighed, and went back to code cracking. The FBI must have programs that could work on breaking codes. She could simply turn the whole problem over to them. Of course, if Harrison knew what he was doing, he'd have used upper- and lowercase letters mixed with numbers to make it very tough to crack, even for the most sophisticated programs. But eventually it would yield its secrets.

She glanced at her watch. It was four o'clock. She'd give herself an hour more to work on it, then she'd report her findings to Jake and her mission would be—

not accomplished, but over. Oh, but if she could crack the code herself...

Once the investigation was complete, no doubt Jake would move out of Mrs. Jorgensen's house and back to wherever he came from.

If he didn't move, she darn well would. His accusations on Saturday night, his belief that she was "easy with her favors" as her mother might have put it—well, if he believed that was possible, he couldn't love her as she loved him. And the new Cyn wouldn't accept less than complete love and trust. Somewhere was a man who would love her as she deserved to be loved.

Who knew where she might find him? Once she'd finished up here, she'd follow Harrison's example and hop a plane somewhere exotic for a well-earned vacation. She was absolutely not going to hang around Seattle moping.

She had her pride.

It was pride that made her redouble her efforts to crack Harrison's code before the end of the day.

"Think, think," she chastised herself.

She refused to be daunted by the endless possibilities. She got up and began to pace the small office. She knew herself that passwords were difficult to remember. That's why so many people made themselves vulnerable choosing their middle names or wedding anniversaries, and used the same password for everything.

A combination of numbers and letters, upper- and lowercase, were the hardest to crack, and the toughest to remember. At home she'd taped a note to the underside of her keyboard reminding herself that her banking password was her high school locker combination and the initials of her grades one and three teachers. Who but an accountant would remember such things years later?

Might Harrison have had his own little reminder system somewhere handy to his computer?

She felt like slapping herself upside the head. She'd never thought of the obvious.

In a flash she crossed back to the computer and flipped up the keyboard. Nothing but the manufacturer's name and a serial number appeared there. With a mental shrug, Cyn tried several combinations of the letters and numerals, but got nothing.

She tapped her fingers on the desktop. *Think.* She flipped the monitor around, checked underneath and then began searching desk drawers for clues.

Nothing.

She turned her chair this way and that, then got on her hands and knees and checked the undersides of the armrests and seat. While she was on all fours she crawled under the desk.

"Cynthia?" At the sound of Neville Percivald's puzzled voice, her head flew up and with a loud thwack banged the underside of the desk.

"Ow," she cried, and with tears of pain blurring her vision, she emerged. She could just imagine how she must look, her red leather derriere twitching as she crawled backward...that's if the brief skirt hadn't hiked up so high—

A gentleman would turn his back. Unfortunately, she could feel Neville's ungentlemanly gaze glued to her backside like a branding iron. She gave an extra wiggle to her hips to camouflage her actions as she fumbled one of her red beaded earrings out of her ear.

By the time she'd dragged herself to her feet, rubbing the bump on her head, she was able to display the jewelry in her other palm. "Dropped an earring," she said breezily.

He nodded. His eyes looked dazed and he was breathing a bit rapidly. It made her feel like the star attraction in some cheesy peep show.

"It appears Father's date was more successful than ours the other night," he said, jerking his head in the direction of the floral boutique that used to be front-office accounting.

"Yes. Your stepfather and Agnes seem well suited."

"I was hoping to find out how, um…*well suited* we might be, the other night." The door of her office clicked shut behind him, and instinctively she moved closer to her phone. If he tried anything, she could call security, or failing that, bash him with the receiver. Her ick antenna was on full alert. It was amazing that he could look so very upright and newsanchorish and be such a perv.

"Yes, well. Some other time." Like when they were hosting skating parties in hell.

He moved a step closer and her fingers inched nearer the phone. "How about tonight?"

"Sorry, I already have plans." Plans that did not include whips, chains, leather or private rooms in some sleazy club. She suppressed a shudder at the thought.

"Tomorrow night?"

If she hadn't already planned to blow this joint, she'd be planning it right this second. She debated going with the I'm-not-sure-it's-a-good-idea-to-date-people-at-work routine, but she'd already accepted a date with him once, so that was out.

She could claim she was planning on entering a nunnery, which, given her recent experiences with men, wasn't such a bad idea. But she wasn't Catholic, which made the whole thing sound fishy even to her own ears.

There was always the lesbian angle, but Neville seemed the type who might want to watch—as in the "Ladies Choice" fantasy in the "Erotically Advanced" section of *Raunch.*

Double ick to that.

Instead she sighed and said, "Can I let you know tomorrow?"

His lips pursed in annoyance. "I suppose so," he answered stiffly.

Darn. She should have gone with the nunnery. Now he probably thought she was playing hard to get, when in fact she planned to be *impossible* to get. She didn't plan on working here tomorrow—or any other day.

She was itching to get back to sleuthing. This was her last chance to crack Harrison's code and prove to…*herself* that she had what it took to be a great undercover agent.

Marching to the door, she held it open. "Well, thanks for dropping by. I do need to get those month-end reports finished up."

Petulantly, he snapped, "Till tomorrow, then."

Apart from a grade A extra-large egg on her head, she had nothing to show for her attempts to guess Harrison's password. There'd been nothing under the desktop but a couple of rocklike lumps of ancient chewing gum.

Hopelessly, she punched in every flavor and brand of chewing gum she could think of and got the same response to each. *Invalid Password.*

If she were a woman of violence, she'd throw the computer out the window. The words *Invalid Password* seemed to have burned into her retina. She had a feeling she'd see them for the rest of her life, every time she closed her eyes.

Time was running out. She knew she could outsmart Harrison, if she could just *think!*

The answer was probably sitting right in front of her nose, and she couldn't see the forest for the trees.

She gazed ahead, a vague imprint of *Invalid Password* stamped across her vision like a neon aura. She blinked a few times, focusing on the Grand Prix poster on the wall in front of her. Funny, of all the things people had mentioned about her predecessor, nobody had commented on his passion for racing. If she were staying here she'd replace the framed poster with something more to her taste.

She stared at it for a moment. Had Harrison attended the Grand Prix in 1997? Her eyes widened and she gasped. Large letters, small letters, numbers. It was so obvious, it couldn't be.

Could it?

Had the code been literally staring her in the face all these weeks?

Taking a shaky breath, she typed in "Grand Prix 1997."

Invalid Password.

"1997 Grand Prix."

Invalid Password.

"Grand 1997 Prix."

Invalid Password.

Oh, well. It had been worth a shot.

As a last resort, she typed the whole thing backward: "7991 xirPdnarG" and hit Enter.

Like a key turning in a well-oiled lock, the password opened Harrison's secret file.

Her cry of delight could have been heard at the

German deli two blocks away. She wanted to jump up and down and shout her success to anyone who'd listen. Then she clamped her lips shut, remembering this was top-secret stuff. Quickly, she opened one of her month-end statements on screen, covering over the telltale file. After five minutes, when her scream had drawn no curious visitors, she dared to take a peek at Harrison's secret file.

Her stomach had tied itself into knots of excitement and her fingers trembled slightly on the keyboard as she studied the columns of numbers on her screen. It was a set of books, all right, but she knew immediately they weren't for Harrison's home accounts. They were for the company.

It didn't take her five minutes to realize that this was Aladdin's cave, the treasure trove of secret evidence she'd been looking for. These books contained categories not listed in the "cover books" she'd been working on.

Harrison had been clever, she had to give him that. Her accountant's mind appreciated the subtleties that had allowed him to create a set of phony books that probably would have passed muster during an IRS audit.

She lost herself in the document, the way a mystery fan gets lost in a thriller. Grabbing her notebook, she made notes as she went. When she reached the bottom of the document, her eyes bugged out. She couldn't believe it!

A list of names and addresses in the U.S. And in Colombia.

"Good night, Cynthia. Don't work too late," Agnes said, popping her head in the open office door, the Chintzware pot of roses in her hand.

"Hmm?" Cyn glanced up, stunned. It couldn't be the end of the day—could it? "Oh, good night, Agnes."

"I'd stay late to help you with the month end, but I've got a date tonight," the older woman said with shy pride.

Cyn grinned at her. "Month end? Oh, don't worry about it. Have a great time."

Once Agnes left, Cyn's face sobered suddenly. There was a good chance that George's stepson was up to his bland eyeballs in crime.

Doug Ormond and Lester Dart were clearly part of it.

Harrison had used an abbreviated code, kind of a personal shorthand, but D.O. and L.D. seemed clear enough.

Not wanting to call any suspicion to herself by working too late, she crossed to the supply cupboard for some blank disks so she could transfer a copy of the suspicious files. Then her job would be done and Jake and the FBI could take over.

She wouldn't gloat, she decided, as she began copying files. The words *I told you so* would not pass her lips. Instead, she'd be coolly professional. Cyn the Bold reporting in—mission accomplished. Well, maybe she'd polish up her mother's sterling tray so she could literally deliver the goods on a silver platter.

She popped one full disk into her bag and inserted another. The outer offices were hushed, and now that she was filling her bag full of incriminating evidence, she wanted to get the hell out of Dodge as fast as possible.

"Come on, come on," she encouraged the computer, as though she could make it copy the files faster.

She glanced at her watch. Almost six. It would look

strange if she didn't leave soon. Almost there. She was almost there....

Done. She dropped the last disk in her bag and sighed with relief.

A knock sounded on her open door and she jerked her head up to see Neville, a bland smile on his face.

"Hi, Neville," she said brightly, while panic seized her chest. With a jerky mouse click, she pulled up her month-end file to cover the incriminating evidence of her snooping.

"You're working late, my dear." He stated the obvious, moving closer.

"Just finishing up a few things for month end," she chirped, standing and turning to face him so her body shielded the screen.

He came even closer and toyed with a pencil on the corner of her desk. "Agnes had a word with me before she left."

"Agnes?"

"Yes." His face flushed slightly. "She said you'd been crying."

"Of course I haven't been crying." Not for hours, anyway; she'd been too caught up spying to even think about Jake's defection.

"Your eyes are rather puffy, and a bit red," he pointed out.

"That's just, uh, allergies," she managed to murmur.

He dropped his gaze. "Agnes was under the impression that I had, um, hurt your feelings by leaving the other night."

Oh, Agnes, you didn't. "No. No, of course not. Agnes must have made a mistake."

There was a pause. And when he spoke again his tone had changed so completely, he didn't even sound like the same man. "She wasn't the only one who made a mistake." Neville's voice was cold as lead.

She turned to him in surprise and found him staring at the notepad on her desk—the one she'd used to jot down the most incriminating pieces of information from Harrison's file.

"Neville, that's not—" She reached for the pad of paper, but his hand slapped down on it so hard she felt the impact quiver through her palm.

"I think you've made a very big mistake, my dear."

She heard voices from the hall, voices she recognized. Eddie from shipping, and Doug Ormond. Maybe they could help her? Even as she thought it, Neville strode to the door to call them in.

While his back was turned, she grabbed the phone and frantically punched in Jake's emergency number, her fingertips slipping with sweat.

"Put down the phone, Cynthia," Neville said in that same cold, inhuman tone.

She glanced over her shoulder. The man she'd once thought so harmless and pleasant had a gun trained on her back. He was flanked on either side by Eddie and Doug Ormond, all three looking grim and murderous.

She put down the phone.

13

JAKE FOUGHT A RISING sense of unease, sipping tepid coffee that tasted like toxic waste—as though that would calm his gut.

About a dozen agents were gathered in the meeting room, along with some guys from the Drug Enforcement Agency, customs and the local cops, working on a plan to widen the net and catch as many drug-dealing fish as possible.

As pumped as he felt that they'd found hard evidence at Oceanic, right now he didn't give a rat's ass about anything but getting Cyn out of there. Today. Now.

But he was too well trained, too experienced an agent to do something stupid. He couldn't phone her at her office or show up there. He'd have to wait until she left for the day, then make damn sure she didn't go back. Nobody in the meeting had referred to her, probably because they'd forgotten she existed—all except Carl, who'd glanced over at him a couple of times with a questioning expression, but kept his mouth shut.

Cyn was a volunteer; no reason for her to be involved now there was a possibility of danger. Damn it, Jake should have handcuffed her to the bed this morning to prevent her going to work. Worry, sharp and acidic, churned in his gut along with the god-awful coffee. He stood suddenly, unable to sit still any longer.

Adam gave him a quizzical glance, but Jake shook

his head sharply. He didn't have anything to contribute to the conversation, because he hadn't heard one word in ten. He glanced at his watch. A couple of hours before she'd be through. He slipped out. They would assume he'd visited the john.

Instead, he checked his messages. The sick feeling of unease didn't let up. No messages from Cyn. There was one from an Agent Wong of Interpol in Hong Kong. The man had left both work and home numbers, and, since Jake couldn't begin to figure out what time it was over there, he tried work first.

"David Wong," a soft voice answered in English on the first ring.

"This is Special Agent Jake Wheeler, FBI."

"Ah, yes, Agent Wheeler. You have been inquiring about a Thomas Harrison?"

"That's right."

"I believe we may have found him. A body was pulled from the harbor late yesterday. Fits your description."

Jake's limbs felt like they were frosting over. "How did he die?"

"A bullet in the back of the head."

Execution style. "Any sign of torture?"

There was a short pause. "It is impossible to say at this time." A discreet cough traveled the miles between Hong Kong and Seattle. "The body was badly decomposed. Perhaps the autopsy results will tell us more."

"Are you certain it's Harrison?"

"No. Not one hundred percent. He was wearing a watch engraved with his name, and a wallet containing identification was found near the body. But we will not be able to confirm identity until dental records can be matched. However, we know he was Caucasian and his height and clothing match your description. I believe these to be the remains of Mr. Harrison."

Jake rubbed a hand across his churning gut. "Looks like the killers didn't care if he was identified." Maybe they were sending some kind of a warning? Harrison must have double-crossed or stolen. "Any idea when death occurred?"

"We believe several weeks ago. As soon as all the tests are completed, I will forward you a full report."

"Thank you."

"In return," the courteous voice continued, "I would very much appreciate any information you might have about Mr. Harrison's known associations."

"You will have our full cooperation, Mr. Wong. Thank you for this information. I'll be in touch."

"Good day, Special Agent Wheeler."

As he hung up, Jake noted his hand wasn't shaking. It must be the only damn part of him that wasn't.

He spared a glance at the meeting room as he jogged by. His sense of urgency was too keen to stop and brief the troops. He could do that from his cell phone.

He knew damn well he'd essentially broken ranks by hightailing it out on his own, but he couldn't worry about breaking a few lousy rules now. And while he was at it, he broke another one and called Cynthia's direct number at Oceanic.

"Come on, baby. Pick up," he muttered, swearing with vicious helplessness when he got her voice mail.

He tried her home number, but he wasn't surprised when he got her answering machine. He cursed the air blue, pushing harder on the gas pedal.

"LOOK, I CAN EXPLAIN," Cynthia protested for about the fifth time as she was forced at gunpoint into the warehouse.

She was pleased to find her voice steady, but then she'd already moved beyond the first panicky fear to a surreal feeling that this couldn't possibly be happening. No way was the man with the cold eyes and colder looking gun the one who reminded her of a trusted anchorman, and no way were they going to shoot her in cold blood. Things like that only happened in movies...didn't they?

Now that she had confirmed Harrison's involvement in the drug smuggling and money laundering operation, she began to wonder about his "vacation" in Hong Kong. No one had received so much as a postcard from the previous accountant. Had he ended his tenure at Oceanic staring at a deadly weapon just as she was doing? A shudder rippled through her.

As though he'd read her mind, Doug Ormond asked, "Did Harrison put you on to us?"

"Harrison? Do you mean the man who held my position before me?"

"Yeah, Harrison. Dude with the expensive habit and the sneaky fingers."

Her stomach felt a little odd, like she might be coming down with something. "I'm not sure I follow. I thought Harrison was in Hong Kong."

It was Neville who answered her. "He was, for a day or so, until some friends of ours caught up with him." He mimed with his gun.

"Dead?" she squeaked.

"I'm afraid so, darling. Everybody who crosses us winds up dead." He glanced at her significantly. "But in your case that won't happen right away." He motioned to Eddie. "Tie her up."

"What with?"

Cyn scanned the area for any kind of weapon, any means of escape, but there didn't seem to be any. On the bright side, she couldn't see anything suitable for tying people up, either. The boxes were all taped, the wooden crates nailed; there was some kind of a chain thing on one of the machines, but it looked like it would be a lot of work to get it off.

Exasperated, Neville passed the gun over to Doug Ormond. "Wait here."

Once he'd gone, Cyn attempted a confident smile. "Hey, guys, I know Neville's under a lot of stress right now. Why don't you just turn your backs for a few minutes, I'll slip out and we can all pretend this never happened?"

"Shut up," said Ormond.

Well, it had been worth a shot. While they waited in silence, she had time to wish she'd taken boxing or karate to keep in shape. What good was deep water aerobics when your life was on the line?

Around her, piles of boxes and sacks loomed, hulking and menacing. The cement was cold and hard through her thin-soled shoes. But not as cold and hard as the knowledge that her predecessor had been shot dead. Even as her mind tried to focus on that one horrible fact, she skittered away from it. She couldn't afford to panic; she had to think.

And all she could think about was how much she wished she'd listened to Jake when he'd told her to stay away from this place. At least she could count on him to search Oceanic when she disappeared. They'd find something. Agnes would remember her asking about Dominic Torreo—that was the only clue Jake would need. It was definitely cold comfort, but at least she felt her death would be avenged along with Hank's.

She had another futile wish. She wished she could tell Jake she loved him before it was too late.

But it seemed like too late was on its way when the heavy doors opened and Neville Percivald strolled in—her leather bag under one arm, a pair of handcuffs swinging from the other.

At the sight of the handcuffs, she gulped. It was one thing to be helpless when in bed with a man like Jake, quite another to be helpless in front of the three evil stooges.

She struggled, twisting and scratching, when Neville grabbed hold of her. He grunted when she managed to kick him in the shin, and if Eddie hadn't joined in, she really felt she might have got away. But the two of them managed to cuff her right arm to a water pipe.

She glared at them both and raised her chin, determined not to give in to the panic squeezing her chest. Common sense told her they weren't going to shoot her right there in the warehouse, and she still had one fist and two feet left to defend herself.

That and her wits. Which she'd better start using.

There was a strange moment, sort of like an awkward lull in dinner-table conversation, when none of them seemed to know what to do next. Ormond was still pointing the gun her way, his arm beginning to quiver from holding it up for so long.

Neville stared at her warily, standing out of kicking range. "I should have brought rope," he grumbled. "I think the best thing is to take her to my place."

The metal handcuff clinked angrily against the metal pipe as she yanked hard. She knew the kind of stuff he was into. If he thought he was going to strip her naked and do disgusting things to her, he had another think coming.

"I don't know." Eddie shuffled his feet. "I don't mind taking somebody out, but I don't want to get involved in any of that kinky stuff of yours."

"Yeah." Ormond jumped in. "Let's just do it quick and clean." Since he was the one with the gun, she had to force herself not to shut her eyes and cower.

"I saw her put something in here," Neville said, picking up her bag and upending it over the coffee-break table a few feet in front of her.

Out tumbled her wallet, breath mints, makeup bag, keys, an old nail file, an open package of tissues and, finally, clattering to the scratched Formica tabletop like a couple of dirty secrets, two black disks.

Neville shot her an evil look, then picked up one of the disks, turning it in his hands and gazing at it as though he had X-ray vision. "Well?" he demanded.

When Jake was around, danger acted like an aphrodisiac, but right now she didn't feel turned on at all. She felt angry. These men had taken a good company and turned it into a shameful thing. What would happen to George and Agnes and Marilyn and all the other decent people who worked here?

Damn it, she wasn't going down without a fight.

They'd find out what was on the disks soon enough. All she could do was stall as long as possible and wait for an opportunity to escape. "It's, um..." She shrugged. "Just some month-end files. I wanted to work on them at home."

"Go get a laptop," Neville ordered Ormond, who put the gun down on the table, massaged his right biceps and headed off without a word.

She exhaled slowly. Without the gun pointing at her,

she could think better. Now there were only two of them against her, so the odds were one-third better, but there remained the sticky problem of her being handcuffed to the damned pipe.

"Please, could I use the bathroom?" She directed her question at Eddie, who she figured was her best shot at any sympathy. But even as Eddie blushed and harrumphed, Neville said, "No."

Time ticked by and Neville took the opportunity to rummage through her makeup bag. As she watched him paw through her cosmetics, she couldn't believe she'd once thought him gentlemanly. Her arm was starting to lose all feeling. She began to clench and unclench her fingers to keep the blood flowing.

"Was Harrison your boyfriend?" Neville asked while twisting open her lipstick.

"No. I already told you, I never knew him." Was he really dead? Had these awful men killed an accountant?

"Let me guess. He was supposed to call from Hong Kong, and when he didn't, you figured he'd double-crossed you and you decided to come in here and help yourself."

"No. That's not right at all." In the back of her mind, she was at least grateful they hadn't a clue as to what she was really doing here. She was determined to protect Jake and the operation. "I took the job because I wanted a change. While I was doing the month-end books, I just, um, found this file that didn't seem to match the one on my computer. That's what you saw on my screen. I'm a very conscientious employee."

"A bit too conscientious, I'm afraid."

"But I don't understand. What did Harrison do?"

Neville gazed at her for a moment, then shrugged. "As I'm certain you already know, Harrison began to sample the merchandise we were bringing in from Colombia, more and more as his cocaine habit grew worse.''

''He was a drug addict?''

''It's an expensive habit. Then he tried to set up his own operation on the side. He must have figured out we were on to him, because he stole a large sum of money and left the country.'' Neville shrugged.

If he'd tried to set up his own operation, Harrison couldn't have been alone. Things started to fall into place. ''Was that what happened to Dominic Torreo, the murdered drug dealer? Did he cross you, too?''

''Well, well. She is a clever little girl, isn't she, Doug? Yes. Dominic was working with Harrison. Now they're both out of business. I just can't work out what your role was, and if anybody else is going to come crawling out of the woodwork.''

''Of course I wasn't working with them. I don't know them. I really don't know anything,'' she said, kicking herself for revealing that she'd caught the connection between Harrison and the murdered drug dealer. Her brain didn't seem to be working as sharply as usual.

Neville booted up the computer and inserted the disk. In less than a minute, the incriminating pension file stared at her from the laptop screen.

''I didn't know he'd kept a set of everything for himself,'' Neville mumbled, scrolling through the numbers, then glancing sharply at Cynthia. ''Maybe it wasn't drugs you were after. What was it, Cyn? Blackmail?''

''No. I stumbled on the file and wondered what it was, that's all.''

''Right. And you were taking the file home because...?'' He gazed at her with phony inquiry.

"I wanted to look it over at home. I didn't want to make any rash accusations against my predecessor."

"Well, aren't you the Girl Scout. You weren't going to ask for a sizable contribution to your *own* retirement fund to encourage you to keep quiet about our operation?"

"What operation? All I know is the pension plan seems inefficient. I have some ideas for improving it."

"Hey, man," Eddie said. "Maybe she doesn't know anything—"

A snort of disbelief silenced him. "Have you forgotten the packaging she hid under the pallet just over there?" Neville reminded him, jerking his chin toward where she and Jake had checked out the chopstick shipment.

"This is about packaging? What, I forgot to recycle?" She began to wonder if the blood had not only drained out of her right arm, but her head as well; nothing was making any sense.

"Don't play dumb, Cynthia. It doesn't suit you. Let's just say we're big believers in recycling here at Oceanic. Those sheets of packaging coming up from Colombia get recycled in a friendly lab into top-grade cocaine—street value in the millions. But you already knew that. Why don't you just tell us who else you're working with, and we can put this unpleasant incident behind us. No hard feelings."

No hard feelings? She had the strong feeling that *she'd* end up recycled as fish food. If she could get them to release her, even if they planned to take her to Neville's house, at least she'd have a chance to get away. It wasn't much of a plan, but it was the best she could come up with.

She tried to look scared, which wasn't that difficult

under the circumstances. She bit her lip and glanced right and left, then dropped her voice to a stage whisper. "If I tell you, they'll kill me."

"Tell us everything you know, Cynthia, and we'll see if we can find a place in our operation for you."

As a doorstop? She tried to look relieved and gullible. "I won't let you down, Neville. Can you take off the handcuff now?"

"First tell us what you know."

"Hey, look. Oreos." Ormond had grown bored with the interrogation and was opening drawers. The bag of cookies rustled loudly as he stuck his meaty paw in and withdrew a cookie. She noticed his hairy knuckles and recalled the superintendent's wife had said one of the movers had hairy knuckles. Too bad Cyn hadn't made the connection earlier.

"Mmm. I love Oreos," he said, chomping loudly. Little black crumbs tumbled down his chin like volcanic ash.

"Could you manage to hold on to the gun?" Neville admonished him.

"Oh, yeah. Sorry." He slumped into a chair, pointing the gun in her general direction. His other hand, which grasped a fresh cookie, hung down like an ape's.

Out of the corner of her eye, Cyn saw something scuttle. Something black and furry with a snaking tail. Just when she thought things couldn't get any worse, the damn rat had to join the party. A little cry escaped her, and with her free hand she pointed to the cookie-addicted vermin. It ran toward the sound of the rustling bag like a hungry farmhand to the dinner gong.

"Whaa?" Ormond jerked his head in the direction she was pointing and suddenly all hell broke loose. He gave an overweight, middle-aged thug's version of a squeal of fright, and the rat, which was just about to take the cookie, ended up taking a bite out of his knuckle instead. He knocked the rat flying with one hand, roaring in rage, and then the gun went off.

Cynthia closed her eyes and instinctively recoiled, trying to make the smallest possible target. Was this it then? Her life was about to end in this horrible warehouse?

A hoarse scream rent the air, but it wasn't coming from her throat. Eyes jerking open, she realized it was Eddie doing the screaming. He fell to the floor, grabbing a bleeding thigh. "Son of a bitch, you shot me."

And then an explosion rocked the front of the building. Almost immediately she heard the howl of an alarm.

The rat darted back among the boxes, taking Ormond's dropped Oreo cookie with it.

"What the—" Neville glanced at her, then his eyes narrowed into ugly slits. "Keep an eye on her," he ordered the groaning Eddie, grabbing a gun out of his suit jacket pocket. "Come on!" he ordered Ormond, who followed, sucking his knuckle and cursing.

Cyn didn't have time to worry about whether the explosion was caused by friend or foe; all she knew was this was her one and only chance to escape.

Along with the other contents of her purse, her key ring was on the table, the little silver key winking at her like an unreachable star. It was the key Jake had put there. The key to her sex-shop handcuffs. She knew Neville shopped at the same store. Was it possible that's where he'd purchased the cuff currently on her right hand? She gazed up at where she was attached to the pipe. The handcuff looked identical to the ones she had at home. Did they have a universal key? She had no idea, but this was her best bet for an escape.

Eddie groaned, more interested in his problems than hers. If she could just get rid of him… "Eddie, let me help you."

He muttered a curse.

"You could bleed to death. Those two just ran off and left you. Unlock these handcuffs so I can bind your leg."

"Don't got the keys." He stared helplessly at his own sluggishly bleeding thigh.

To trust or not to trust? She glanced down at him and realized he had a gun in his hand. It didn't bode well for trusting him. "You need to put pressure on that. I think there are some towels in the bathroom, and maybe a first aid kit."

He gazed up at her, obviously assessing the risk of leaving her there. But it was clear she couldn't go anywhere without the key to the handcuffs. With much grunting and groaning, Eddie managed to haul himself upright and hop painfully to the bathroom.

Come on, come on, she urged him silently, knowing the other two could return at any moment.

Eddie made it to the bathroom, but didn't shut the door. He couldn't see her, but she imagined he'd be checking on her from time to time. Quickly, she reached forward with her free hand, yanking and straining, but there was a good six inches between where her fingers ended and the table began.

Trying a move she'd seen in an action movie, she raised both arms, gripped the water pipe and swung her body forward. And what she learned immediately was that those movie stunt people must do a lot more sit-ups than she. Her stomach muscles screamed in protest as she tried to hook her foot under the table, missed and swung back with all the grace of a sack of onions.

She sobbed with frustration and tried again. Failed again.

"FBI! Freeze!" Even through the thick fire door, she recognized the voice.

"Jake!" she cried, shuddering with relief. He was here. He'd rescue her. Everything would be all right.

Gunfire exploded.

Seconds later the alarm was silenced.

"Oh, my God. Jake. No." He wouldn't have turned off the alarm; he wanted the authorities to investigate. Neville must have turned it off. Which meant Jake could be bleeding, hurt, needing her. She took a deep breath and jackknifed forward once more, gritting her teeth with the effort. She hooked her toes under the table and with every muscle in her body screaming, managed to pull the table inch by agonizing inch toward her.

Gasping, she reached forward, and this time was able to grasp her Pacific Northwest Accounting Association key ring. With no time to worry about whether the rattling would alert Eddie, she grabbed hold of the little silver key and inserted it into the lock.

Her hands were shaking and sweaty, so she fumbled and the key wouldn't turn. *Please, please,* she whispered urgently, almost sobbing with nerves. Jake needed her. She had to get to him.

Frantically, she turned the key left and right with her trembling fingers. Just when she was certain the key wouldn't fit, she heard the click as the lock gave. She thought that metallic click was the most wonderful sound she'd ever heard.

She pulled her arm free and ran forward, glancing

into the bathroom to see Eddie sprawled on the floor, passed out. She hesitated only a second. Jake, too, could be lying on the floor, bleeding. It was no contest as to whom she'd tend first.

As she raced for the door, she noticed an open toolbox beside one of the hydraulic lifts. Thinking she might need a weapon, she grabbed a wrench, then paused. Eddie had a gun; she could go back and take it from him. Then she remembered she didn't even know how to use a gun.

Against the arsenal out front, a wrench wasn't much, but it felt reassuringly heavy in her hand.

She opened the door just wide enough to squeeze through. All the lights had been turned off in the main office; there was only the dim illumination from the emergency lights to guide her. She crept down the corridor, eyes adjusting, ears superalert. She heard nothing but the low hum of the building's heating system and her own shoes scuffing the carpet.

She rounded the corner and heard voices. "This is the last time I'm asking. Where is she, you son of a bitch?" It was Jake's voice, angry and menacing and very, very alive. Her heart pounded and her knees sagged. He was all right. Jake was all right. They were going to get out of here. She'd be able to tell him she loved him, after all.

She sped down the corridor and stopped. There he was, healthy and commanding, his big, scary black gun pointing at Ormond's privates.

The big man cowered. "Who?"

Both men were in profile to her and she saw Ormond's eyes move. He had to be looking for Neville. Where *was* Neville?

As she opened her mouth to warn Jake, Ormond said, "She's—"

"She's dead." Neville rose just behind Jake, his own gun now trained on Jake's back.

"No." Jake said the word softly. Then he roared, "No!"

"I'm afraid you're too late, old boy."

But Jake didn't seem to take it in. His face was suddenly ashen, his eyes lifeless. "Not...not Cynthia." His voice sounded hoarse and old.

"Don't worry, lover boy. You'll be joining her shortly." Neville laughed, a wry chuckle. "She had me fooled. I thought she was working with Harrison, when all the time she was a stooge for the FBI. Very convenient."

Jake shook his head, as though a bee were buzzing around his ear. He seemed to pull himself together, stashing the raw pain she'd witnessed behind the granite mask. "Drop the gun and place your hands on top of your head," he ordered Neville.

"I don't think so."

Jake jerked his head toward Ormond. "Then your friend here'll be singing soprano."

"Nev, for Chrissakes, man." Ormond's voice rang out in horror. With his hands on top of his head, she saw him try and cross his legs to protect himself.

"That's right." Neville went on as though Ormond hadn't spoken. "You shoot him, and I shoot you. Then I'll make it look as though Ormond here killed an FBI officer as well as engaging in smuggling, right under my innocent nose. I'll be very upset, of course, and will cooperate fully with the FBI. I must remember to order a new suit from my tailor. Something I can wear to both your funerals."

Do something, Jake, Cynthia urged him silently. *Say something.* But he didn't seem able to concentrate. "Tell me what you did to Cynthia," he said at last.

And in that moment she knew he loved her. So much he couldn't think straight even with his own life in terrible danger. Tears filled her eyes.

"He didn't do anything to me," she said, loud and clear, stepping forward and throwing the wrench at Neville.

"Get down!" Jake shouted, even as she saw Neville's gun swing her way.

She watched the wrench arc through the air in slow motion like a bad shotput, and heard the twin explosions. She dropped to the floor, heard the bullet zing past. Neville reared back, eyes wide and mouth open on a groan as he clutched his shoulder and keeled over.

Jake swung his gun back toward Ormond, but the man hadn't moved. He looked as if all the fight had been knocked out of him. He couldn't stop staring at Neville. "You were gonna let him kill me. I thought we were partners."

In two steps, Jake had crossed to Neville's side, kicking the gun from his lax hand and retrieving it.

"You all right?" he all but shouted at Cyn.

She nodded, not trusting her voice.

Jake dropped to his knees to check Neville's pulse.

"Is he…is he dead?" Cyn managed to ask, her voice trembling as badly as her legs.

He shook his head. "Doesn't deserve to, but he'll live." Glancing around, he stalked over to a computer, pulled one end of a cable out of the machine and the other end from the wall socket, then swiftly hog-tied her former boss. Neville's eyes fluttered open and he groaned.

She retrieved a second computer cable and passed it to Jake. Without a word, he took it and tied up Ormond.

The trembling that had begun in her legs spread upward. She wrapped her arms around herself and tried to breathe while Jake ignored her and got on with business. Grabbing his cell phone, he punched in numbers and gave orders. She heard words—*ambulance...local cops...DEA*—but her mind wouldn't decipher them. Everything was coming from far away and she felt as if she had water in her ears.

Her gaze cut to Neville, groaning on the floor. There was a big red patch on the front of his shirt. She looked away. The sight of the gunshot wound reminded her of Eddie, lying there in the bathroom. "Eddie's hurt."

"Who?"

She was shaking so badly she could barely stand. "Eddie."

"Where is—" Jake glanced at her and he was at her side in an instant.

"Hang on, Cyn, don't faint." His arms wrapped around her, warm and strong. "Hey, baby. It's okay. It's all over now." He rubbed his big hands up and down her arms.

A dark shape materialized, then another. She gave a squeak of alarm, then noticed the FBI insignia on the black jackets. "Eddie's in the warehouse bathroom. Shot," she told Jake softly, unwilling to talk to anyone else, unwilling even to move from his arms.

"We'll get him. You all right?"

"Yes."

"Good." After a final squeeze around her shoulders, he said, "I'm going to have someone drive you home. I've got a few things to take care of."

"My keys, my purse. They're in the back."

Jake gave low-voiced orders over her shoulder, and before she knew it, she'd been ushered out of the building and was on her way home.

She hardly noticed the drive with a fresh-faced young man who was obviously dying to get back to the excitement at Oceanic and resented being put on chauffeur duty. Still, once they'd arrived at her house, he opened her front door for her and, after she punched in her alarm code, walked her through the house.

"This isn't necessary," she assured him. The official tour only reminded her of the other night, when the police officer had done a walk-through as well, just before Jake had dumped her.

The rookie's skeptical look said he agreed with her completely. "Jake's orders, ma'am."

She would much rather Jake had escorted her home himself, but at least he'd been thinking of her safety. That warmed her cold limbs somewhat.

"Can I make you some tea or something?" the young man asked, shuffling from foot to foot.

She felt old enough to be his mother. "No." She smiled at him reassuringly. "I'm fine. I'm going to have a hot bath and go to bed early. But thanks. You go on back now."

If she'd given him a gift-wrapped box from Tiffany's he couldn't have looked any happier. Come to think of it, he was probably the type who'd rather risk life and limb than fool around with jewelry, anyhow. "If you're sure."

"I'm sure. Thanks for bringing me home."

He was gone in an instant and Cyn was alone. She still felt shaky and hollow, but part of that had to be hunger.

She warmed a can of soup and forced herself to eat

it, knowing she'd feel better. Then she brewed a pot of chamomile tea and poured a cup, pale as weak sunshine.

After the day she'd had?

Crossing to the liquor cabinet she dug through dusty bottles until she found brandy that was probably older than she was. A liberal dose gave a certain body to her herbal tea and started a slow warmth spreading through her.

Next, she dragged herself upstairs, noting how each and every muscle in her body ached, and drew herself a hot bath, letting the faucets run until the tub threatened to overflow. Lavender bath crystals perfumed the steam coming off the top, and with a sigh, she lowered her body into the lusciously hot water.

Her mind drifted to Neville Percivald and she gulped hot tea, shuddering. Hot water outside, hot liquid inside, and still she shivered. Forcing her mind away, she focused on the moment when Jake had believed she was dead. Right then, she'd been as certain he loved her as she was certain she loved him right back.

Once this business was behind them, maybe they could start over. Have a real date or two and conduct a romance like normal people. She sighed with pleasure at the thought. She'd like to date Jake. He owed her some major wooing.

The steaming water was beginning to relax her and she sighed deeply, inhaling the scent of lavender. Some wooing would definitely be on the menu. Mmm. Menu. Jake loved cooking. She let herself drift for a moment, fantasizing about the two of them in his kitchen, wearing nothing but aprons.

The sooner they could wrap up the Oceanic case, the quicker they could get to the wooing part. Now that they had Harrison's secret file, it should be easy to close down the drug ring and convict Neville and his buddies. Bits of Harrison's file swam in front of her eyes like dream images.

She sat up, sloshing water over the side of the tub. Darn it, Jake didn't know what she'd found. She hadn't had a chance to tell him.

She got out of the tub and dragged her robe over her still-wet body. After a quick, frantic search, she found her purse and dumped everything out. Yep, whoever had repacked it for her had included the diskettes with the pension files.

She had an idea. It was crazy, but it just might work.

14

Jake's eyes were gritty from lack of sleep. He supposed it hadn't been a bad haul: one shipment of coke and one piece of the pipeline—Oceanic—removed. It wasn't enough. He'd hoped to infiltrate the entire network.

In the predawn darkness, he let himself quietly into Cyn's house. He knew she'd be sleeping, but he needed to check on her. He needed to watch her sleep, watch the rise and fall of her chest and know she was alive. For a second his heart stalled as he recalled the moment when he'd thought he'd lost her. He never wanted to live through anything so devastating again.

He rubbed his tired eyes. When had it happened? When had he fallen in love with that kinky, stubborn, irritating… He sighed. It was hopeless trying to figure out when she'd sneaked under his guard. She had. That's all. The woman had taken his heart hostage and he hadn't so much as put up a fight.

He swallowed hard and moved stealthily toward her bedroom. Light spilled out of her office doorway. He imagined she'd forgotten—or felt too afraid of the dark—to switch it off.

But she was there, sitting at her computer wrapped in her white terry robe. Her hair stuck out all over the place, as if it had been toweled but never combed. As she tapped intently at the keyboard, love squeezed his heart. Love for the brave, nutty woman with a head for numbers and a heart for giving.

A wry smile—part admiration, part frustration—twisted his lips. Why wasn't she sound asleep after the trauma she'd been through?

He wondered what she was doing. Maybe she was writing a complaint letter to his boss.

He'd done some stupid things before, but putting this woman's life in danger topped the list. No doubt when she told her tale, he'd be headed for a disciplinary hearing. Which he richly deserved. They could do anything to him, take his badge, he didn't care. She was alive, and that's all that mattered.

He just hoped he hadn't screwed up so badly he'd never get a second chance at the only woman he'd ever loved.

"Hi," he said softly, so as not to startle her.

She gasped and turned his way. As their gazes connected, he felt her warmth; it was as if she'd leaned right over and kissed some secret part of himself only she could reach.

He dragged a hand over his unshaved face, felt his eyes mist. He must be more tired than he'd thought. He hated botched operations. And he felt personally responsible for this one. He'd been the one to push, determined to prove Oceanic was the next link in their take-down. He'd discovered he was right and the same day blown the whole operation sky-high. Talk about snatching defeat from the jaws of victory.

"Hi, yourself." Her eyes were red rimmed from strain and lack of sleep, her face pale and free of makeup, her hair in total disarray, but right then he'd never seen anything so breathtakingly beautiful as the smile that curved her lips.

It was only a botched undercover operation. Compared to Cyn's safety that was nothing.

In the past he'd prided himself on his self-control and discipline, but in that moment he knew he'd been fooling himself. He could no more have stayed away from those lips than he could have stopped himself loving her. In a heartbeat he was spinning her chair until she faced him, bending to kiss her.

With a throaty sound of pleasure, she opened her lips beneath his, and his tiredness was blasted out by a rush of need as powerful as any he'd ever known. He felt her arms wrap around his neck, leaving her robe gaping. He reached beneath the terry and touched the firm round swells of her breasts. The nipples blossomed as he caressed her. She was so warm, so blessedly alive. Each beat of her heart beneath his hands, each sigh, each flutter of her pulse reminded him that she was full of life. And that life had become so very precious to him.

He felt trembling, and realized it was coming from him. "I thought I'd lost you," he murmured against her lips.

"I thought he was going to shoot you."

"I'm sorry."

"Me, too."

"I need you."

"Oh, yes." She smelled of lavender and woman, her skin warm and silky beneath the rough terry. He wanted to go slowly, to savor every blessed, living inch of her, but his patience had deserted him along with his self-control. He eased her thighs open with his knees and trailed a hand over her belly, finding her slick and ready.

His blood felt fevered within him, and his own eagerness almost embarrassed him. Damn it, he was acting like a horny teenager; he just could not wait.

Her hands came down from his neck and started working his buckle, while frantic little moans spilled from her lips. "I need you, now."

Not any sooner than he needed to be deeply and completely inside her. The fumbling with his belt was taking way too long. With his hands in her armpits, he hauled her to her feet, hoisting her onto the desktop.

While he dealt with the belt and unzipped, she shoved the keyboard out of the way, and a dim corner of his mind found enough attention to be amused that she remembered to push the save key. Then he gripped her upper thighs, spread her wide and plunged into her, groaning as the slick heat enveloped him.

Her eyes widened with shock at the impact, then he lost sight of them as her head fell back. Her legs wrapped tight around his hips and her body arched right up against him, balancing on her hands, behind her on the desk. Her robe hung open, the sash looped lazily across her belly. He pulled it wide and pushed back the lapels to watch her belly and breasts as she gyrated against him.

He tried to hold himself back, slow things down, to prevent himself coming inside her in a humiliating nanosecond, but it was hopeless. She'd picked up the frantic rhythm, and since every shred of his self-control was history, he gave up and plunged into ecstasy.

But his helpless groan only triggered her climax, and he watched, mesmerized, as shudder after shudder rippled through her, matched by the high-pitched cries that rippled from her throat.

He collapsed into the chair, dragging her with him so she sprawled across his lap, her legs hanging over the armrest, her head against his shoulder, arms wrapped once more around his neck.

"I love you," he murmured against her hair.

A sigh whispered against his neck, then he felt her lips in the same spot. "I love you, too," she answered, a catch in her voice. They stayed in that position for several minutes, and he thought he'd never felt so…so content, so complete.

"I acted like an ass the other night. I'm sorry."

She stirred and her hair tickled his chin. "I wanted to explain, but you wouldn't let me. I'm *not* wild. I've just been pretending. Neville stuffed his tongue down my throat before I could get out of the limo." Jake felt her shudder of revulsion and hoped it was a long time before the groaning Neville got a whiff of anesthetic. "And my dinner date last night was with Walter. He's found someone new and she told him he has to right all the wrongs of his past."

"What?"

Cynthia chuckled. "I think she's a kind of New Age person. So anyway, that's the story."

"You're lying," he said with great conviction.

"What?" Usually she said "pardon" or "excuse me." He must have ruffled her feathers but good. Her lips were parted in indignation, an expression of puzzled anger on her face.

"You just said you're not wild. That, lady, is a lie. You're the wildest woman I've ever known."

Anger turned to smiling pleasure as a pink blush colored her cheeks. "Really?" She sounded distinctly complimented.

He couldn't resist kissing her again.

She sighed, and put her head back on his shoulder.

For a while they just sat, slumped together in her office chair, content.

After a few minutes, she stirred. "Did you talk to George Percivald?"

Jake sighed heavily. He didn't want to talk about this, but he respected her right to know. "Yeah. He was pretty upset, but I got the feeling maybe it was a relief. I think he'd known something wasn't right, but couldn't bring himself to mistrust his own stepson."

"Is he going to be all right?"

"Agnes was with him."

Cynthia nodded, understanding everything that meant, so he didn't have to explain how Agnes had held the elder Percivald's hand throughout, then quietly gone to make tea. When she came back, Jake could see she'd shed a few tears in the kitchen, but she'd remain strong for her man's sake, he was certain.

"He wants to do everything he can to help the investigation. Not that there's much he can do unless he can convince his stepson, or Ormond, to start talking." Jake yawned, leaning back and closing his eyes, acknowledging the bone-deep exhaustion. "We should go to bed."

"I have an idea," Cyn informed him in a clear voice that didn't sound sleepy at all.

"I think I'm too tired." He opened one eye and gazed down at her exposed breast. "Unless you're planning to be on top. Then...maybe."

She chuckled. "It's not about sex. I didn't get a chance to tell you, but I found the real set of books. Harrison had hidden a copy. Very incriminating stuff. Neville and his buds will get put away for sure." She sounded just like a cop, which made him smile.

Then her words sank in and he sat up straight, so fast

he almost ejected her right off his lap onto the floor. "You found evidence?"

"And a list of names," she said, smug as anything. "I'm also pretty sure the pension's being used somehow to launder money. That's what I was working on when you came in and, um, distracted me. I'm going to check the personnel files more carefully tomorrow."

"You brought them home?"

She gave him a look he was getting accustomed to, and he dreaded it. It meant he wasn't going to like what was coming next. "At the office, tomorrow."

"Absolutely not!"

She leaped off his lap and glared. "I've thought about this, Jake. I say we keep the company open, send the shipments out, just like nothing's wrong. Agnes and George and I can keep things going, and if anyone asks, we'll say Eddie's off sick and Neville and Ormond had to go away on business. Of course, we'll replace the packaging sheets with dummies, but I say we follow those shipments and see what happens."

Her eyes shone with eagerness. "In the meantime, we start investigating some of the pensioners and track down the other names Harrison listed."

"But you—"

"If we close the company down, the rest of the criminals will get suspicious. They'll have time to disappear. But if we pretend to carry on as usual, you and the rest of your team can do your jobs. Maybe you'll find out who killed your friend." She stuck her chin up and glared at him. "I plan to be at my desk tomorrow morning."

He jumped right out of the chair and shook his finger at her. "You were almost killed tonight. You're not trained for this stuff."

"You recruited me, Jake," she said in a calm voice that only made him madder. "Besides, you were almost killed, too. And you're trained."

"That's different."

"Because you're a man?"

"Because I can't do my job if I'm worried sick about you."

She sighed and wrapped her housecoat closer. She glanced up at him and he noticed a furrow between her eyes. She had that expression on her face again, the one that made him nervous. "I've been thinking about this a lot, Jake. I think I've found my new career."

"As an agent?" He groaned the words.

"No. A forensic accountant. I'm really a great accountant, I've just been bored. I figure I can use my skills and still get a little adventure." She shot him a mischievous glance that immediately put him on his guard. "Would you put in a good word for me at the FBI?"

He started to splutter. "I can't even begin to tell you what a terrible idea that is."

"Why?"

He tried to find a coherent thought and managed to grab a fleeting one. "The bureau frowns on interoffice romance."

"We don't have to tell them."

"I think they might get suspicious when we start having kids."

She thought about that for a second and her eyes got all teary. "Are you saying what I think you're saying?"

He huffed, intensely uncomfortable with the teary thing. "It's not a misplaced decimal point. I'm talking about us having kids. You and me." His stomach felt like he'd eaten a boulder. "Or don't you want kids?"

"Of course I want children. But—" she blushed rosily "—isn't there something else we should be doing?"

He felt distinctly smug. The woman couldn't get enough of him. "Morning, noon and night, honey. We can spend every Friday night at the neighborhood sex store stocking up for the weekend. We'll work through every fantasy in that damned magazine of yours."

Her eyes sparkled, but a little frown line marred her forehead. "But—but isn't there something else?"

"You mean where we'll live?" He shrugged. Man, she could be anal sometimes. "Your house, my house, a sailboat in the Mediterranean, I don't care."

"No, that's not—"

"Oh, you're worried about your job? You'd be a terrific forensic accountant. I can introduce you to some people." And he'd make damned sure not to let her get into anything dangerous.

By now she was deeply flushed. He had the uncomfortable feeling he'd gone off the trail somewhere, but he couldn't quite figure out where. Finally, she took a deep breath, as if she had to say something unpleasant. "I mean, shouldn't we get married?"

"Well of course we'll get married. What do you think I've been talking about?"

"Well, you never said the words," she insisted.

He sent her a grin that had her backing away swiftly. "I talk better with my hands." He grabbed the cord of her robe and pulled her to him, taking his time to restore perfect communication between them.

"SO, WILL YOU?" he asked sometime later.

"I might be too tired."

He nipped the soft inner slope of her breast, just to let her know he got the joke. "Will you marry me?"

“Mmm, yes, please.” She chuckled softly. “You know, we could start our own tradition—an entire family of FBI agents.”

“Where are those handcuffs?”